Praise for these incre

JENNIFER E

Forget You

"The romance in this book is outstanding, the story is superb, and it's a story you can't put down. *Forget You* is a must read!"

—Chick Loves Lit

"Certainly a book to be read again and placed at the top of the favorites shelf. . . ."

—A Good Addiction

"Sexy and full of surprises . . . an enchanting tale of searching and finding. Each of their shared moments are addictive and special, and oh-my-God, so searingly sexy, unmasking qualities they would not have otherwise discovered in each other."

—Girls Without a Bookshelf

"Lets just put it this way, Jennifer Echols has a way with words . . . beautiful, intelligent, and downright sexy!"

—Princess Bookie

Going Too Far

"A brave and powerful story, searingly romantic and daring, yet also full of hilarious moments. Meg's voice will stay in your head long after the intense conclusion."

—R. A. Nelson, author of *Teach Me* and *Breathe My Name*

"Naughty in all the best ways . . . the perfect blend of romance, wit, and rebelliousness. I loved it!"

—Niki Burnham, author of *Royally Jacked* and *Sticky Fingers*

"Powerful . . . a thoroughly engrossing look into two people's personal stories of loss and strength. . . . The two characters grow and change together. . . . Mesmerizing to read, whether you're a teenager or adult."

—*Parkersburg News and Sentinel*

"None of us in the office could put the advance copy down."

—*Lipstick*

"A tremendously talented writer with a real gift for developing relationships between her characters."

—*Romantic Times*

"Powerful without being over-the-top, and reveals universal truths while still being a very personal story."

—Teen Book Review

"Edgy, tense, and seductive, with a very tough-tender, wounded heroine who is trying to figure out who she is, and an intelligent, thoughtful hero who thought he had that all figured out. . . . Humor and sarcastic wit alternating with terribly tender and sneakily seductive scenes."

—Smart Bitches Trashy Books

"An amazing book . . . you will still be thinking about days after you have read it."

—Flamingnet

"What a powerful read. . . ."

—Coffee Time Romance

"A big roller-coaster ride . . . a torrent of different emotions. . . ."

—YA Book Realm

"Fast paced, detailed, and addicting. . . ."

—Lauren's Crammed Bookshelf

"*Going Too Far* has everything a teen love story should have."

—Book Loons

"An amazing writer. I can't wait to read more of her books!"

—The Book Girl

"An absolute pleasure to read. I couldn't get enough of it."

—Pop Culture Junkie

"A compelling novel about the choices teens make, the consequences, and uncontrollable things that happen. . . ."

—Ms. Yingling Reads

"I stayed up late and most likely failed two tests simply because I could not physically put this book down. It was way worth it though."

—Addicted to Books

"Deeply rich characters with many layers that need to be peeled back before the reader is exposed to the real Meg, the real John After."

—YA Reads

These MTV books by Jennifer Echols are all also available as eBooks

Other romantic dramas by Jennifer Echols

Forget You

Going Too Far

Available from MTV Books

Love Story

Jennifer Echols

Gallery Books MTV Books
New York London Toronto Sydney

Gallery Books
A Division of Simon & Schuster, Inc.
1230 Avenue of the Americas
New York, NY 10020

This book is a work of fiction. Names, characters, places, and incidents either are products of the author's imagination or are used fictitiously. Any resemblance to actual events or locales or persons, living or dead, is entirely coincidental.

First MTV Books/Gallery Books trade paperback edition July 2011

For information about special discounts for bulk purchases, please contact Simon & Schuster Special Sales at 1-866-506-1949 or business@simonandschuster.com.

The Simon & Schuster Speakers Bureau can bring authors to your live event. For more information or to book an event contact the Simon & Schuster Speakers Bureau at 1-866-248-3049 or visit our website at www.simonspeakers.com.

Manufactured in the United States of America

10 9 8 7 6 5 4 3 2

Library of Congress Cataloging-in-Publication Data

Echols, Jennifer.
Love story / Jennifer Echols. — 1st MTV Books/Gallery Books trade pbk. ed.
p. cm.
Summary: A rival for her grandmother's inheritance arrives in college freshman Erin's creative writing class, unaware that he plays the main character in one of her steamy short stories.
[1. Creative writing—Fiction. 2. Authorship—Fiction. 3. Love—Fiction. 4. Inheritance and succession—Fiction.] I. Title.
PZ7.E1967Lo 2011
[Fic]—dc23 2011024708

ISBN 978-1-4391-7832-4
ISBN 978-1-4391-8048-8 (ebook)

Acknowledgments

Thanks to my brilliant editor, Jennifer Heddle; Nicole James; Catherine Burns; NYPD Lieutenant Steve Osborne; Laura Bradford; my dad; and as always, my critique partners, Catherine Chant and Victoria Dahl.

Love Story

1

Almost a Lady

by Erin Blackwell

Captain Vanderslice was something of an ass. He took Rebecca's gloved hand and kissed it at the lowest point of a deep bow. "Miss O'Carey, you are blooming into quite the young lady."

"And you, sir, look as fine as always," Rebecca lied, watching him straighten before her. Tall and dark, he might have been handsome but for a stray bullet that had caught his cheek during the War Between the States ten years before, burrowing a thick scar from nose to eye.

Rumor had it that the visible wound wasn't the only one he'd suffered during the war—and that despite his status as a bachelor in a border state deprived of many of its young men by the ravages of war, this disappointment with regard to offspring was the main factor that had kept several ladies from accepting his hand in marriage. However, the prospect of the bloodline ending mattered not to Rebecca's self-centered and business-minded grandmother, who thought the match advantageous, for someday it would merge Captain Vanderslice's vast horse farm with her own.

It mattered to Rebecca. She racked her brain for something to say to the captain that would be neither rude nor an encouragement of his amours. "Wasn't Colonel Clark's derby a delight! He talks of making it an annual event."

"It will never catch on," said the captain with hauteur, swirling the mint julep in a tumbler in his gloved hand.

"Oh! I'd consider the races a success, with ten thousand in attendance," Rebecca maintained. She continued to exchange unpleasant pleasantries with the captain while her eye roved about the rich ballroom, searching for an escape before the captain's small talk turned to courtship, as it had at every social gathering of late.

Luck was not on her side. At a typical country dance, one of her friends from the neighborhood would have strategically interrupted the exchange, drawing a grateful Rebecca away from the gentleman's attentions. This was no country dance. Colonel Clark had organized a race of the area's finest three-year-old colts on the outskirts of Louisville, and this exclusive ball in his mansion included only the richest families. In a gathering of perhaps a hundred, Rebecca was alone.

Almost. She spied movement out of the corner of her eye. Framed by the arched window that let in the cool May night, beyond the patio, David's dark jacket blended with the shadows, but his golden hair and crisp white shirt glowed in the soft candlelight reflected from mirrors in the ballroom.

She had asked him to meet her. She had retreated to this corner of the ballroom with a view of the garden early in the evening, and had glanced casually through the archway in search of him after every dance for four quadrilles, three reels, and a round dance. As she spied him at last, she felt as if her heart with its insistent throbbing were actually moving the lace of her bosom.

"Miss Rebecca!"

She started, nearly bursting from her tightly laced corset in surprise. But it was only the elderly Mr. Gordon, stepping between herself and Captain Vanderslice. She smiled gratefully at him for the interruption. Recently on a turn about the garden at her grandmother's estate, she had shared with him her opinion of the captain and her grandmother's plans. "Mr. Gordon." She bowed and gave him her hand.

"Gordon," the captain said shortly.

Mr. Gordon merely nodded to acknowledge the captain. To Rebecca he said, "I was most pleased with the performance of your horseflesh in the third race today. I hear you trained this filly yourself?"

"*You* trained!" the captain gasped, aghast at Rebecca.

Rebecca kept her eyes on Mr. Gordon, which seemed a good policy if the captain was intent on merely being shocked by everybody instead of participating in the conversation. "You heard this from our stable hands," she said, "but they give me too much credit. Our young David Archer has done most of the work. I merely took an interest."

"And picked this filly out of the barn to train," Mr. Gordon prompted her.

"Well, yes," Rebecca said, "after discussions on the subject with David."

"Young, you say," Mr. Gordon mused. "Looking for a place of his own, out from beneath the long shadow of his famously talented father, perhaps."

Rebecca's heart throbbed again, this time with alarm. She knew Mr. Gordon was only making conversation to distract the captain from wooing her, and she appreciated his efforts. If only she could keep her servant-lover from being hired away from her grandmother's farm in the process. "Well, I don't know that Archer is all that," Rebecca backtracked. "I probably have more of an eye for horseflesh than I give myself credit for. It is not ladylike to accept the accolades."

"Nor is it ladylike to take such an interest in horseflesh in the first place!" the forgotten captain exploded. "Rebecca, are you mad? Hanging about in the barn will ruin your reputation! I shall speak with your grandmother!"

"What an excellent idea!" Rebecca said. "Mr. Gordon, would you be so kind as to help the captain find my grandmother?"

"And you must accompany us!" the captain exclaimed to Rebecca, offering his arm.

Rebecca hung back. "No need. I am quite incapable of disciplining myself. You had better get to the root of the problem, and I shall stand here by myself in the corner and think remorseful thoughts about what I have done."

"Come, Captain!" Mr. Gordon feigned outrage. As he put a hand on the captain's shoulder to turn him, he crossed his eyes at Rebecca.

She winked at Mr. Gordon. She appreciated his help, and she felt a twinge of guilt at deceiving him. If he had known he was not only extracting her from an embarrassing courtship, but also clearing her for an illicit one, he would not have been so helpful.

She watched the elegant backs of the two men weave among the partygoers and disappear into another room in search of the matriarch. With a last stealthy glance around the party, she backed to the arched doorway. She moved with excruciating slowness due to the damned fashion of the season, a bustled gown with an impossibly tight skirt, allowing steps of only a few inches at a time. The dress was flattering for marriageable women, she supposed, but extremely inconvenient when one had designs on a stable boy.

Finally she passed under the arch and outdoors. The cold air made her shiver in her sleeveless gown, but she must hide her discomfort. The only way to pull off this affair without being cast into her bedchamber until her coming-of-age, and without causing David to be let go, or, much worse, to become a victim of country justice, was to have an excuse available at all times. Her excuse at the moment was that she had felt light-headed in the party and needed fresh air. Such a thing had never happened to her—the stable hands had told her she could hold her liquor admirably for a lady—but there was a first time for everything.

Then, if she ever reached David beyond the patio, her excuse would be that she had left her fine riding gloves in her favorite filly's stall at the races, and David, recognizing them and mistrusting the rough workmen to send them after her, had brought them to her at the colonel's party.

At least, that was the excuse Rebecca had invented, and those were the orders she had given David to follow. But David had been known to disobey orders, and to escape the consequences with a charming smile. He might have grown tired of waiting and left for home after all.

Normally Rebecca would not have attributed such disrespect to a servant. But David was not normal. Devoted he was not. Patient he was not, either. In fact, arranging a romantic tryst with him had been a bit like herding cats, and at several points she had been ready to give up on him entirely and attempt an affair with the son of the greengrocer, and had told David as much. That he seemed hardly moved by the threat only made her want him more.

The War Between the States had begun when they both were but four years old, and though it had not ravaged Louisville, it had been a preoccupation of the community, with threats of evacuation and concerns about beloved menfolk gone. Rebecca's father had been commissioned as an officer of General Bull Nelson and had died of a bullet to the gut at the Battle of Richmond, and her mother had slowly expired of heartbreak.

Rebecca missed her parents terribly, but she did not remember much of this period, save the sea of white tents at the Union Army training grounds on the outskirts of the city. Any parenting to which she'd been subjected had come from her aloof grandmother, grown bitter with grief at the passing of her daughter, perhaps, but Rebecca suspected her grandmother was naturally acrid, for a disposition of such intensity and consistency surely was born and not made. Rebecca had found solace in sun-filled romps through the pastures playing at army and other inappropriately tomboyish pursuits with David, the son of the stable master—a friendship that would have been harshly discouraged if anybody had been paying attention.

But nobody had. And looking over her shoulder and past the troublesome white frills on her gown, she saw that nobody watched her even now as she stole away from the grand mansion with candlelight spilling from its arched windows, across the patio, into the cool night.

David stood before her, broad shoulders and slim hips appearing all the more gentlemanly tonight in her farm's special-occasion finery: long jacket, tight breeches, and tall riding boots. When he spied her, he ducked behind the hedgerow, where they could not be seen by anyone stepping out on the patio for air. She rounded the hedgerow and peered about the yard on the other side. Satisfied that they would not be discovered here, either, she gazed way up at him.

He smiled down at her, his eyes tracing the plunging neckline of her gown. So enraptured was she with studying his face after days caught up in the whirlwind of balls and races, and so distractingly did her heart beat against her breastbone, that some moments passed before she remembered to greet him. "Hullo, David."

"Hullo, Miss O'Carey." His words were the proper address to a daughter of the landed gentry from a stable hand. Indeed, his words always had been proper—in public at least. It was the attitude behind his voice that told her he did not consider himself her inferior. And that is what drew her to him, over and over.

What he said next was not proper at all. "Would you care to walk behind the stables?"

She should have laughed. Never would they get away with such a thing. A witness would happen upon them and report the tragedy to her grandmother before it could happen, saving Rebecca's womanhood and ruining her evening.

Rebecca did not laugh. David watched her expectantly, no humor in his steady blue gaze.

"I would soil my slippers," she murmured, "and the maid would notice in the morning." She kicked the toe of one gold shoe beyond the hem of her gown to show him.

"Then I suppose we can't go far." His strong hand encircled her wrist, and he pulled her.

She looked up into his eyes in surprise, wondering what he meant.

"Come with me into the bushes, Your Highness," he said. "Come with me into the darkness. Isn't that what you wanted when you asked me to bring you a glove you hadn't forgotten?"

Of course that was what she had wanted. But she was not prepared to admit this, much less to follow through.

He pulled. And in that instant, heat burst from her heart and flooded her bosom, splashing a blush across her cheeks and rushing in a tingling trail to her fingertips and her toes. This stable boy—or whatever he had grown into when she wasn't looking—was strong enough to take her into the bushes whether she wanted to go or not. There was nothing for it but to trip after him.

Even as she did so, he whispered over his shoulder, "I'm beginning to think you don't know as much about love as you claim. You seem astonished that I've called your bluff." He stopped under a leafy bough laden with fragrant white blossoms that glowed in the moonlight.

"I'll wager I've learned as much in my boudoir as you in your stable," she countered. "My maid was previously employed by the chorus line—though if you speak a word of that to my grandmother, you will find ground glass in your coffee."

He exhaled shortly through his nose. Rebecca was unsure whether this was a laugh or a sigh, because her presence tended to elicit both reactions from David.

Then he placed his fingers on her bottom lip—pointer finger on one side, thumb on the other—and gently squeezed as if plumping her lip to ready it. "I'm going to kiss you now, Rebecca. Don't scream."

Her nervous laughter was cut off as his lips met hers.

Since those long-ago summer days of play, she had considered David her dear friend. He was important enough to her that she had hidden their friendship carefully from her grandmother. But now they were both eighteen. Over the recent months, the very secrecy of their relationship had turned dark in her mind, and needful. David was a man now, she a woman pursued by others, driven toward this kiss. She opened her mouth for everything she had dreamed of and expected.

What she had not expected was David's hands upon her bodice. They first grasped her waist, then smoothed up her back and wandered to her front. When one thumb traced her neckline, dangerously close to her bosom, she broke the kiss with a gasp.

DID I GASP MYSELF? I WAS terrified that I'd made a noise while reading my own story, surrounded by my classmates. My copy of "Almost a Lady" stared up at me from the long table of dark polished wood, just as it stared up at the other six students seated around the table, only half the class. But none of them were reading it. Two of them whispered together, two read textbooks, two typed on their laptops. And none of them were staring at me. To disguise my gasp just in case, I took another long breath as if I simply couldn't get enough of the good, fresh New York City air. Then inhaled again and held it while I concentrated on my heart, which seemed to be palpitating.

I was nervous. Me, nervous! My story, by the luck of the draw, would be one of the first three critiqued in class. I only hoped it wouldn't be the very first. I was confident in my writing, but nobody wants to go first. And nothing mattered more to me than my stories.

This one especially. I'd written it from life, sort of, about my very own, very real stable boy back home in Kentucky. We'd started out as friends, like David and Rebecca. Then something awful had happened and for years I couldn't get past it. Now we never would.

We could in my story, though. I could set up obstacles to love, just like in real life—and then, unlike in real life, I could knock them down. Making every piece slide into place for my characters, writing them an unrealistically happy ending, gave me a rush and made me high. This was why I wanted to be a novelist.

The people in my high school creative-writing classes hadn't felt this way. But now I was in an honors creative-writing class at a New York university famous for its programs in creative writing and publishing. Granted, every freshman in the honors program had to take this class, and most of them weren't English majors and might not care about writing fiction, but surely some of them would see what I saw in my story and love it as much as I did.

If that were true, they would not be able to tear themselves away from reading and rereading my delicious romance. Yet strangely, they seemed to be getting on with their lives. I could hardly hear their breathing over their taps on laptop keyboards and the noise of late-afternoon traffic outside the window, but I was pretty sure nobody gasped. The girl nearest me texted on her insidious-looking black phone as if reading my story had been just another homework assignment and had not changed her life.

Screw all of them. I dove back into my story.

* * *

"Shall I stop?" David whispered, kissing the corner of Rebecca's mouth. "If we're caught, you may be confined to your room, but I will lose my position. My father may lose his position, too, and then he will shoot me." David kissed her chin, left a trail of kisses down her neck, and mouthed her breastbone. Placing one kiss at the lowest point of her neckline, between her breasts, he paused and glanced up at her, his blond hair catching in the frills of lace upon her dress. "Better make it worth the trouble."

"By all means," she breathed—none too easy a feat in her corset. If this kept up she might swoon of tightly bound excitement.

With her leave, his tongue lapped at the tender skin between her breasts. He licked his way up the other side of her neckline, blazed another trail of kisses up that side of her neck, and nuzzled past the smooth ringlets of hair that her maid had arranged so artfully.

"Some things will have to wait until we are truly alone," he growled in her ear, sending chills down her neck and across her arms in the cool night. "I should like to put my lips here." His hand wandered down her bosom again, and cupped her breast. His thumb moved back and forth across her nipple, hard beneath the lace.

Now it was she who grasped him, her fingers finding his white shirt beneath his riding coat, her palms sliding over the warm, hard muscles of the chest that lay beneath. She kissed his lips.

Then he took charge of the embrace, grasping her shoulders to hold her still while he explored her mouth with his tongue.

Rebecca had no concept of how long this ecstasy went on before he pulled back, panting, and set his forehead against hers. "Well, that satisfies my curiosity, Miss O'Carey. Thanks for a lovely evening."

"Cad." She shoved him lightly.

Smiling like a scoundrel, he backed against the boughs. White petals rained down upon them both.

He fumbled with something in his breeches. She had thought the past few minutes the most intense of her life, but they were nothing compared with the alarm and ashamed delight now rushing through her veins—until she realized he was only bringing out his pocket watch.

Glancing at it, he said, "You'd better go back before you're missed."

"All right." She backed a pace away and observed him, calmly now that her heart had quieted. He carried the watch for timing the horses, of course, but it was easy to imagine him a gentleman, with a gentleman's pocket watch, his clothes the fashion of a young dandy rather than the uniform of a stable hand. He could so easily have been the great catch of the neighborhood, and in that case they could have been married.

But it was not to be. She shook her head to clear it. It was one thing to arrange an assignation with the stable boy, and another thing entirely to fall in love with him.

"I had almost lost the wherewithal to ask," she said, "but did you bring my glove after all?"

He stared at her blankly for a moment, and she thought he had not brought it, and that her grandmother would demand some fine explaining if Rebecca had the misfortune to meet her on re-entering the party.

But this was more of his usual stonewalling to frighten her. With a grin he pulled her glove, tightly rolled, from another trouser pocket.

"I suppose I can't stroll into the party with my excuse flopping about," she said. "That would look odd." She fished her reticule from her own pocket and attempted to work the rolled glove through the small opening. It would not go.

"Here, let me."

Instinctively she pulled back, not wanting him to soil her glove and her reticule with his dirty fingers.

She looked up at him in embarrassment. Of course he had

washed before meeting her. His fingers were not dirty, as usual in the stable. She was horrified that she had instinctively thought such a thing, as if he were dirty permanently. From his somber expression she could tell he knew exactly what was going through her mind.

Gently he took the glove and the reticule from her. As she watched, he worked the glove through, careful not to open the reticule too far and tear it. "I saw a snake eat a rat once," he commented, "out behind your grandmother's north barn. Unhinged its jaws to do it."

"That may be beyond the capacity of this snake," she said—and just then the reticule gave, and the glove slipped inside. They both sighed their relief.

He fastened the jeweled top and handed the reticule back to her, his fingers brushing hers. "When will I see you again?"

At dawn, when you drive us in the coach back to the house, she could have said cattily. But he gazed seriously at her, and something told her the kiss they had finally shared had changed everything between them. She might not love him, but she could not disappoint him.

"My grandmother leaves for business in Frankfort tomorrow," Rebecca said. "Let's look for an opportunity."

"Let's do." He touched the tip of her nose with one finger, then her bottom lip again. "Take care, and watch out for captains."

She laughed and whispered, "Always." Then she fled the bower.

She returned to the party, furtively examining the revelers as she entered. No eyes were upon her, not even those of her grandmother, across the room, or Captain Vanderslice, conversing with elderly Mrs. Woodson, boring her ever closer to death. Everybody seemed involved in their own pursuits. The mint julep was Rebecca's friend tonight, throwing a shroud over others' powers of observation. Nobody saw her come in or commented on her reticule, obviously full to bursting.

She would not even need to use her pin money to pay off her maid, as she had done several times in the past when David had met her in the barn. They had simply played then, not kissed. He had taught her to swing on a rope from the loft down to the hayrick below like a pirate conquering the poop deck. The issue had been that she was too old to be playing, and much too old to be playing with the stable boy.

The latter had not changed, she thought as she gazed out the doorway she had just entered. Blinded anew by the candlelight, she could not make out shapes in the darkness as she had earlier, but she did detect a flash of blond head keeping its distance across the patio. Watching her, and waiting.

I LET OUT A LONG, SATISFIED sigh. This story set up a grand adventure for Rebecca and David, with a fairy-tale ending—everything I'd longed for with my stable boy. It was perfect. The class would love it.

I only wished they would reassure me by telling me so. But they kept their heads down, focused on their own work, as if we were waiting for the subway. Maybe later in the semester we'd be comfortable enough with one another to start a group convo as we waited for the whole class to trickle in. But it was only our second meeting. Even so, normally I would have started the group convo myself. I hated silence.

Today was not normal. To get my mind off the impending judgment of my goal in life, I pulled my calculator out of my book bag. My boss had offered me a double shift at the coffee shop on Saturday. If I took it, I wouldn't be able to go to the Broadway matinee I'd scoped out. If I didn't take the shift and I bought the cut-rate Broadway ticket, I might have to dip into the reserves I'd saved over the summer to make my first payment on my dorm room. My scholarship covered tuition only, and I'd been able to talk the university into a payment plan for my rent since I'd unexpectedly become destitute the night of high school graduation.

A Broadway ticket might have been a frivolous expense when I was faced with eviction. But I'd wanted to study writing in New York City as long as I could remember. Now I was afraid I wouldn't be here long. And if I didn't make the most of my experience, it would be like I was never here.

As I crunched numbers—God, my hourly pay was low, and tips were abysmal no matter how low I wore my necklines—I resisted looking up at the students entering the room. I especially avoided meeting the eyes of the two noisy guys who blustered in and sat directly across from me, just as they had on the first day of class. They knew each other from elsewhere, obviously, and the Indian one in particular was the cocky type who might give me a hard time about "Almost a Lady." People had made fun of me for writing romantic stories before. I hoped he and his friend wouldn't gang up on me.

Summer was the last one in, and I felt my shoulders relax. I'd never been one of those timid girls who couldn't take a step without the shadow of her best friend crossing her path. But putting my story in front of these strangers was like stripping naked in a men's prison rec room. I turned to Summer, expecting a friendly roommate-type question designed to set me at ease, such as, *How did calculus go?*

She looked me up and down and shrieked, "Where did you get that scarf?" drawing the boisterous guys' attention.

Busted! I tried to mix my expensive clothes from home with the cheap replacements I could afford. I was aiming for a gradual, graceful decline into poverty. But when I'd gotten dressed that morning after Summer had left for her eight o'clock, I'd been tired.

I'd thrown on a T-shirt, a scarf, and my most comfortable jeans—all of which happened to be designer. I should have been more careful. Summer did not own any designer labels, but she wanted them. And she knew them when she saw them.

I gazed at her blankly. "I have no idea what you're talking about." I meant that I knew *exactly* what she was talking about, and we should discuss it *later*.

But we'd been friends only five days, too short a time for her to decipher my unspoken messages. She looked me up and down again. "And those jeans," she murmured.

"I beg your damn pardon?" I asked, still telegraphing for her to shut up.

She dumped her book bag in her richly upholstered chair, grasped my wrist, and dragged me out of my own richly upholstered chair. We both tripped on the edge of the Oriental rug as she pulled me toward the door.

Most of my classes were held in modern buildings, like you'd expect at any college. But the honors freshman creative-writing class met in a converted town house. Our classroom was a long boardroom, the dark wooden paneling hung with portraits of dead scholars staring down at us from their frames. The thick, carved table and big comfy chairs replaced student desks. The stately room made the class and our writing seem important—until Summer and I tripped over the rug, which reminded us that we were just freshmen after all, wearing shorts and hooded sweatshirts. Or, in my case, a designer scarf and—

"Designer jeans!" At least we'd reached the hallway and she'd pressed me against the wall before she hissed this at me, out of our classmates' hearing. "I thought you said you shopped at the thrift store."

"I *do* shop at the thrift store." The only thing I had actually purchased there was an outfit for my belly-dancing class. A little flamboyant but a lot cheaper than new workout clothes would have been. And I often browsed in the thrift store, which counted as shopping.

"There is no way you got a two-hundred-dollar scarf in a thrift store," she whispered. "And those jeans. They're from last year. A size-four woman did not drop dead and give her almost-brand-new designer jeans to charity. I thought you didn't have any money. You told me you were working at the coffee shop because your scholarship is tuition only. You didn't say you have a line of credit from back home!"

"I don't. The scarf and the jeans were gifts." Not a lie. My grandmother had bought all my clothes for the six years I lived with her.

Summer pointed at me. "I knew all that detail in your story was a little too realistic. You're really Rebecca, aren't you? Just in the present day? You own a horse farm in Kentucky."

"What? No! Why would you think that?"

"Last weekend when Jørdis brought the Sunday *Times* to the dorm, you went straight to the horse section."

"There is no horse section of the *New York Times*."

She poked my breastbone. "You know what I mean. The horse-race part of the sports section."

I drew myself up to my full height and looked down at Summer, trying to impress on her the ridiculousness of her theory, which was of course pretty damn close to the truth. I said haughtily, "I certainly do not own a horse farm." My grandmother owned it. Even when she died eventually, I would never own it. She'd made sure of that.

Summer stared stubbornly up at me. Then her eyes drifted down to boob level. "And that shirt. I should have known nobody looks that good in a regular old T-shirt, not even you. Who made it?" She grabbed my arm, whipped it behind my back, and rammed my face into the wall. Holding me there, she fumbled with my neckline to read the label. "We've only known each other a few days," she muttered, "but I always assumed I would share everything with my college roommate, and we are not getting off to a good start."

She was a poor girl trying to look rich. I was a former rich girl suddenly poor. As a tall redhead, I could not have looked more different from Summer, tiny and African-American—but we were both Southern and struggling to fit in here in New York. I had sensed this about her immediately, and I had liked her a whole lot until she dragged me out into the hall and threatened to blow my cover. I was just about to jab my elbow into her ribs to get her off me—I had to hide that designer T-shirt label at all costs—when a voice beside us purred, "Good afternoon, ladies."

Summer and I jumped away from each other. Gabe Murphy was our writing teacher, a stubby man with a bulbous nose and lots of snow white hair. He would have looked jolly, like Santa Claus, except he dressed in a hoodie and cargo shorts and flip-flops like most of the class. I figured he'd been a surfer in California until one day he glanced in the mirror and realized he was forty pounds overweight and nearing retirement age, and he thought he'd better come to New York to pursue the writing career he'd always thought he would have plenty of time for later.

I called him our writing teacher rather than our writing professor because I wasn't sure he was a professor. That was a special designation the university gave to personages with fancy degrees. I doubted it applied to Gabe. I wasn't sure whether to call him Dr. Murphy or Mr. Murphy or just plain Gabe. He hadn't introduced himself, and the syllabus was labeled GABE MURPHY. No clue there. None of the other students had taken a stand on the issue, so I coped by calling him *Excuse me,* or—

"Hello," I said noncommittally. "Summer was just straightening my shirt before class. I want to look professional when we discuss my story."

"We're writers," he said. "We're prone to eccentricity." He tilted his head toward the classroom, indicating that we should follow him inside.

When he'd disappeared through the doorway, the grin Summer had worn for him dropped away. She pointed at me again. "I am not through with you."

"I can tell!"

We crossed the classroom threshold and bounced into our chairs. We couldn't slip into them because they were huge and upholstered. Pulling them out and dragging them back up to the table caused a commotion in the quiet room. Even the noisy guys across from us had hushed with the entrance of Gabe. Now they watched us reprovingly, as if we were five-year-olds playing jacks in a church pew at a funeral.

Ignoring the noise, Gabe said a few words about appreciating those of us who had been brave enough to share our stories first. As if we had volunteered for this. He shuffled through the stapled stories in front of him, making sure all three for the day were there. He had said during the first class meeting that nowadays, writing students were paranoid about sharing because they were afraid someone would nab their work and publish it on the internet. So our instructions were to place one copy of our stories on reserve in the library for the other students to read. Then we brought copies for everyone. The class made notes during the discussion and passed the copies back to the original author. I couldn't wait to read my classmates' glowing praise.

"These stories have a natural order and flow nicely from one to the next," Gabe was saying, "so let's start with—"

There was a knock on the door.

I heard my sigh again in the stillness of the regal classroom. This one was not a sigh of satisfaction but a sigh of what-species-of-tree-slime-dares-knock-on-the-door-at-a-time-like-this.

Gabe got up from his upholstered chair. This was not instantaneous because of the weight of the chair and the girth of his own belly beneath his La Jolla T-shirt. He opened the door a crack and talked in a low tone to the interloper. Summer and I were closest to the door. We couldn't look over our shoulders and stare at Gabe without being obvious, but we could hear most of what was being said. The interloper wanted to transfer into our class. Gabe was telling him we did have space for one more, but a creative-writing class was a family unit, and before the interloper joined, the other students would need to approve. The interloper said he was sure that would not be a problem.

I recognized his voice. Or rather, I recognized the tone of his voice. The Indian dude was cocky, but the interloper's cockiness would make the Indian dude look modest in comparison.

"Are you okay?" Summer whispered, managing to make even those breathy words sound high pitched. "Are you that worried about the class discussing your writing? You look really pale all of a sudden. I mean, you're already pale, but it's like your freckles have faded."

A dry "Thanks" was all I could manage. I was not okay. I was gripping the edge of the carved table so hard, I would not have been surprised if my fingers snapped off.

The interloper was my stable boy.

And I could not let him read my story.

2

"We have a new student," Gabe announced, closing the door. He pulled out his wingback chair at the head of the table and sat down. "A potential new student. He's out in the hall drawing a horse. In the meantime, where were we?"

I did not care where we were. Gabe reviewed the rules for critiquing the stories. I should have cared, but in my mind I was out in the hall with Hunter Allen, jogging his elbow so he messed up his horse.

All of us had drawn a horse as a creativity demonstration on the first day of class. Gabe's point, I think, was that each person had a unique perspective and something to bring to a creative-writing group. The cocky Indian guy definitely had a unique perspective. He had drawn a horse's ass. Summer had drawn the underside of a horse—inaccurately. It seemed to have no gender, or at least no genitalia, like a Barbie or a Ken doll. But it was a perspective I wouldn't have thought of, and I was impressed with her. I was not an artist, but I had tried my best to capture a horse in motion, not in a race of some human's devising, but running for the sake of running, a horse being a horse. I had loved looking out my bedroom window first thing in the morning with the mist rising from the bluegrass, watching the yearlings race each other when nobody was betting, because that's what horses did.

I crossed my fingers that Hunter would draw a horse the class wouldn't like.

"And that's how our in-class critiques work," Gabe said. "We need to be sure we understand this process up front. The classroom dynamic is very important." He looked around the table as he said this, eyes lingering on each student in turn like a seasoned writing instructor. He'd probably been teaching writing part-time at the junior college in So-Cal for years to finance his surfing addiction. "You need to trust one another in order to do your best work. Once the classroom dynamic goes sour, it's almost impossible to sweeten. Are there any questions?"

His eyes rested on me, as if I had been daydreaming. Who, me? I actually did blush because I wanted Gabe to think well of me. The college arranged for the outstanding freshman honors creative-writing student from the fall semester to work as an intern for one of the major publishers during the spring semester. That could be my foot in the door for an editorial job when I graduated, even publication of my own novel someday. Plus it paid more for fewer hours than my current coffee shop job, which was killing me, and I would not have to work standing up.

Gabe didn't look like the type of guy who would have a lot of sway over a publishing internship committee, but after the decision makers reviewed my portfolio, they might ask him whether I was easy to work with. Maybe getting along with other authors was the most important criterion. Then again . . . whoever heard of authors getting along with each other? Look at Hemingway and Stein, or Hemingway and Fitzgerald, or hell, Hemingway and anybody.

Another knock sounded at the door, and in walked my stable boy—sans the riding jacket and breeches. His eyes were an intense blue, exactly the color of his polo shirt. He could have been accused of vanity, wearing that color on purpose, except that his disheveled appearance made it clear he didn't care about that sort of thing. Except he did. His dishevelment was carefully planned.

I waited for those eyes to meet mine. Of course he saw me. I had long red hair. I practically glowed in the dark. And as he stood before us at Gabe's right hand, he met everyone's gaze in turn, just as Gabe had, working the room. Everyone's gaze but mine.

"Tell us your name," Gabe said to Hunter, "and why you want to be in this class. Be convincing. This is your big chance."

Hunter nodded. "My name is Hunter Allen." Most college freshmen would have mealymouthed their way through this self-introduction, but Hunter embraced it as if he were on tour promoting his self-help DVDs. "I want to be in this class because the other freshman honors creative-writing class I'm in conflicts with my chemistry class. I can't be in two places at once, a concept that seems beyond the grasp of this institution of higher learning. My schedule is fucked up."

A guy snorted laughter because Hunter had cussed in class, and several of the girls gasped. Hunter was testing Gabe. Hunter liked to test people.

Gabe passed the test. He didn't raise an eyebrow, just sat with his chair pushed back from the table, gazing at Hunter, giving him the floor.

"Also," Hunter went on, "my roommates Manohar and Brian"—he gestured to the Indian dude and his friend—"told me this class wasn't full, but it did have lots of beautiful women."

Now all the guys burst into laughter, and one of the girls on the other end of the table exclaimed, "You're in!"

Summer turned to me. "I heart this person."

"You would," I muttered. Girls always did. Including me.

"Your horse, sir," Gabe said.

Hunter handed Gabe a sheet of paper. He had the nerve to give us a grin over his shoulder and salute us with two fingers as he left the room again.

Gabe examined the paper, then held it up for us to see. Everyone leaned forward, squinting. It was a horse's tack—bridle, reins, saddle—all placed as if a stable boy had put them on a horse. There was even a broom for manure. Only the horse was missing.

It was a message. To me. He'd been teased about being my stable boy for the last six years at our school, and finally he was out from under me. He did not want to be called a stable boy anymore.

He was not going to like my story.

"All in favor of Hunter Allen joining the class," Gabe said, "raise your hand."

Everybody in the room raised a hand except me.

Summer turned to me and asked out loud, "Why aren't you raising your hand?" Afterward Summer and I were going to have a talk about subtlety and secrecy, because damn.

I said, "I think we have enough students already. It's an honors class and we're trying to keep the class size small. It's capped at twelve."

"It's capped at thirteen," Gabe corrected me.

"It ought to be capped at twelve," I said. "And we've already arranged the schedule for discussing our stories."

I could feel Summer staring at the side of my face. "Are you on crack?"

I raised my voice over the guffaws of the guys across the table. "I am working my way through college, and I am concerned about getting the best value for my hard-earned money."

Summer gave up on me and turned back to Gabe. "Can I have Erin's vote?"

"No," Gabe said.

"Then can I vote twice?" asked Brian.

The class tittered. Manohar gave Brian a look of outrage.

"Because he's my roommate!" Brian exclaimed at Manohar. "Just because I'm gay doesn't mean I like men, perv."

Hunter opened the door and leaned into the classroom. "I'm

going to pretend I didn't hear any of that." He backed out again and closed the door.

"She's outnumbered anyway," Gabe said. "Looks like we have a thirteenth student." He glanced at me and pursed his lips, perplexed. Then, amid a smattering of applause from the class, he scraped back his weighty chair and went to the door to let Hunter in. Violins screeched repeatedly, as when the heroine is about to get stabbed in a horror movie, but I don't think anybody heard them but me. The violins were drowned out by the escalating applause as Hunter followed Gabe into the room. Gabe sat at the head of the table and gestured toward the only empty chair, at the foot.

As Hunter rounded the table, he paused to put out both hands and slap Manohar and Brian simultaneously in the back of the head. "You didn't warn me about the horse."

Brian lunged after him from his chair. Hunter instinctively sped up, jogged a step, then slowed to his customary saunter. He collapsed into the comfy chair at the end of the table as if the whole episode had taken a great deal out of him. Leaning over one armrest, he eyed the girl on his right from underneath the blond hair in his eyes and said loudly enough for the whole class to hear, "I'm so glad to be here." Guys laughed, girls giggled, and the entire chemistry of the quiet classroom had changed from scared freshmen to friendly writing class, just because Hunter had joined us.

Gabe was busying himself with administrative duties again. Copies of the stories had to be found for the additional student. The dude whose story we were reading today, Kyle, didn't have an extra copy of his story for Hunter. Neither did the other girl. I did, but hell if I was volunteering that information. No matter. The girl sitting next to Hunter, Isabelle, had already read the stories in the library, like we were all supposed to, and she slid her copies in front of him.

"I explained this," Gabe said, "but it bears repeating. When your story is being discussed, you are not to join the discussion. Creative writing tends to be very personal. We are more defensive of it than we realize. If you were allowed to respond to everything your fellow writers said about your work, discussion would quickly break down into an argument. You'll have a chance to respond to the critique, but only at the end."

Gabe was still talking. He was saying that we would discuss Kyle's story first, then the girl's. Ten minutes before, I would have been relieved that I wasn't absolutely first, but now the delay meant two-thirds of a class period of torture until Hunter read my story. I pretended to turn my attention to Kyle's story in front of me, but out of the corner of my eye I watched Hunter. He shuffled through the three stories. Paused over one, examining the title. Or the byline. Slipped it out of the stack and put it on the bottom.

I TRIED TO RESPOND INTELLIGENTLY TO the first two stories. I had read them in the library and made notes on them. They were not to my taste. Kyle's story was told from the point of view of a wolf whose ecosystem was disappearing, an environmental apocalypse tale, although I could tell from his description of the forest and his accent in class that he'd rarely explored past the boundaries of Brooklyn. The girl's story was about an old man sitting in a café and mulling over his regrets about things left undone in his life. I would have gone to sleep if the man hadn't been taking in so much caffeine. But constructive criticism was part of this class and part of our grade, so on behalf of the writing community and my internship, I did my best to say something helpful in a shaky voice that told Hunter my heart was doing acrobatics in anticipation of my turn.

Finally everyone slid "Almost a Lady" out of their short stacks and put it on top. My stomach dropped as if I'd just crested the tallest peak on a roller coaster and was about to barrel down the other side. Hunter's head was bent. If he hadn't been reading my story before, now he was.

"Manohar," Gabe said, "why don't you get us started?"

Manohar glanced up at me and smirked.

Uh-oh.

"First of all," he said, "I wanted to check something. Am I reading this right? Did this Captain 'Vanderslice'"—he made finger quotes—"get his family jewels shot off in the war? Isn't that stolen directly from Hemingway's *The Sun Also Rises?*"

"I beg your pardon," I said haughtily. "That's like saying you can't have somebody cross the street in your scene because James Joyce wrote about somebody crossing the street one time. All of literature and only one character can get shot in the nuts?"

Everyone around the table leaned in. I focused my anger on Manohar, but I could see the other students in my peripheral vision and feel them as the air in the room got hot. Only Hunter lounged in his rich chair, reading my story, cool as ever.

"Now you're using the term 'literature' very loosely," Manohar said, with more finger quotes. "It reads like a romance novel." He tossed imaginary long hair over his shoulder. " 'She saw him from across the room and knew he was the one for her, the stable boy.' "

"Do you read a lot of romance novels?" Summer asked him.

Several guys hooted with laughter. I would have smiled, too, if I had not been on my deathbed.

Manohar turned bright red, but he was laughing. "I—," he began.

Summer was not laughing. "Because you would base that judgment on something, right?"

I felt bad that she was talking out of turn instead of me, disobeying Gabe on my behalf. On the other hand, she was a lot cuter than me, and harder to be angry with. Manohar only tilted his head while she ranted.

"Everybody knows how a romance novel goes—," he began again.

"Not if they've never read one, they don't," she insisted.

He talked over her. "All I'm saying is that there's no place for that kind of crappy writing in an honors creative-writing class." His voice rose at the end of his statement because several girls gasped when he said *crappy*. "I know I'm not the only one in this class who thinks so. You're not supposed to write a romance novel for an honors creative-writing class."

"I didn't know that," I said, trying to keep my voice even, wishing the angry tears out of my eyes.

"How could you miss it?" he insisted. "In high school, didn't people make fun of you for writing romance novels? Even for reading them?"

"Of course they did." My hand pounded the table. Everyone jumped, including me. I removed my hand from the table and sat on it. "My mistake was assuming that when I got to college, people would not be such assholes. Heaven forbid I pursue a career writing romance novels. Romance is only fifty-three percent of the paperback market, and I would hate to earn a steady income while the rest of you are living in your parents' basements, writing novels about dead wolves—"

"Hey!" Kyle exclaimed.

"—getting rejected from *The New Yorker*, and cutting yourselves."

Two boys on the other side of Summer laughed together. I could see them over her head. One of them said a little too loudly in a faux drawl more reminiscent of Tennessee than Kentucky, "Heaven forbid!"

"You're assuming this is publishable," Manohar told me. He'd seemed cocksure before, a superior intellect cutting down a Southern girl in class. Now his black brows pointed down in a V. "This is not publishable. You could read it out loud and make a drinking game out of knocking one back every time it says *bosom*. And I don't think any story you turn in for an honors creative-writing class should contain even a single instance of the word *nipple*."

"Correct me if I'm wrong," I shouted over the laughter, "but there's nothing in the syllabus for this class that says we can't write *nipple*."

"Because that's understood!" Manohar exclaimed.

"Is it?" I asked. "Maybe you're just bothered by nipple personally."

"Everybody is bothered by nipple," he said, karate-chopping the thick table with each syllable. "Serious writers know this. You would not find a nipple in *The New Yorker*."

"She didn't write this story for *The New Yorker*," Summer said.

Manohar gestured widely with both arms. He hit Brian in the chest and didn't seem to notice. "Exactly!"

I shook my head. "I don't think this is about my story at all. I think it's about you, Manohar. I can tell that reading this story made you uncomfortable, and I wonder why that is. Either you're a very curious virgin, or you want a stable boy of your own."

Manohar's mouth dropped open. He didn't say anything. He didn't have to. All the guys in the class moaned, "Oooooooooooh!"

Except Brian, who raised his hand and said, "Um, no, that would be me."

And except Hunter. I was fairly certain Hunter hadn't joined the moaning. I dared not turn my head to look at him. My face burned with anger at Manohar, and shame that he'd made me lose my cool and attack him with a joke worthy of my grandmother's stables, and worry about what Hunter would say.

I read Gabe's lips rather than heard him. "We never discussed what kind of writing was acceptable for this class."

The students hushed themselves as if he'd stood up and banged his fist on the table, even though he'd spoken in his usual soft voice, like he was out having coffee with one of us and telling us about catching a wave in the Pacific. Now there was a little murmur of question: *What had Gabe said? Had he said something about Erin's kind of writing?* But nobody wanted to be the one to admit they hadn't been paying attention. After all, it was only our second class.

"To Erin's point," Gabe said, "there is no genre specified. I hope each of you will feel free to explore the kinds of stories that move you, and to hone your craft for your own purposes. To that end," he turned to Manohar, "our critiques of each other's work need to be constructive." He turned to me, and I tried not to shrink back. "And we need to respond to those critiques in a manner that leaves the floor open to honest communication."

The air was thick with tension, all eyes on me. If this had been high school, I would have sat there in silence and mortification.

But you know what? One year of age—I won't say maturity, considering how I'd just lost my temper, but at least age—had changed me. And the publishing internship was a carrot held just beyond my lips, motivating me. Gabe had been taking notes the whole time Manohar and I argued. I should have been more careful about what I said in front of him. I had written a story about Hunter and I didn't know whether he was going to blow my cover.

So I forced a smile and said, "Gabe, I'm truly sorry. I see now how I sounded, and I promise I'll do better next time. It's hard to be one of the first!"

He nodded, and Summer and some of the other girls laughed nervously. Manohar sneered down at my story.

I wrote INTERNSHIP in block letters in my notebook, as a reminder.

"Brian?" Gabe prompted. "What did you think of Erin's story?"

"I enjoyed it," Brian said. "That was some stable boy."

I swallowed and did not look at Hunter and doodled curlicues around INTERNSHIP.

The girl next to Brian said the first line of my story was the funniest thing she'd ever read. Beside her sat Kyle, the guy who'd written about the wolf. He said my first line ruined my whole story for him. The next two people made similarly contradictory and therefore useless comments, and then came Hunter.

But Gabe skipped right over Hunter to give him more time to read, and asked for commentary from Isabelle.

The remaining girls said they liked my story. The remaining guys did not. I didn't care anymore. My debut as a New York author was ruined already. Now I was only concerned with whether they'd noticed that the stable boy I'd written about was actually the stable boy sitting at the end of this very table. An uncanny likeness, they would say! An amazingly accurate description! Obviously written by someone infatuated with Hunter Allen!

But slowly I realized that nobody would figure out this story was about him. Nobody would suspect me of putting a character in my story who, one class period later, randomly showed up in the class. They wouldn't even know we knew each other.

Unless he told them.

Summer took her turn, rushing to my defense with such enthusiasm that it was clear she was speaking as my roommate, not as a fellow writer. "Oh, and one more thing." She looked straight at Manohar. "Nipple!"

The class laughed. I grinned at Summer and she beamed back at me. At that moment I loved her very much and almost forgave her for the brouhaha over my clothes earlier.

"Hunter, what did you think?" Gabe asked.

Everyone in the room looked at Hunter expectantly.

I looked down.

"Oh, I shouldn't comment," Hunter said, one side of his mouth curved up in a charming smile and one dimple showing.

I did not actually see this because I was staring down at David thumbing Rebecca's nipple. I did not have to see Hunter's charming smile to know it was there.

He went on, "I haven't had a chance to read it closely enough."

"You commented on the first two stories," Brian pointed out.

"They were shorter," Hunter said.

"This was a long story," Isabelle affirmed. "I nearly had a heart attack when I saw it in the library. It's thirteen pages long. For me, writing five is like pulling teeth."

Through the general murmur of approval that ensued about the wondrous length of "Almost a Lady," Manohar spoke to me across the table. "Congratulations. You have written a very long story."

I shot him the bird.

Gabe grabbed my hand, lowered it gently to the table, and patted it twice without looking at me. He cleared his throat. The class quieted, and he prompted again, "Hunter?"

Hunter had been talking to Isabelle. Now he glanced up at Gabe, then turned his shoulders deliberately to me and met my gaze. He smiled.

I had known Hunter for a long time. This wasn't his charming devil-may-care smile. It was tight and false.

He would never deliberately show it, but I suspected he was furious with me.

"Erin," he said, "I am from Long Island, but I've spent some time around Churchill Downs, in Louisville, and I've been to parties with horse people. You've captured that experience perfectly."

Isabelle said, "Her story's set in the eighteen hundreds."

Hunter nodded, eyes still on me. "The parties haven't changed."

"All right, Erin," Gabe murmured. "It's finally your turn to talk."

I opened my lips. I'd had so much to say in defense of my story thirty seconds before. But I could not think of a single retort with Hunter watching me through those clear blue eyes, wearing that tight smile. He had never been to a race party as far as I knew.

The closest he'd come was the night of the Derby last May, when he whistled to me from the yard and handed me my music player and earbuds, which I'd left on the shelf in the stable office. Now he was reminding me that my horse farm was his now. My horses, my house, my parties. Over the summer he'd probably thrown the parties himself.

I looked down and drew fireworks exploding out of INTERNSHIP. "I said everything I wanted to say when I spoke out of turn."

"You're sure?" Gabe asked me. "Going once, going twice . . ."

I bit my lip and nodded.

"It's a big deal to go first," Gabe addressed the whole table, "and I think all these authors deserve a round of applause."

There was applause, and cheering, and somebody shouted, "Nipple!"

"Write hard," Gabe said, "and I'll see you Thursday."

Chair legs raked back on the hardwood floor. Everyone burst into the conversations they'd been too repressed to have with each other on their way into class—before Hunter had arrived to loosen them up. Amid this bustle of leaving, Gabe inhaled deeply through his nose, portly chest expanding. He fished a tie-dyed bandanna out of his pocket and touched it to his forehead.

"Aw"—I was about to say "Gabe" but stopped myself since I still wasn't sure what to call him—"is that because of me? I'm very sorry to make you mop your brow."

He chuckled. "The first critique session is always the hardest. And some semesters are harder than others. I'll make it. Don't worry about me." He was still smiling as he slid me his copy of "Almost a Lady," rolled out of his chair, and left the room. But I wondered: did he mean I should be worried instead about myself, my writing, my grade, my career?

As people passed behind me to escape the room, they dropped

their copies of my story in front of me. Normally I would have paged through them immediately to read the comments, even though I'd be late for work. But I needed to speak with Hunter. And he was flirting with Isabelle. I strained to hear them over the babble of other voices.

"Calculus is kicking my ass," he told her.

"Going too fast for you?" she teased him.

"No, it looks vaguely familiar from high school. This TA, I don't know where he's from, but . . ."

"He has a very interesting accent in English?"

"Was he speaking English? I honestly do not know."

Isabelle laughed. "Complain. He shouldn't have been put in front of a class if his students can't understand him."

"I don't want to be the one who strips this guy of his fellowship."

Yeah, right, play the empathy card. Hunter was good at making people think he cared, until he stabbed them in the back.

"Get one of those computer programs that teaches you a foreign language," Isabelle suggested.

"That would be a really good idea if I knew what language he was speaking."

Hunter was funny. This was a funny conversation I should have been having with him instead of this bitch, and who did she think she was?

Standing, I forced the copies of "Almost a Lady" into my book bag along with my thirty-pound calculus book and my fifty-pound book for early American literature survey (not my favorite period, lots of puritanical preaching about virtue, bleh!) and my laptop. Manohar was standing next to his chair, too, watching me and still smirking at me.

I dropped my book bag in my chair and leaned across the table so swiftly that he stepped back. I managed not to laugh that I'd spooked him. I extended my hand. "No hard feelings," I told him. "I don't agree with your critique, but I do appreciate it."

I think he took my hand only because he was so surprised. "No problem," he said. Then he seemed to recover, and he grasped my hand hard enough to hurt. "I'm sorry if I was out of line."

I pulled my hand out of his grip. "Don't be. I carry a grudge. If you write some macho ultraviolent action-adventure crap for your first story, your ass is mine."

I had thought Summer was deep in discussion with the guy next to her, but when I said this she shrieked with laughter, then giggled a quiet "Sorry" and turned back to the other guy.

"Game on, Kentucky," Manohar told me. Grinning as if he really did look forward to the game (that made one of us), he shrugged one strap of his backpack over his shoulder and walked out.

Isabelle had finally left Hunter's side. I hefted my bulging book bag and walked the length of the table. Hunter sat in his mighty chair like the head of the table rather than the foot, writing on his copy of my story. As I approached, he looked up and offered it to me. He didn't smile as he said, "Hullo, Miss Blackwell."

Taking the story from him, I noticed for the first time that his five-o'clock stubble glinted golden on his hard chin. I croaked, "Hullo, Hunter."

He smiled then, the charismatic smile I recognized from school. "Thanks for not blowing my cover about being from Louisville. I told my roommates I'm from Long Island."

"Why?" I asked. *'Cause that is kind of strange, considering that you have stolen my Louisville horse farm,* I wanted to add. I traced the s from INTERNSHIP with my fingertip on the thigh of my jeans and kept my mouth shut.

"Because people here think that the South is stupid," he said. "Besides, I really am from Long Island."

I frowned at him and turned around to make sure everyone else in the room had left. Only Summer waited for me outside the door, leaning against the frame and talking to Brian. I faced Hunter again and said softly, "You moved from Long Island to Kentucky before the seventh grade."

"I never felt like I belonged there."

Until now. There was so much irony in the unspoken words between us. Somehow I had to step past it and connect with him.

"I overheard you complaining about your calculus instructor," I said. "As long as you're rearranging your schedule, maybe you could transfer into my class. I have to go to work now, so I can't stay and tell you about it—"

This was a flimsy excuse. It would have taken me an additional thirty seconds to give him my instructor's name and class time.

"—but I take a break at nine. If you want to come by, I'd be glad to talk with you. I'm at the coffee shop on the corner of—"

He nodded. "I know the one. I've seen you there. I'll come by at nine."

He'd seen me there? I hadn't seen him since graduation night, when he and my grandmother delivered the blow.

I wanted so badly to slap him. Or kiss him. But there was no physical show of the emotion passing between us, layer upon layer, the upper strata putting the lower ones under enormous pressure. I simply turned and left the classroom, "Almost a Lady" flopping about in front of me.

But I would need to mine those layers when I met him alone. I had to shut him up before he said anything about me and my stable boy to Gabe. I could not let Hunter Allen ruin my life.

Again.

3

"I can't believe you!" Summer exclaimed.

"Really?" I gave her a wary glance as I passed her in the hallway outside the classroom. I hoped she would follow me down the stairs. Brian had disappeared, but Hunter, sitting at the foot of the table, could still hear us.

"Yes, really!" She followed me down the stairs. "You are an attack dog. I've seen you in action. I'll never forget how you barked at that cabdriver the other day."

"You have to bark at cabdrivers or they'll take advantage of you." Actually, I had never talked to a cabdriver before, because I'd never had the money to take a cab. But right after I'd met Summer four days ago, I'd agreed to splurge and share a cab to MoMA with her, and ended up arguing with the cabbie about the expensive fare. Ever since, I had wished for that money back.

"But we start discussing your story and you melt down?" Summer asked. We'd reached the bottom of the staircase, and she pushed through the door ahead of me, onto the street. The twilight surprised me—as always. In Kentucky at this time, an hour of daylight would have remained, gently retreating across the grassy hills, into the trees at the edge of the western pasture. Here the five-story buildings created an artificial canyon, walls blocking out the sun. Night came early.

Summer didn't seem to notice. She was on me. "I had to come to your defense. Gabe finally gave you a chance to talk and you didn't say a thing. If I didn't know you, I'd say that at one point, that ass Manohar made you cry! You must have had something in your eye."

"Must have." I glanced back at the entrance to the building to make sure Hunter hadn't followed us. Then I pointed her down the sidewalk in the direction of the coffee shop. My five minutes of damage control with Hunter had already made me late. There was no leeway in my schedule.

"I don't want you to get discouraged because of somebody like him," she insisted. I was walking fast, and she had to skip to keep up with me. People hurrying home from work sidestepped us and watched the commotion out of the corners of their eyes as they passed us. "You're going to finish writing the whole novel, right?"

"No."

"Why not?" she insisted. "I loved that story! All the girls in the class did, not that you listened to their comments. After Manohar was so harsh, you were in outer space. You only heard the negative comments. I was watching you. Your ears pricked up when Wolf-boy Kyle said he hated your first line. But a lot of us enjoyed your story. Why don't you finish the novel and try to get it published? Forget Manohar."

"The market for historical romances is tighter than it used to be."

She shrugged. "I'm sure they still publish brand-new authors."

"Right, if those authors play by the rules. For a new writer trying to break in, that's very important. 'Almost a Lady' doesn't follow the rules."

"What's the matter with it?" She sounded genuinely curious, but as she asked, she twisted her neck to look up at the tops of the buildings. Nothing said *Southern* like her awe, and I hoped she got over it before she made me look like a hick by association.

"A historical heroine needs to be all innocent and virtuous and shit," I told her. "She can't just want some like Rebecca. And my hero, David, is completely wrong. A historical hero can't be the same age as the heroine. He's a lot older. He is respected in the community—or he *would* be respected, if only he had not been unjustly suspected of murder."

"What?" Summer was listening now.

"That's how these stories go," I said. "But the historical hero will be cleared of the murder in the course of the story. Maybe the heroine will help him with that—at her peril! And the historical hero has tons of money. He might have inherited a title, too, because historicals are generally set in England in the eighteen hundreds. Setting it in America is asking for a rejection. So is making the hero a stable boy."

"Then why'd you write it that way? I thought you were trying to get a novel published."

"I wrote the story that's been in my head." I took a deep breath and finished with, "Hunter is the stable boy."

"Hold that thought. I saw a rat." She darted into the side street we were passing, toward a Dumpster. "My first New York rat!" she called to me over her shoulder. "He's so cute!"

"Watch out," I called back. "They jump."

The adorable varmint must have jumped at her by then because she came screaming out of the street. She reached up and shook me by both shoulders. "Why didn't you warn me?"

"Because you were chasing a rat, telling me how cute it was."

She let my shoulders go but continued to scowl up at me. "Hunter is the stable boy? I thought David was the stable boy."

At the mention of Hunter, New York City sharpened for me: The blue street tattooed with faded yellow lines. A building of brown brick on one side of the street and another of gray marble on the other. Small trees planted in the sidewalk, leaves already blushing red in mid-September. A shop window reflecting my hair, a blur of orange in the midst of the city. I had thought my summer here had been the experience of a lifetime, but the mere thought of Hunter intensified it—because he had almost taken it away from me. And he could take it away now.

"Come on," I called to Summer. "I'm going to be late." When she trotted beside me again, three steps to my two, I explained, "David is the stable boy in my story. He is modeled on Hunter, from class. Hunter of the piercing blue eyes and dreamy good looks and the invisible horse."

"Oh, Hunter!" She slapped both hands over her mouth, then moved them to gasp, "How did this happen? You met him in the dorm and based this character on him, thinking he would never read it because he wasn't in our class? How mortifying!"

"Not exactly," I muttered. "I mean, yes, it's mortifying, but I knew him before."

She squinted up at me. "From your summer here?"

We'd come to the edge of the park, where two police horses, a chestnut and a gray, were tied several lengths apart. While they waited, they whinnied to each other to reassure themselves that they weren't alone in this strange city.

I felt a pang, and a sudden drive to touch a horse, to run my fingers across a tough coat. I would get arrested.

I turned away from the horses and swallowed. "No, from home."

"In Kentucky?" she shrieked. "But when he introduced himself in class, he said he's from here. Long Island!"

I nodded. "His dad used to work with the horses out at Belmont. That's why my grandmother hired his dad in the first place. He and Hunter moved to our farm when Hunter and I were in middle school."

"You mean, they moved to your town and worked on your farm? No, you mean they actually moved to your farm, don't you? Oh my God."

"Well, we have small houses for the stable hands, and it was just the two of them. Most families wouldn't want to live on the farm, but they did."

"You have small houses for the stable hands," she repeated in disbelief.

"Hunter and I were friends at first, and then our parents had a falling-out." I shook my head to keep from dwelling on that awful night. "He and I avoided each other for the rest of the summer. And when school started in the fall, somebody figured out that his dad worked for my grandmother, and that Hunter helped out at the farm, too, sometimes, and everybody started calling him . . . wait for it . . ."

"Stable boy," Summer intoned. Then she grabbed my arm. "I was right! You're Rebecca from your story! You're loaded!"

"Was loaded," I murmured.

"But Hunter's loaded, too," Summer insisted. "He was wearing a Rolex."

"I noticed. That was a nice touch on my grandmother's part. What happened was—"

She looked at me as she stepped forward. I saw movement beyond her shoulders. In a flash I threw my arm in front of her just before she walked off the curb and into the path of a taxi.

"Hey," she complained. Then she saw the taxi. Her eyes widened. "Whoa."

I put my hand to my heart and breathed through my nose to calm the adrenaline rush. "Be more alert until you're used to walking around the city," I scolded her. "Accidents happen."

"Everybody at my high school talked about a girl who was newspaper editor there a long time ago," Summer exclaimed. "She went to New York City on scholarship and got killed in a crosswalk by a taxi her first day. I was almost that girl!"

"My high school told the same story," I assured her. "It's an urban myth designed to scare you and keep you at home. Just look both ways before crossing the street, okay?"

She blinked at the traffic whizzing in front of us until the light changed and we stepped into the crosswalk. "What happened was . . . ," she prompted me.

I glanced up the street again, paranoid now about speeding taxis. We were crossing Fifth Avenue. The five-story town houses grew into elegant twenty-story hotels here, carved stonework on every corner of the buildings. Ten blocks up, the Empire State Building, already glowing white against the pink sky, peeked around the shoulders of the smaller buildings in front of it.

I stepped up on the opposite curb. "When my grandmother was our age, she earned her business degree here in New York so she could run her family's horse farm. She wanted me to do the same and take over someday."

"I thought you're majoring in English," Summer protested.

"I am. A few days before high school graduation, I admitted to her that I did want to come to college here, but I would not major in business. I would major in English so I could write romance novels."

"And she freaked?" Summer asked.

"My grandmother does not freak." I felt my nostrils flare as I thought of her. "She waited until graduation night, when I'd come home to change between the ceremony and the parties. She called me into her office. Hunter was already there. She informed me that she didn't need me anyway. Since blood clearly was not thicker than water, she would give Hunter my college money. He would major in business here, then run the horse farm. And when she dies, he will inherit the horse farm for his loyalty."

"What!" Summer squealed. But she had to step behind me, single file. We'd reached a portion of the sidewalk with scaffolding overhead so the construction workers in the building didn't brain pedestrians with falling cement blocks.

I kept talking over my shoulder as I entered the passageway packed with people forming two lanes of traffic. "The worst part is, I should have seen it coming. Our high school classmates would mention going to the University of Louisville or the University of Kentucky. Hunter would always shake his head and say, 'I am getting out of here.'"

The passageway narrowed to one lane. A huge puddle from last night's rain blocked half the width of the sidewalk, cigarette butts and a fortune cookie wrapper floating at the edge like timid waders in a cold ocean. "So it doesn't make sense to me that he would accept my grandmother's offer to take over the farm," I said as I pushed my way through the crowd around the puddle. "Yes, he'll get a free education, and he's getting out of Kentucky for a few years. But then he'll have to go back. For the rest of his life. Knowing how he feels about Kentucky, I'm astounded he would agree to this plan. Even for money. Even for her."

It had been a while since Summer had interrupted me, which was unusual. Standing firm against people shoving me. I looked back and saw she was stuck on the other side of the puddle, politely waiting for a break in the oncoming pedestrians.

"Go ahead," the sari-clad woman behind Summer scolded her in a singsong accent, "else we'll be here all day."

I stepped back into the current of the crowd, let it sweep me back to Summer, and grabbed her by the wrist. I pulled her roughly against the current, ignoring the mean looks of other pedestrians. My book bag socked one man in the shoulder and he told me sharply to watch it. I held fast to Summer's hand and dragged her out from under the scaffolding. We popped into the open twilight. She sighed with relief. I suppressed my own sigh.

"How long did it take you to change from a nice, normal Southerner to a hardened New Yorker?" she demanded.

"A couple of hours, but I was living in a tiny two-bedroom

apartment in Hell's Kitchen with five roommates." I glanced at my own cheap watch—I'd left my Rolex in my jewelry box at my grandmother's house. I was way late for work. I increased my stride, and Summer practically ran beside me.

"During the summer, I worked two jobs and socked away money. I was too busy to dwell on what my grandmother and Hunter did. But in the past week, I've started obsessing about Hunter. I knew he was here. I suspected he was in the honors program and lived in our honors dorm. Maybe I even entertained a little fantasy that we could hook up, which would somehow solve all our problems rather than making them worse. I wrote the story to indulge that fantasy. I had no idea he was going to show up in the class."

Though the coffee shop was in sight now, I stopped on the sidewalk and turned to Summer in exasperation, remembering what she'd done. "I tried to keep him out of the class, Miss 'Can I Have Erin's Vote'! We've got to develop a better silent language if we're going to be friends. When I groan like I'm dying, that means, 'Don't let the hunk into the creative-writing class. My story is about him.'"

Summer winced. "I'm sorry. And you're sorry. You can apologize to him."

"I don't care about him," I lied. "I care about winning the publishing internship I told you about."

"Oh, no!" She slapped her hands over her mouth. She knew how badly I needed that internship.

"I don't want Hunter to tell Gabe he is the stable boy," I explained, "because then Gabe will think I'm not serious about this creative-writing class. All Hunter has to do is open his mouth and he will ruin every chance I ever had at that job!"

"Don't cry in the street," she whispered, stepping close to me. "They say it attracts muggers."

That's when I realized my voice had escalated into a hysterical wail that echoed against the glass storefronts. Businesspeople never even glanced at me as they hurried past. I looked all around us and made sure Hunter was not among them. He was not.

"I'm meeting him at the coffee shop at nine," I told Summer, "to try to persuade him not to say anything to Gabe about it. But I'm not like you. People look at you and want to go over to your side and help you. People look at me and want to win whatever game they're playing with me."

I'd half-hoped I was wrong about this, but Summer did not deny it. "Only because you're so strong-willed. You ask for trouble. It's a good sign that Hunter agreed to meet you, at least. That means he can't be too mad at you."

"Yes, he can. Hunter can be furious with you, but he will still be polite." Just like my grandmother.

I was late. I gave Summer a wave and called over my shoulder, "Thanks for listening!" as I dashed across the street and into the employee entrance of the shop. Dropping my book bag and ducking through the neck hole of my apron, I hollered, "I know! I'm late! I'm really sorry!" at the same time my boss shouted, "You're late, Blackwell! We talked about this!"

Hastily I tied my apron strings behind my waist and headed up front to the counter. Minimum wage jobs were a dime a dozen in New York. I'd already held seven of them. But hunting for another would cost me time and money—money I couldn't afford to lose, especially if Hunter decided to ruin my life.

Again.

I STEAMED MILK AND POURED COFFEE for hours before business slowed enough for me to take a peek at the copies of "Almost a Lady" burning a hole in the bottom of my book bag. I wasn't supposed to do homework in the shop. My boss would probably lump reading comments about my story into that category, rather than the category in which this activity belonged: the *Someday When I Am a Best-selling Author You Can Take Your Soy Milk and Shove It* category.

But this time I didn't care what he thought. He was in the back of the shop, and this was important.

First I read Gabe's copy of my story because his comments mattered most. I closed my eyes for a moment and allowed myself to frame what I wanted him to say about my writing. I had used this technique a lot during the summer. If I pictured myself successful, I was more likely to find success. Every time I had done this over the summer, I had opened my eyes still unpublished, still poor, living with five dirty roommates, and about to get fired from my job walking dogs. Hope springs eternal, though, and before I read Gabe's comments on my story, I envisioned him raving about my writing and suggesting that I apply for the publishing internship. *Oh, really?* I would say. *I hadn't thought of that!*

I opened my eyes and flipped through my story. Not one slash of bloodred pen stabbed my prose. Page after page was clean. He'd reserved his comments for the blank half of the last page, where he'd scribbled in soft pencil:

Erin,

I have read many stories for freshman honors creative writing classes. Compared with the talents of past students, your grasp of dialogue and pacing is remarkable. You have a gift, and you have worked hard at honing it. I look forward to reading what you write for the rest of the semester and seeing how far you can push this.

As for Rebecca . . . I had difficulty connecting with her and caring about her because you never say what she wants out of life. It isn't just the stable boy.

My cheeks tingled as if Gabe had slapped me. In the back of my mind I knew he'd given me a compliment of some sort in his first paragraph, but I registered only the insult in the second. Of course all Rebecca wanted was the stable boy. That was the whole point. What did Gabe want her to want? Was I supposed to make her a girl alone in the world, struggling to make ends meet in the big city? What a Theodore Dreiser–ass laugh-and-a-half that would be.

Feeling that I was being watched, I snapped my head up. I would have thought the shop was funky and adorable with its mismatched chairs, exposed brick walls, and art from students at my college, exactly the type of place I'd always wanted to work, except that my boss had yelled at me enough here in the past two weeks to ruin that effect.

The shop was empty. My coworker for the shift had disappeared into the back along with my boss, and not a single passerby wanted caffeine at this time of night.

I put my head back down. While my stomach was tied in a knot, I might as well read Hunter's comments, too. I sifted through the stack of "Almost a Lady" until I came to his copy, which he'd commandeered from Isabelle and signed his name across like it was his, not hers, not mine. Paging through it, I saw there was a lot of writing in blue pen on a page near the end of the story, his scrawl almost illegible, like he'd already been in business for himself for forty-five years and if other people couldn't read it, that was their problem. I kept flipping through and saw nothing else, even on the backs of the pages. I returned to the offending page. He'd circled "I saw a snake eat a rat once" and scribbled in the margin,

> *David would not say this. It's gauche. He would not utter a sexually loaded metaphor at the risk of repulsing a lady. In*

fact, he would not risk his job, his father's job, and this "country justice" you mention for a girl in the first place. He has other girls.

"What are you thinking so hard about?"

I jerked my head up at Hunter's voice. He stood at the counter, blond hair in his blue eyes, watching me. I wondered how long he'd been there, and whether my lips had mouthed "ouch" as I read.

I shoved the stack of papers under the counter. He might have seen what I was reading and recognized his handwriting, though. So I admitted, "I was thinking I'm not going to enjoy freshman honors creative writing as much as I expected."

"Give yourself a break and a little time," he said in the soothing tone girls loved. "You're invested in that class, and you had a hard first critique."

What nice advice, and how innocuous. Clearly he was editing himself, just as he'd said David would have left out any sexual metaphors when easing a glove into Rebecca's reticule.

I could have asked Hunter what variety of caffeine he wanted. I didn't. I shooed him to a table at the window looking out on the neon-lit street, then whipped him up a latte. That's the drink with the foamy head that a talented barista makes a design in, like a flower or a delicate palm frond. Note that I said *talented barista*, not *chick who had been working in a coffee shop for two weeks*. I had been shown how to make a heart. The bottom of it came out too rounded, and when I turned it upside down, it looked like an ass.

I poured a cup of black for myself, slid Hunter's heart latte from the counter, and called to my boss that I was taking my break. I started from behind the counter and across the floor of the shop with full confidence. But as I neared Hunter, I realized that besides class, this was the first time I would be facing him since graduation night in Kentucky, when he stood behind my grandmother.

He turned from the window and focused those blue eyes on me. I slowed down. My heart thumped so loudly in my chest that I was afraid he would hear it if I sat down across from him. Note to self: I should not snag so much coffee while working in the coffee shop if the ticker went into palpitations every time a stable boy gave me a glance. As I sat down across from him with my cup of black, I pushed the latte across the table to him, ass cheeks down.

Only then did I realize the significance of bringing Hunter a latte with a heart drawn in the foam after I had just gotten it on with him fictionally. I should have attempted the palm frond.

It was too late then. But he didn't notice the heart—at least, not right away. He looked out the window and tapped his toes under the table as if he was anxious to leave. This was so unlike him. He looked comfortable in every situation, whether he wanted to be there or not. The charm was always on.

A bell tinkled. Laughing students pushed through the coffee shop door and approached the counter. Hunter followed them with his eyes and then finally, painfully slowly, looked down at his mug. He frowned at it and turned it around on the saucer, trying to figure out what the picture was. "Oh!" he exclaimed. "How appropriate. You drew me a little heart."

"It's an ass."

He tilted his head to one side to get a different view of it. He spun the mug around into its original position. "I see now." He winked at me. "What you mean is, it was supposed to be a heart, but you realized too late that drawing me a heart in my latte would be embarrassing after I read your story."

4

He had a strange way of pronouncing *coffee,* with a rounded *o.* He'd never had much of a New York accent, not even when he first moved to Kentucky. It only came out with certain words. I found myself dwelling on this to keep from running from the shop in mortification.

"No, the picture in your coffee is an ass," I blurted in defense. "I also draw a mean spleen."

His eyebrows moved up ever so slightly—one of the few ways I could tell I'd gotten to him. "Can you do a liver?" he asked. "With bile?"

This talk was not going as I had planned. To convince him to keep his mouth shut about the stable boy, I needed to be nice. I wished I could write INTERNSHIP on the surface of my coffee in foamed milk as a reminder.

I grinned at him with all the pretend friendliness I could muster. My cheeks hurt. "Give me another week of training. I've been working here for only two."

His brows went down. "I thought you took a bus up here the day after graduation. My dad told me he drove you to the bus station."

You mean the day after you stole my life, I thought, grinning hard. Out loud I said, "I did. First I worked at a deli, but they were always trying to tell me what to do, which takes some getting used to."

I meant it as a joke, but Hunter didn't laugh. He just blinked at me across the rim of his coffee cup.

"Then I heard about a dog-walking job," I hurried on. "That didn't work out."

"Why not?" Hunter asked. "You love animals." He sounded as if he was trying to convince me.

"Dogs aren't horses," I told him. "But they *should* have bits in their mouths." I held my hand in a claw beside my mouth to represent a horse's bit.

Hunter looked blankly at my hand and then at me as if he did not get it.

I put my hand down. "I loved my job at the library, but I got fired when they caught me with weed."

He gaped at me. "Erin Elizabeth Blackwell!"

I dismissed his concerns with one hand, nearly knocking over my coffee. "It wasn't my weed. I had a lot of roommates and they were a mess. One of them hid his weed in my book bag and then forgot about it. Getting fired was the last straw. I was lucky I got fired, not arrested! I stomped all the way back to the apartment building, but as I stood on the sidewalk looking up at the window, scripting my dramatic exit from the apartment, I thought, *Where am I going to go?*"

I was back in the street that hot and lonely day in July, neck aching from looking up, eyes stinging from tears. Summer and Jørdis had complained for the past few days about living in the dorm, the crowding, the noise. I did not complain. Five dirty roommates had taught me the value of two clean ones.

"Are you sure you weren't smoking just a little?" Hunter touched his thumb and finger to his lips, toking up.

"I don't have time for that!"

His blue eyes opened wide. I realized that my hands were

open wide, too, gesticulating in exasperation. I was still caught in that horrible July day. I needed to get my mind out of there. This conversation with Hunter was a completely different horrible situation, and I was not as desperate as I'd been back then. Not yet.

I cleared my throat. "Do you want the info on my section of calculus?"

"Yes," he said quickly. "These sections are a crapshoot. If I'm not careful, I could transfer out of Eastern Europe, straight into Thailand." He produced the latest-model cell phone, a giant step up from the bare-bones model he'd carried back home. As I gave him the name of the class instructor and the time, he entered the info with his thumbs. Several times his thumbs stumbled and the muscles of his strong jaw clenched, which was Hunter's way of muttering "fuck" in frustration. Either he'd just gotten this phone and wasn't used to it yet, or he was truly out of sorts.

"Why are you taking calculus anyway?" I asked. "Shouldn't you be in business math, since you're majoring in business?"

"Same reason you're in calculus when you're majoring in English." He ended his data-entering session with an especially forceful hammering of his thumb, and dropped the phone into his backpack. "The university doesn't want honors students taking easy A's."

"It might be an easy A, but business math would still make sense for a business major," I reasoned.

He rotated his neck until it popped. "Why are you taking belly dancing? That makes no sense for an English major."

I felt a flash of suspicion. How did he know I was taking belly dancing? But he'd also known where I worked before I told him. He must have seen me around in the past week without my seeing him. Clearly we'd been circling each other.

"I'm taking belly dancing because I can," I said casually. "But if you're taking calculus, you're missing out on a business math class you need for your major. I looked at the catalog. I actually considered majoring in business like my grandmother wanted me to."

This time he reacted. There was no other way to describe it. He seemed very surprised. And since Hunter never showed his surprise, I was more convinced than ever that there was something wrong with him. "You did?" he asked.

"Yes, for about five seconds."

Recovering his cool, he took a slow sip of his latte, watching me over the rim of his cup as if waiting for a sign from me that I'd slipped in some poison. "Not that you would know this," he said, setting his cup back down, "but running a horse farm is extremely complicated. It involves more than adding columns of numbers. I need to know the derivative of Horse of Course and the linear transformation of Boo-boo."

I was sipping my own coffee, and I hoped the cup hid my face as I winced. Boo-boo was my horse.

Hunter leaned forward and looked straight at me. "This stable boy needs an education."

If Hunter never showed surprise, he never, ever showed anger. And right now he seemed angry with me. Despite my stomach twisting into knots, I nonchalantly took another sip of coffee as if I were calmly considering him. I'd put this off long enough.

"Hunter," I began, "I'm truly sorry about the stable-boy business in my story. I hope you didn't take it the wrong way."

He watched me steadily, his brows down in what I could have sworn was barely controlled outrage. I noticed for the first time that the rims of his eyes were red. "What way did you want me to take it, Erin?"

My fingertips hurt from pressing hard against my hot mug. "Maybe I had you on my mind because I assumed you might live in my dorm or register for some of my classes. But I never intended for you to read my story. I wasn't baiting you, if that's what you think."

He continued to stare me down. Between my hot face and the coffee below my chin, I felt like I was sitting in a sauna.

Finally I asked, "Why are you angry with me?"

He sat back in his chair. "Why do you say I'm angry?"

"I can tell. For some reason, you're slipping a little."

He gave me a wry smile. "I'm angry because what you've done is insulting. There are only two possibilities. First, you knew I was going to be in that class, and you wrote that story deliberately to mess with me. But the story was dated several days ago and I just transferred classes today. I don't see how you could have known."

"I didn't know," I assured him. Boy, didn't I.

"Which brings us to the other possibility. You wrote the first assignment of your creative-writing degree about me. Which means I was on your mind. Which means you liked me in middle school and high school, just like Rebecca carried a torch for David, through six years of those asshole kids at school calling me your stable boy, and you never said a thing."

I could hardly believe what I was hearing. Not only was he angry, he was also admitting for the first time that he cared how people talked about him in relation to me. This scared me. When Hunter and I had started seventh grade, he was the new kid at my school. I could have made things easier on him and introduced him to my friends. I didn't. I pretended he didn't exist. That probably contributed to the asshole kids making fun of him when they found out he was living on the grounds at my farm.

And I had always felt guilty about that. But right after what happened between our parents, I could hardly look at him, much less maintain the friendship we'd started or pal around with him at school. I still couldn't talk about it. My own anger welled up in defense.

"I don't understand why you think there are only two possibilities for what is going on in my mind," I seethed, "when we are not even friends. Sounds like an oversimplification on your part, to make yourself feel better about what you're doing. Even you would feel bad about stealing the birthright of a girl who had a soul. But as long as I'm a shallow girl, starkly drawn in black and white, hell, steal away."

Color crept into his cheeks underneath his tan. "I am not stealing anything. Not yet."

"Oh, yeah?" I challenged him. "What time is it?"

Reflexively he glanced at his Rolex. Score!

I struck again. "Where'd you get the money for the outrageously expensive T-shirt you're wearing? Did I drop it in Boo-boo's stall before I left home? Because the last I checked, you were shopping across the river in Indiana, at the thrift store next to the mall, just to make sure you didn't wear something to school that one of your friends had thrown out." I had passed by the parking lot and seen the farm truck my grandmother let him drive to school. I knew what was going on.

I'd pushed him too far, and I held my breath for his reaction. I'd never seen him lose his cool completely. Now I was about to see it at my workplace and get fired from my job again.

His glare zeroed in on me. His jaw hardened—

And then he laughed. He threw back his head and let out rich, rumbly, boy chuckles as if I was the funniest girl in the world and I made him happy.

Hunter losing himself in laughter—this I had seen. But he used it strategically, as when the high school chemistry teacher or the president of the bank or the guidance counselor helping him apply to this college was the one making the joke.

I asked him suspiciously, "Have you been drinking?"

He beamed at me. "Drinking?"

"Did you go out drinking after the writing class?"

He shrugged. "Manohar and Brian and I had a few beers."

I thought he'd had more than a few beers. "And when you had a few beers with Manohar and Brian," oh God, I could just picture the guffawing, "what did you chat about?"

He maintained that same politely jovial expression, like he couldn't quite catch what I was saying.

I gripped the edge of the table with both hands. "You didn't chat about stable boys, did you?"

He grinned at the ceiling. "I might have mentioned it."

"Hunter." I gazed down at my mostly full mug of crude oil, stomach sinking. "That's what I wanted to talk to you about."

"Really?" His handsome face wore an ironic smirk. "I thought you wanted to talk to me about calculus."

I felt like such a fool. I'd psyched myself up for this conversation, worried over it because it mattered so much, and he'd prepared by getting buzzed. I said gravely, "I think I have a shot at the publishing internship they award at the end of the semester. It would take a lot of pressure off me. But to get it, I need to do well in this class. I need Gabe to take me seriously. I don't want him to find out there's a real stable boy."

Hunter picked up his mug. He tipped it ever so slightly toward him. I could still see the surface of his latte, and I watched him suck the heart into his mouth.

"You're going into business with my grandmother," I said. "I know you want to leave the stable boy behind. I'm trying to leave that whole life behind and get out of your way. The internship will help me do that."

His tongue peeked out of his mouth. He licked a bit of the foam heart off his upper lip.

"I know you're angry with me, Hunter, and I understand why. But I honestly never meant to offend you. My only real crime is to step aside and give you a stab at millions of dollars and a hundred and forty-two horses."

"A hundred and forty-seven," he corrected me. Of course they'd bought and sold and bred them over the summer. Because he was buzzed, he couldn't resist reminding me that the farm went on without me.

He set his mug down. "I won't tell Gabe."

I ignored his patronizing tone. I was growing more desperate by the minute. "Don't tell anyone else, either. It might get back to Gabe."

The corner of his mouth quirked into a smile. "I won't."

"And ask Manohar and Brian not to spread it around."

"I'll ask. I can't promise anything. You may owe them a favor."

I stared dumbly at him. He was blatantly toying with me now. Hunter was very persuasive. He could have convinced Manohar and Brian of anything if he'd wanted to. He did not want to.

And what kind of favor could I possibly do for them? Unlike last spring when I could have gotten them admitted to the Churchill Downs clubhouse, I had no clout, no money, nothing left to offer.

Maybe that was Hunter's point.

I'd done all I could do to save my internship, though. My boss was standing at the counter, reminding me that my break time was almost over. I raked back my chair. "Thank you, Hunter. And again, I'm really sorry about this. I know we both wish we could go back to enjoying New York and pretending each other didn't exist." I reached for my mug to take it back to the counter with me.

Before my fingers touched the ceramic, Hunter grabbed my hand and gazed up at me.

I hated how my body responded as if he were my boyfriend, not my classmate or even my sworn enemy. Maybe heat would have shot across my chest regardless because he was handsome, confident, a force of nature. But I was afraid I had done most of this damage to myself. In real life we hadn't engaged in a friendly conversation since the summer before the seventh grade, save one sparkling night last May. But in my mind I'd already written *Almost a Lady,* the entire novel. In my mind, we'd slept together.

His hand still squeezed my hand. His thumb swept across my palm, and as I watched, the pupils dilated in his bright blue eyes. I wondered whether in his mind we'd slept together, too.

He released my hand and nodded toward my chair. "Sit down another sec. Your grandmother wanted me to bring you something you left at home." He reached around for his backpack.

Obediently I collapsed into my chair because my legs felt weak, and because I really did need him on my side. But I said quickly, "I don't want it."

He broke into a playboy grin, as if we were flirting instead of dancing around a sensitive topic. "How do you know you don't want it? You haven't even seen what it is."

"Whatever it is, I left it on purpose."

He pulled it from his backpack and placed it on the table between us. My music player and earbuds.

The last time he'd handed me my music player, at my grandmother's Derby party last May, he'd saved me from a convo with Whitfield Farrell, a twenty-one-year-old college dropout who would inherit the famous farm next door. Whitfield was widely known for his drunken exploits at the horse parties, and widely rumored to want in my pants. My grandmother had ordered me to be nice to him because she did business with his dad.

So Whitfield put his hand on my ass. I was not far from slapping him and then taking whatever punishment my grandmother dished out, when Hunter tapped on the window and held up my music player, which I'd left in the barn. When he saw I couldn't get away from Whitfield, he came inside the mansion. Made a big commotion of it, too, stomping in his stable boots across the antique Persian rug. Whitfield wandered away to find another bourbon. Hunter watched him go, then turned to me. And he flirted with me like he would flirt with any girl at school until my grandmother stalked up and asked him in an angry whisper what the hell he thought he was doing inside her house.

Thing was, this had seemed completely in character for Hunter. He was the charmer, the savior, the leader, every girl's hero. When the neighborhood boor targeted a girl for the evening, of course Hunter would deftly intervene, even against the boss lady's wishes.

For anyone else. Not for me. For years, Hunter and I had kept our distance. When he stepped in, I started thinking about him differently. Thinking hard about him. Casting him not as everybody else's hero but as my own. The prom had passed already, but graduation was coming up. We were headed for the same college. Because of our past together, we would have a lot to work through, but maybe college was our time to do it.

And then he stole my life.

I managed a tiny smile for the several-months-older, quite-a-bit-drunker Hunter, as if the music player represented a long-ago period of my childhood rather than last May. "I definitely left that in Kentucky on purpose," I said. "It'll do me no good here. I can't afford new songs."

His golden jaw dropped. He rolled his eyes. He must be plastered. "Songs aren't that expensive," he said.

"Every little bit helps," I said, "when I'm trying to pay the rent and experience New York."

He talked right over "New York" as if he hadn't heard me. "You love your music."

"I did when I was trying to shut everything out. Now I'm trying to let everything in. I want to hear New York rather than some song I downloaded. I want to smell New York. Well—New York smells like garbage. Vietnamese garbage, Mexican garbage, Lithuanian garbage, Nigerian garbage, all within a three-block walk. Even the stench is part of the experience. I want to pay attention."

Leaning forward, he covered my hand and the music player and earbuds on the table with both his big hands.

My face flushed hot like he had thrown his latte into it.

"You don't want your music player because your grandmother gave it to you," he said. "Admit it."

I tried to pull my hand out from under his. The corner of the music player dug into my finger. I stood up.

"Sit down." He sounded authoritative, and suddenly very sober. He squeezed my hand on the table. "We're not done."

"Yes, we are." I loosened my hand from his and placed it on his shoulder. "Some of us work for a living." I turned for the counter.

Before I could slip my hand away, he grasped it again. "Give me your new cell phone number."

I laughed shortly at the irony: dreamy Hunter asking for my number, when I couldn't give it to him anyway. "I don't have a cell phone."

He closed his eyes and kept them closed for several seconds, as if hoping that when he opened them again, my second head would have disappeared. In the light of two mismatched lamps on nearby tables, each of his blond lashes cast two long shadows down his tanned cheeks. He opened his eyes. "How can you not have a cell phone?"

"Too expensive."

Shaking his head, he pulled my hand until it lay flat on the table in front of him. He drew a pen out of his pocket and clicked it open. "Here's my number, then. If you ever need me, find a phone and call me."

I was pulling hard all this time. Despite my best efforts, by the time he stopped talking he'd already written HUNTER across my palm, in case I forgot whose phone number was written there, and his area code.

"Hunter." I looked around the coffee shop, afraid of making a scene at work, but truly not wanting Hunter's number tattooed on my hand. "Hunter, this may be hard for you to understand when you are on the stealing end of the inheritance rather than the victim end. If I needed help, you are the last person on Earth I would call." I gave my hand one last, hard jerk and reeled back a couple of steps. His pen had left his entire phone number on my palm, plus a line down my middle finger and off the tip.

"My break is over and I'm already in trouble for getting here late." Scooting my mug from the table, I hurried away, weaving among the now crowded tables filled with a second wave of late-night coffee addicts. My boss glowered at me with his fists on his hips. I could only hope Hunter, the future president of a multimillion-dollar equine enterprise and the heir to a fortune, understood where I was coming from as a girl alone and struggling financially. I hoped he would cut me some slack about the stable boy.

As if.

NEW YORK IS THE CITY THAT never sleeps, but it does get tired. Its eyelids grow heavy and it wants to veg in front of the television. When my boss let me off work at eleven, all the other shops were closed. Traffic was sparse. Only a few pedestrians passed me on the street. The lights were no less bright, but the night had formed a dome over them, as if I were walking through a movie set made to look like the city rather than the real thing, and I would never see very far down the dark side streets even when dawn broke.

I felt like the only person in the world awake and walking by the time I reached the honors dorm. But every window on the front was still lit, even mine, dimly, with light filtering through the doorway from Summer and Jørdis's outer room. I might even encounter Hunter in the stairwell. This should have been the last thing I wanted, but it wasn't. I lingered over my mailbox in the lobby, sifting through endless pamphlets for campus events scheduled when I would be at work and tossing each one in the recycling bin.

Finally I shuffled up one flight of stairs and opened the door to my room. The first thing I saw was Summer and Jørdis sitting cross-legged on Jørdis's bed, cutting out pictures. The second thing I saw was my green-sequined belly-dancing outfit hanging on the back of my door. When I'd first brought it home from the thrift store, I'd planned to keep it in the closet I shared with Summer, but Jørdis asked me to hang it in full view of the room because she liked the glitter. She was an art major.

Maybe this was how Hunter had known I was taking belly dancing. Growing warm, I wondered when in the past week he'd been in my room.

Summer looked up from her scissors and grinned at me. "Well? Did the stable boy make it to your assignation?"

I glared at her, then looked pointedly at Jørdis. Summer and I really, really needed to work on our silent language.

Summer dismissed Jørdis with a flourish of her scissors. "Jørdis knows all about it. Brian stopped by. He said he and Manohar and Hunter went out and got wasted, and Hunter told them he was the stable boy."

Usually I was very careful with my belongings because they would need to last me a long time. My book bag was a large leather designer bag I'd seldom used back home. I needed it to take me through college and beyond, because I'd never be able to afford another one like it. And I dropped it to the floor with a thud, unable to hold up the weight of my books and "Almost a Lady" for another moment.

Jørdis produced a third pair of scissors—her supply of sharp instruments was limitless—and held it out to me. "While we are discussing this, come and cut for me. It will help you with your aggression."

Jørdis was Danish and no nonsense, softened only by the silk scarves she dyed herself and tied around her hair to keep it out of her paint. She seemed like a nice enough person and she hadn't yet complained about me tromping back and forth across her room at strange hours to get to mine when I worked late. She only seemed distant because of her harsh Scandinavian accent, her flattened affect, and the fact that she was always either gone, with her bed made tightly, or sitting carefully on her bed so as not to muss it, holding scissors. When she and Summer and I first met, she had told us right away how her name was spelled, that the *o* in her name contained a slash. Summer and I had called her "Jørdis with a slash" behind her back for several days until we decided she wasn't so bad.

One thing she was very good at, surprisingly, was making friends. She'd already decided her project for her college gallery show at the end of the semester would be a series of huge collages composed of tiny cut-out faces. This meant that whenever Summer or I had a spare moment, Jørdis shoved a pair of scissors in our hands and dumped a pile of old magazines or photographs in our laps. She also recruited people she met in the lobby or the hallway to come back to the room and cut out faces with her.

Tired as I was, I didn't think handling a sharp instrument was a good idea. But I knew from experience that there was no arguing with Jørdis. I slunk to her bed and accepted a pair of scissors and a ten-year-old copy of *Rolling Stone*. "Hunter promised not to say anything to Gabe," I murmured, "but since he got drunk with Manohar and Brian and told them, I'm screwed already. They'll spread it everywhere because I'm the honors program joke."

"Brian didn't make it sound that way at all." Summer placed a neatly clipped face on the pile in front of Jørdis and turned the page of her copy of *Tiger Beat.* "Hunter was shocked and flattered by your story, and he got drunk with Manohar and Brian because they were discussing whether you have a thing for him."

For a long, delicious moment, I believed Summer. Then my memory of my conversation with Hunter kicked in. "Did Brian tell you that's what went on," I asked her, "or is this your interpretation of the events?"

"It's my inter—"

"Right," I butted in. "Do me a favor and stop interpreting. Hunter could not care less whether I have a thing for him, because he doesn't have a thing for me."

"I'm not so sure." Jørdis bit her lip and carefully cut around someone's ear for an achingly long moment before she continued, "I caught your Hunter outside in the hall several days ago, reading our names on the door. I made him come in and cut for me."

Wow. I nodded toward the door to my private room. "Did he ask you whose belly-dancing costume that was?"

"He did," she said. Mystery solved.

"Did he peek into my room?" It was tiny, only the width of the bay window that took up one whole wall, and exactly large enough for a single bed and a miniature dresser and desk. Every room on the front of the honors dorm housed two roommates in the outer chamber and one in this alcove. I'd heard around the dorm that students killed for these bay window rooms, and the older students called dibs. But Jørdis said the tiny room made her claustrophobic and reminded her of her summer in Japan, where she had been made to sleep in a tube. Then Summer didn't jump at it, so I did. I loved the smallness, the closeness, and the door that I could close. It was all very Virginia Woolf—until you remembered that she committed suicide, which took some of the fun out of it.

No, I loved my little room, but I had to store most of my stuff in Summer's closet in this larger room. There wouldn't have been much for Hunter to see inside my room. I still wanted to know whether he'd seen it.

"He did not peek," Jørdis said, "but he pumped me for information about my roommates, especially you, until I asked him whether he knew you."

Summer leaned forward expectantly and dropped magazine and scissors. "What did he say?"

"He said, 'Not really.'"

Summer turned to me. "See? He's confused by your swift exit from Kentucky. Jørdis asks him whether he knows you and he wistfully says, 'Not really,' like he wants to reconnect with you but doesn't know how."

I sliced through the center of the picture I was trimming. I was too tired to argue with Summer, but I wished she would quit picking up the broken pieces of my life and trying to build something romantic out of them. That's what I'd tried to do in "Almost a Lady," and that's what had gotten me in this mess.

I pointed at Summer with my scissors. "Hunter said he would ask Manohar and Brian not to tell Gabe or anyone else about the stable boy, but he couldn't promise anything. That's where you come in. You're friends with Brian. Ask him to keep quiet about this as a favor to you. Make friends with Manohar and do the same thing."

"Whoa!" She held up *Tiger Beat* as a shield. "I already defended your story. Haven't I done enough?"

"Five words." I counted them on my fingers for her, the scissors hanging from my thumb. "Can. I. Have. Erin's. Vote?"

Summer cackled. "I can't imagine asking a favor from Manohar. You heard him in class. He hates me."

"Then you're going to have to do a one-eighty and stop antagonizing him in class," I said. "If he wants to tell me that romance novels aren't fit to wipe his ass, you just go ahead and let him say that. My internship is more important than my pride." I wasn't sure this was true. My pride was pretty damned important. But I was tired, cutting with only one eye open now. If I had that internship, I wouldn't need to work for six hours on top of attending class and studying for twelve.

Summer winced. "My father specifically warned me not to get all citified at college and bring home a white boy."

I exchanged a brief glance with Jørdis. I was more fluent in my silent language with her than with Summer. Jørdis and I were wondering how Summer had made the leap from not antagonizing Manohar to taking Manohar home to Mississippi.

I went with it. "Manohar isn't white."

"He's worse," Summer said without looking up from her magazine page. "To my father."

"I'm not asking you to enter into a serious relationship with Manohar and take him home to meet your racist daddy."

Summer's lips pressed into a hard line. She looked forward to showing her daddy who was in charge of her life. I had her already.

I continued, "I'm asking you to flirt with Manohar and get some info out of him. And if you break his heart—well, that's romance novel fodder, and only what he deserves, right?"

"Right," she said with fake reluctance. Suddenly she seemed absorbed in carefully clipping a new face. She was determined not to look up and let us read in her expression what we'd already guessed: that she was crushing hard on Manohar and was thrilled to have this excuse to go after him.

Jørdis sat back against the wall and smiled at me in admiration. The silent message was so obvious I would have been concerned that Summer would read it, too, except that Summer was clueless. Yes, I was good at reading people. I studied them so I could put them in my novels.

If only I could read stable boys.

5

After a few more minutes of cutting out faces and silently laughing with Jørdis about Summer's utter lack of subtlety, I said good night, closed myself in my own room, and studied. I sat there for three days. At least, that's what it felt like.

I did leave during these three days. I went to class, and I spent long hours at the coffee shop. But the New York experience I'd longed for was slipping away from me, not because of my lack of cash, but because I was so overwhelmed with the homework I couldn't get done while I was busy making coffee.

And I did love my tiny room. True, there was hardly any space for storage, but I hadn't brought a lot of stuff with me from Kentucky anyway, and I didn't have the money to buy the cute wall organizers I'd seen in other girls' rooms on other floors. My walls were tacked with colorful abstract oils I'd borrowed from Jørdis. And of course most of the space was filled with the bay window: a wide wall of glass on the front of the building, and a narrow one diagonally on either side. I could open the shades and watch people approach on the sidewalk, pass the building, and continue down the sidewalk until they disappeared into the endless rows of nineteenth-century town houses. I could imagine the many students before me who had drifted off from their calculus homework watching the foot traffic. I could picture the young men and women in their finery who had stood at this very window when it was part of their family's parlor. They had looked out into the dusty street, their bellies fluttering with butterflies, waiting for the carriage drawn by spirited matched bays that would take them to the ball.

My one small shelf over the desk was piled with my textbooks. I didn't junk up my shelf with New York trinkets like Summer did. I needed to focus not on being here but on staying here, studying hard, writing well, getting that internship. The one folly I allowed myself was the New York City magnet I'd brought with me from Kentucky—the Empire State Building, the Chrysler Building, the Brooklyn Bridge, and the Statue of Liberty stacked together and reproduced in the finest painted plastic. I'd had it for years. I'd stared at it as a kid, longing to come here someday. And now it stuck to the metal filing cabinet that doubled as my bedside table, reminding me I'd better not throw it all away.

The music cranked up several floors above me, signaling a party. I'd overheard Manohar and Brian talking about it in creative-writing class a few days earlier. I'd felt the obligatory blush flood my face, and the obligatory drive to glance at Hunter at the end of the table, where he chuckled with Isabelle. If our dorm was throwing a party, surely he would be there.

But the farther I stayed away from Hunter, the better for both of us. I even smiled at Manohar during class when he shot a few barbs at me about the romantic elements of Isabelle's awful story. After class, as I was walking out with Summer, I thought I heard Manohar whinny at me. I ignored him.

Now that the bass line of the rock song shook my bay windows, I turned the page in my history textbook. And wished for my music player after all.

I'd almost regained my concentration, focusing on the words rather than the beat, when the door burst open and banged against my desk. "We're going to a beach party!" Summer announced, already bouncing away. "Put on your bathing suit!"

I peeked around the door frame into the larger room, where she was pulling a bright yellow bikini out of her dresser. "The coffee shop takes up so much of my time," I said. "I need to study while I ca—"

She whirled to face me and shook her fists, a piece of bikini swinging in each. "You wanted me to flirt with Manohar and bring him over to your side. This is the perfect opportunity, and I am not going to a party in the men's bathroom in a bikini by myself!"

Reluctantly I pulled my own bikini from my dresser. It was designer, from last year. Luckily it was solid steel blue, not a bold pattern that would date it to a particular collection. And it wasn't too worn. I'd gotten no use out of it at all during my long, hot summer working in New York.

One of the differences between expensive clothing and cheap clothing, I'd discovered now that I'd actually tried on something in a New York department store's bargain basement, was that expensive clothing could make the wearer look better. My bikini was no exception, draping in graceful folds reminiscent of a 1950s starlet.

But a glance in Jørdis's full-length mirror reminded me that there was nothing the loveliest designer bikini could do about my freckles. This summer I'd had zero opportunity to acquire a light tan, so my freckles stood out like a pox on my white skin. In *Pride and Prejudice,* Lydia calls a neighborhood girl a "nasty little freckled thing." Silently Elizabeth agrees. The reader is not to sympathize with Lydia, but she is to sympathize with Elizabeth. I loved Jane Austen with all my heart, but I could not forgive her for this.

Summer called, "I guess, if I am going through with this bizarre notion of flirting with Manohar, I need to touch up my makeup and look like I mean it."

This was Summer's hint, I thought, that I'd taken off my makeup for the night, and she did not approve of my look for a party. Reluctantly I pulled my face cream out of my makeup bag. I was almost out. And I would never be buying this particular miracle cream again. It was ridiculously expensive, I realized now that I compared its price with dorm rent. I resented having to waste a dollop on this party, just to silence Manohar on the stable-boy issue.

Summer watched me struggle with the tube. "Fold it like toothpaste."

"I'm past that point. I think I can get another month out of it if I cut it open, but I've tried all Jørdis's scissors. They're not sharp enough." I sighed with relief as I came away with a smear and moisturized my face. Then I reached for my powder.

"Are you trying to cover up your freckles?" Summer watched me in the mirror above her dresser. "I'm not saying you should. But I use a brand of foundation that's a lot thicker than yours."

"No, I'm not trying to cover them up. It's fruitless. I've tried everything and I have made peace with them." Lie. "The most I can hope for is to tone them down with a look of dewy freshness." I passed the powder brush over my nose one more time. I'd lived a hard life and lost my looks already. Or maybe that was the dark circles under my eyes from studying late. Anyway, I wasn't gussying up to catch a man. Summer was saving my internship and I was going with her, in a bathing suit so I would feel even more naked and exposed than I had during that first critique session in the writing class—almost as if Hunter had planned the party this way.

"You look beautiful," Summer told my reflection.

"You *are* beautiful," I said. She glowed with energy in her bright bikini. I wished, at that moment, that I could trade places with her, that I was the clueless Southerner wide-eyed at New York, wanting nothing more out of life than a fabulous professional job and a meaningful love relationship, ecstatic at the prospect of forced flirting with a boy from class.

We locked our outer door and pushed open the door to the

stairs. "I'm so excited," she gushed. Her voice sounded hollow in the stairwell. "Maybe next I could write an espionage story for Gabe. It's like I'm a spy. A spy for love." She kept talking but the music had drowned out her voice by the time we passed the third floor. We kept climbing and pulled open the door to the fifth floor.

I'd been going to horse parties since I was fourteen. In retrospect, I realized this was not because my grandmother thought I was mature enough to handle the alcohol and schmoozing with older boys like Whitfield Farrell. I was not. It was because she was grooming me, even then, to take over.

Four years later, Hunter was taking over instead, and I was destitute, with a lot of partying under my belt. I'd even done shots with a few celebrities who came to Kentucky only during Derby season and who thought they were part of the in crowd if they drank bourbon and wore a hat. And now, walking into a college party on the fifth floor of the honors dorm—could it sound more lame?—I got nervous, chickened out, spread my hands over my bare tummy, and would have backed away down the stairwell if Summer hadn't grabbed my hand and pulled me through the crowd outside the bathroom.

"You like Hunter more than you want to admit," she said in my ear as she tugged the door open. "But maybe he won't be here." She pushed me inside.

The room was dimly lit with a few rotating colored lights, and the hot, swirling mist made it even more difficult to see. The showerheads in every stall sprayed full force—hot water, judging from the fog. The room was more like a sauna than a beach.

But the boys had worked hard on the beach scene. A few potted palms framed the doorway where we stood. About half the thirty people in the room stood in a circle near the sinks and batted a beach ball back and forth. An upperclassman had set up a bar in front of the urinals. He chopped ice in a blender, mixed it with fruit juice and vodka, and garnished the drinks with paper umbrellas.

And over the bare shoulders of boys, right away I saw Hunter stripped down to his bathing suit and flip-flops. For the first time in months and months, here was what I'd seen almost daily for so many Kentucky summers: Hunter with his shirt off. Back home his muscles had worked underneath his skin, stacking bales of hay, holding a bucking stallion. Muscles like that, in a body as beautiful as a machine, should have made noise as they worked, some low grinding music, rather than sliding along silently through their task.

In class or in the coffee shop, I had known those silent muscles were there, disguised in a crisp cotton shirt or a blue polo for another girl to discover. Now another girl had discovered them all right. Bracing one hand against the wet tile wall, Hunter leaned in and talked to a blonde, as confidently and casually as if he'd met a girl from our rival high school outside the pretzel shop at the mall.

I waited for him to look up at me in the doorway, give me a smug smile, and turn back to her. That would let me know he was interested in me and trying to make me jealous.

He never looked at me. He kept talking to her as if I were not there.

Summer noticed, too. Conveniently ignoring his blond accessory, she gasped, "My God—Hunter's body. Are those muscles from being a stable boy?"

"I'm afraid so." Actually, I didn't know. That's how he'd developed the muscles in the first place, but surely my grandmother hadn't made him work for his keep all summer long. He should have grown soft and faded to white in the electric lamplight of her expensively stylish office. He hadn't.

"Do you know what the scar is from?" Summer asked, touching

her side at the approximate location of Hunter's long white scar. Now he would know we were talking about him—if he looked over at us. This didn't seem likely. The blonde gazed up into his eyes and tilted her head, her long hair shifting damply over her bare shoulder.

"Surgery," I said. "He broke some ribs. A horse fell on him."

"What?" Summer exclaimed. "When?"

I shrugged. "Eighth grade?"

"Oh, no!" she cried. "He was so young! Did you visit him in the hospital and sit by his bedside? How sweet!" Hunter was going to hear her even over the throbbing music.

"Shhh," I said. "No, we weren't speaking."

"Erin!" she protested. "Why not?"

Because only a year had passed since my mother died. I had been terrified for him, but if I had visited him, I wouldn't have known what to say.

I nodded at the bar in front of the urinals. "Let's get a drink." I set off across the slippery floor without waiting for her answer and asked the upperclassman for a lime slush with no vodka.

"All right," she said when she'd caught up with me. "But there is way more to this stable-boy thing than you are telling me." She ordered a mango daiquiri with plenty of rum.

I had thought a run-in with Manohar was my biggest fear. After glimpsing Hunter and the blonde again, the prospect of chatting with Manohar seemed downright welcoming. He and Brian lay on lounge chairs in the corner, wearing sunglasses. Summer bounced up to Manohar and unceremoniously told him to scoot over on his chair. That meant I could perch on the edge of Brian's chair. Unfortunately, this meant that I faced Hunter again.

The blonde stood in the shower spray with her eyes closed, hot water splashing off her face and streaming into her hair and dashing onto the tile floor around her perfectly polished red toenails.

As I watched, Hunter reached over and stroked his big hand from the crown of her head down her darkened wet hair, in the middle of the stream of water. Her hair must feel so soft and warm to him, almost like his own body, like nothing. How could he do something so intimate to her? He hardly knew her.

The room was crowded, and when a bare-chested or bikini-clad body passed in front of me and blocked my view, I realized I was staring. I turned my attention back to the conversation with Summer, Manohar, and Brian about the food in the dining hall—which I'd never eaten anyway because I'd begged a university financial counselor to let me off the too expensive meal plan. But the half-naked bodies would move on, and my foolish gaze would return to Hunter.

I could have wondered for the rest of the night whether paying attention to another girl was Hunter's way of telling me he was interested in me instead. I was a romance writer. I spun scenarios the way I wanted them to go.

But that would drive me crazy. I could foresee a whole semester of acting like a seventh-grader, obsessing over whether Hunter liked me—or worse, a whole four years of college. If I was able to stay here that long.

Instead, I used a technique I'd developed to cope after my mother died, putting all that grief into a small box so the rest of my life was clear of it. Chin up, I watched Hunter watching the blonde, his hand sliding down her bare back. I said to myself, *Hunter likes this girl and not me. I should not want Hunter anyway because he stole my farm and he is in cahoots with my grandmother. He has no interest in me romantically. I am still okay.*

And then I turned away. There were plenty of other boys to talk to in the sauna, and some of them looked almost as good as Hunter in the blurring steam. For instance, Wolf-boy Kyle plopped down on the end of Manohar's chair, next to Summer, already drunk enough that he didn't notice Manohar's stony expression behind his shades or the way Manohar slowly and pointedly gave up possession of the chair, drawing up his legs and turning so he sat on it like a bench and his bare thigh touched Summer's.

Kyle leaned toward me across the space between the chairs. "You're the one who wrote the horny story in creative writing. You have got some balls."

Summer shoved him lightly. Manohar barked with laughter. Brian sat up, murmuring, "What'd he say?" The music throbbed and echoed against the tile walls. Holding a conversation involved lipreading as well as listening.

I cleared my throat. "For the sake of polite conversation, Kyle, I will choose to overlook that gender-confused mixed metaphor. And my story wasn't horny."

Everyone, even Summer, gaped at me.

I laughed. "Okay, I guess it was," I acknowledged as Hunter sat down beside me on the end of Brian's chair.

Hunter grinned at everybody but me. "Am I missing class?"

I wanted to ask him where his blond girl had gone off to. Now that I looked, she'd disappeared from the shower, and she wasn't hanging behind him with her hand on his shoulder. But I should not have lusted after him anyway, and he probably had no idea that he was making my skin burn on the side where he sat. I struggled to focus on the group conversation, which had turned to Gabe.

"I'm a little disappointed in him," Summer was saying. "My other roommate, Jørdis—I think you've met her, Hunter—"

Hunter smiled at Summer. He didn't glance at me.

"—she's a sophomore, and she says her honors freshman writing teacher was a willowy lady in a cape who led the class on observation missions through the West Village during class time. I don't think we're going on any observation missions. Gabe sits and listens to us and sips his coffee."

"If it's really coffee," Manohar said. "He's so quiet, like he's in an alcoholic fog."

"Hear, hear." Kyle clicked his plastic cup against mine in a toast.

My stomach turned over. I felt strangely defensive of Gabe. "I know it's coffee," I said. "It comes from the shop where I work. Sometimes he wanders in after class."

"Speaking of which." Hunter reached over, took my cup from my hand, and tasted the lime slush.

The Hunter I knew was not rude enough to drink from my cup uninvited. Was he *flirting* with me? My proper reaction would be outrage, especially after he'd had his hands all over that blonde. I tried not to stare at his wet lips.

"How do you know Gabe's not spiking his coffee?" Brian asked, dragging me back to the conversation.

I didn't know this. But it seemed a stretch to equate Gabe being quiet with Gabe being drunk on the job. And though these drunk boys were just shooting the shit behind their teacher's back, I felt bad for Gabe since he wasn't there to defend himself.

"That's an idea," Hunter whispered in my ear. "Want me to spike this for you?"

I shook my head and said softly, "I have homework to do later." His bare shoulder next to mine sank like he was disappointed. I couldn't waste energy puzzling that out when I needed to rescue Gabe's reputation. Gabe mattered to me, and Hunter did not.

"I like Gabe," I said loudly enough to carry. "He reminds me of someone."

"Who?" Hunter asked. "Tommy?"

Although it had been hard for us to hear each other before, Hunter's one word seemed to have rung out clear as day for everybody. "Who's Tommy?" Kyle asked, and the others sat up to hear the answer.

I did not think this was the time or place or company to state that Tommy was Hunter's easygoing father, and that Hunter and I knew each other from way back when. I could not trust Wolf-boy on top of everyone else with the stable-boy secret.

Hunter was thinking the same thing. He shifted the subject. "I like the way Gabe trusts us to comment on each other's stories."

"He goes too far," Brian said. "Pedagogically speaking, it's one thing to create a student-centered classroom by asking for the students' voices. It's another thing to let them bulldoze each other."

"Is it bulldozing to express your opinion?" Manohar asked. For some reason we were having a hard time hearing each other again. He was shouting. "If you let a creative-writing student think her story is great when it isn't, aren't you doing her a disservice? If she sucks, she needs to know so she can change her major before it's too late."

I opened my mouth and quickly closed it again. My eyes were on the prize, keeping Manohar from going to Gabe with the stable-boy secret. If the price was allowing him to take potshots at me in public, I could pay it.

Summer said what I didn't dare say. "You're assuming that the student making the comment knows what he's talking about. What if he tells another writer that she sucks and discourages her, when her work is very good? What if the student making the comment is, for instance, an economics major and is only taking creative writing in the first place because the honors program requires it, and in actuality he doesn't know shit?"

"This is just a replay of class," Hunter said. "If we're going to talk about creative writing, let's be less specific." I wished he were coming to my aid, but I knew he was only taking control and keeping the peace, as usual.

And I'd had enough. "I don't think it's possible to talk about creative writing without being specific." I turned to Kyle, across from me. "Do you have a really sharp knife?"

He blinked at me, then peered into his cup. "Is this a trick question?"

"No. I only came up here because I need to borrow a very sharp knife, and I thought you might have one." I didn't add that thinking of him as "Wolf-boy" had called to mind the necessity of a knife in the wilderness. This connection made no sense anyway since he was from Brooklyn.

Brian raised his hand and called out, "I have a really sharp knife."

"May I borrow it?" I asked.

"My father gave it to me."

I squinted at him through the mist. "May I borrow it without telling your father?"

"Why don't we go get it from our room," Hunter called across me to Brian. "Then we'll take it down to Erin's room and use it. It will never leave your sight."

I clamped my teeth together to keep from saying anything about Hunter's presumptuous "we," his decision that my use of Brian's knife needed Hunter's input. I could not forget his hands on that girl.

Brian scowled behind his shades, but no one was immune to Hunter's charm. He stood and nodded to Summer. "Save my seat, would ya?"

"Kyle will save it, won't you, Kyle?" Summer asked. "I'm comfortable here." She winked at me.

I assumed that was the signal to me that she felt comfortable with Manohar—more than comfortable. The mango daiquiri was probably helping. I felt uneasy about leaving her there. But after all, half the people crowding the bathroom were chicks, and home was three floors down.

Carefully I crossed the slippery floor, assuming Hunter and Brian would follow. I reached for the handle on the bathroom door, but a man's hand reached past me and opened it first—Hunter, I saw, glancing over my shoulder. I stepped into the hallway, the air dry and freezing in comparison, and told myself the temperature change was the reason I shivered.

"This way." He reached his arm around me and touched my shoulder. He walked ahead of Brian and me, three doors down. Brian fished his key from the pocket of his bathing suit. Hunter reached his own key first and turned it in the door.

Their room was set up exactly like mine but looked completely different. As Brian opened a drawer in his dresser to retrieve the famed knife, I scanned his floor-to-ceiling collage of psychedelic posters. Hunter quietly sat on the opposite bed. His wall was blank, almost as if he and Brian were having an interior design standoff.

I stood awkwardly between them. "Manohar got the small room? How did that happen? I've talked to a lot of people in this dorm and there's always a story behind who gets the small room."

Hunter patted beside him on the bed, an invitation for me to sit.

Blushing, I shook my head.

He spoke without skipping a beat. "I didn't want it. That room is claustrophobic."

"And I came out of the closet when I was thirteen." Brian turned to us, brandishing a glinting dagger. "I'm not going back in." He came toward me with the knife, handle first.

"Brian!" Hunter jumped up from his bed. "Don't give it to her when she's never used one before."

"She asked to use it," Brian said. "Isn't that why we're here?"

"You're going to use it for her. Or I will." Hunter took the dagger by the handle. "Sometimes Erin doesn't know what's good for her." Barebacked and blade down like a jungle man ready to stab the python that crossed his path, he led the way out of the room.

Brian and I exchanged a glance and followed. "What do you need it for, anyway?" Brian asked me in the stairwell.

"I'm almost out of face cream and I can't afford another tube. If I cut it open and put it in a plastic bag, I think I can get another month out of it, maybe six weeks."

Hunter turned suddenly on the stair below us. Brian and I both jumped backward, but Hunter knew better than to turn with a knife point out. The knife was down by his side. "That's what this is about? You don't need face cream. You look fine."

"That's because I've been using it," I said at the same time Brian said, "That's because she's been using it," and rolled his eyes.

We exited the stairwell at the second floor. I unlocked the door, ushered them inside, and opened the inner door to my little bedroom.

"What's your story, then?" Brian asked, already nosing around in my stuff. "How did you end up in the closet?"

"I volunteered," I said from the doorway. "I like it."

Hunter whispered, "You always did like sitting in the closet."

I hugged myself as a chill raced across my skin.

He wouldn't meet my eyes. He was fingering the filmy green fabric of the belly-dancing costume on the back of my door. In a normal tone he said, "I still can't believe you're taking belly dancing for your phys ed credit. It will never do you any good."

"I think it's so cool!" Brian exclaimed.

In the back of my mind I knew I should have thanked Brian for coming to my defense. All I could focus on was Hunter, who had touched another girl in the shower and now had the gall to stick his nose in my business. "What phys ed credit *will* do me any good?" I asked suspiciously. "Horseback riding?"

"You said it," he muttered. "I didn't."

"I liked the idea of getting my abs in shape," I said truthfully.

"I've been doing it for three weeks and look." I thrust my tummy forward to show him. It was flat. Not that he cared.

Brian stuck his head out of my bedroom to see. "You should get your belly button pierced. Say it like you mean it." He disappeared through the doorway again.

"Are you kidding?" I called. "Do you know how much that would cost, not to mention the price of a charm to plug the hole?"

"Your grandmother would be furious," Hunter said quietly, "just like the last time you got a piercing." He touched one finger to the diamond stud on the side of my nose.

We held one another's gaze for a long, electric moment.

I knocked his hand away and whispered, "Everything I do isn't designed to make my grandmother furious. I don't give a damn what she thinks."

I flounced through the doorway, into my room. Brian's rummaging hadn't bothered me at all, but now that Hunter was coming in behind me, I glanced around frantically.

Nothing was out of place. Nothing would betray any more of my secret fantasies to Hunter. He already knew them all anyway.

Brian stood before a cheap frame nailed to my wall. "Wow, a rejection letter. You should take this down. Doesn't it discourage you?"

Ugh, I'd forgotten about the rejection letter. It meant a lot to me to display it. That summer I'd finished the romance novel I'd worked on my entire senior year of high school. I sent it off to the publisher I'd written it for. After only a month, I'd gotten a rejection letter, which was very quick. They must have really hated it.

I searched my dresser drawer for the cream. "No, it encourages me. It's my first firm step toward the writing career I want."

Brian glanced over his shoulder at me. "Isn't a rejection a step *away* from the writing career you want?"

"No," I said. "All writers get rejections."

"Not the ones who are published," Hunter pointed out.

I grabbed the cream from the drawer and wagged it at him between my fingers. "Knife, please."

Instead of giving me the knife, he held out his hand for the tube. I gave it to him. He set it on top of my desk and poised the knife blade above it. Brian and I leaned in to watch. I wanted to make sure Hunter wouldn't mutilate the tube and spill its precious contents—and, I discovered as I edged closer to him, the air around him was so warm. My skin heated deliciously without touching his.

"This is like surgery. With a hatchet." Lightly he slit the tube at the bottom along the crimp, then at the top where it flared out to the cap, then down the middle, connecting the top and bottom cuts. With the tip of the blade he lifted one of the flaps he'd made. "It opens like the space shuttle cargo bay."

"Genius," I said. "My hero."

He straightened and looked at me. Brian and I straightened, too, because when Hunter straightened, the knife came closer to us.

"So, you have a plastic bag to keep it from drying out?" Hunter asked me.

"Yes," I said.

When I didn't move, he looked at Brian, then back at me. "Put it away and come back upstairs with us," he told me.

"You go ahead." I nodded toward my early American literature survey (bleh!) book on my desk. "I have a lot of reading to do."

His face fell. Either he was an even better actor than I'd thought, or he was genuinely astonished that I refused to return to the party with him after he so gallantly performed surgery on my face cream.

"It was lots of fun though," I said. "Quite an eyeful." To Brian I said, "Do me a favor and make sure Summer comes home safe."

"Will do." Brian had already left my room and headed for the outer door.

Hunter stood there a moment longer, blond brows down, disoriented because another man had been put in charge. Then he recovered, resetting his face in the handsome default mode. "Have a great night, Erin. See you in class."

"Thanks, Hunter," I said in a tone that ran right up to the edge of sarcasm without going over. I walked him to the door, shut and locked it behind him, and dashed back to my bedroom to strip out of my damp bikini and bundle into soft sweats before I froze.

As I changed, I listened to their footfalls. Where my bay window ended on one side, my bedroom shared a wall with the stairwell. I didn't want to switch my pillow to the other end of my bed because I would feel vulnerable with my head that close to the door—but some nights I was tempted when students whooped and tramped to the upper floors in the wee hours.

Tonight I was glad I could hear Brian's fast shuffle, holding on to the handrail, and Hunter's slower, heavier amble up the center of the stair tread. I listened to them ascend between the second and third floors, third and fourth, fourth and fifth, their steps disappearing behind the heavy fifth-floor door. This way I knew they were truly gone. The door was closed on the party. Hunter could get back to his blonde, and I could get back to work.

A few hours later, two sets of footsteps skipped back down: one fast as before, the other lighter and halting, tipsy. Brian's voice chuckled at the outer door to my room. The door shut. Only the tipsy steps tripped between the beds, and then Summer was falling through my doorway, pushing my books aside and curling up in my lap.

I brushed her black hair away from her shut eyes. "What's the matter?" I yawned.

"I mentioned the stable boy to Manohar," she mumbled. "He got mad at me. He thinks I don't really like him, and the only reason I was flirting with him was to get something for you."

I could have been coy and said, *I thought you* were *only flirting with him to get something for me. You genuinely like him after all? Gasp!* Instead I said soothingly, "He lives in your dorm and you'll have class with him the whole semester. You'll have plenty of opportunity to work it out. He'll come around."

She rolled over and I scratched her bare back between the straps of her bright yellow bikini until Jørdis came in from the art studio. I meant to read for early American literature survey (bleh!) all this time, but I dwelled on my own words to Summer. For once, I believed them. Summer and Manohar were brilliant and funny, and as long as they could step past the barriers set up by their own egos, there was nothing to come between them.

At least, that's what I hoped. Each night during my fifteen-minute break at the coffee shop, I looked around at the customers, picked two of them to put together, and brainstormed a happy ending for them. Usually they were students because the coffee shop was so close to campus. They had no real problems. Their parents were paying their way through college. The price of one of their nightly mochas could have kept me in peanut butter crackers for two weeks. Any of these young men and women could be perfect for each other. They just didn't know it, and they would never introduce themselves to each other except in a file on my laptop.

But sometimes the customers were young professionals. Guys with the latest haircut, chicks with unruly but strangely flattering hair and no makeup, all wearing the most expensive off-the-rack suits they could afford. I would be this girl eventually. If I played my cards right and won the publishing internship, I could be this girl in January. She loved her job and was set for life. She could hardly believe her luck when the hot guy from the adult nonfiction department at her publishing house walked over to her table and asked to sit down.

I treasured this fifteen minutes a day of writing. Lived for it. So, much as I loved Summer, I felt a twinge of annoyance when she bounced into the coffee shop during my break almost a week after the beach party. More trouble must have bubbled up between her and Manohar. The coffee shop was out of her way. "Hey!" I called. "What's up?"

She slid into the chair across from me. "I was just coming back from the library."

"Headed to the dorm? This is not on your route."

"Yeah. I wanted to ask you something." She suppressed a smile. "Have you read the stories for creative-writing class tomorrow?"

I pointed at her. "No! I've needed to do that, but I got behind in my reading, and when I get off work I have to study for a calculus test tomorrow. I'm going to be down to the wire"—I winced at the unintentional horse racing metaphor—"reading stories right up until class. Why?"

"Hunter's story is about you."

"What do you mean, his story is about me?" I asked loudly enough that my boss peeked through the doorway from the back and put his fists on his hips.

"Uh-oh," Summer whispered. "I'd better go before I get you in trouble."

Too late. But I couldn't let her go yet. My heart was beating so hard, I might actually die of curiosity. "Is there a redhead in Hunter's story?"

"No, but—"

"Okay, thanks for the heads-up. I'll read it tomorrow." I closed my laptop, dismissing her, and went back to work. As I made a cappuccino for my next victim, my heart slowed down. I wasn't in

Hunter's story. This was more of Summer's wishful thinking, mentally writing a story of her own.

That idea got me through my night at work, hours of studying, and a reasonably successful calculus test the next morning even though Hunter sat across the room. But an hour before creative-writing class, alone in the library, absorbed in Hunter's literally and figuratively steamy story, I wasn't so sure.

6

Blurred Vision

by Hunter Allen

His friends created a "beach party" in the men's bathroom on their floor of the dorm by turning on all the showers full force. They said the dorm had a huge boiler that never ran out of hot water, like any converted brownstone in New York City. This seemed strange to him because he was from horse country, where fences were made of limestone boulders that workers had dug up from the ground in 1900, where crops were dried in barns painted black to take best advantage of the warm sun, where the grass was green year-round because of the sun and the rain and the nourishing limestone breaking down deep under the ground. Humans and the elements lived in harmony in the country. He had no understanding of the city, where the sheer number of humans overwhelmed the elements completely, yet the boiler never ran out of hot water.

"This feels so good," said the girl under his hands. His friend tending bar had reported that the girl had downed three strawberry daiquiris already. She was in possession of a fourth, but she had balanced it on the soap dish while she stepped into the hot shower, soaking her bathing suit. She looked up at him through half-closed eyes. He watched droplets from the shower ricochet off the mildewed walls and splash into the clear plastic cup, forming a layer of hot water on top, a second layer of melted strawberry-tinged slush underneath. It no longer looked appetizing, but she'd drunk enough for his purposes anyway.

"It does feel good." He slid his hand around her, toward her latissimus dorsi. He expected this move to go smoothly, but his skin jerked against hers with wet tension. He'd hardly started and he needed lube already.

His friends would laugh at him for thinking this. All men were supposed to come to college experienced. They should know how to massage a girl in the shower in front of half the dorm and act suave about it. They should know how to get this girl into bed shortly afterward and make her think it was a good idea.

He would never have admitted this to his friends or anyone else, but he was not experienced. And the main reason he hadn't gotten around in high school had just walked through the bathroom door directly behind him.

He could not see her with his back turned. He could not hear her husky voice. But he could hear the giggles of her ubiquitous friend. And he watched the mist from the showers settle in layers like the ice and artificial flavoring in the cup on the soap dish set into the wall. The fog from the showers should have swirled with turbulence when she and her friend opened the bathroom door. Instead it calmed and quieted, just as the whole world slowed to a canter, a walk, a halt with its ears pricked up when she came near.

Her stare burned a hole between his shoulder blades. She could stare all she wanted but he would not turn around. Never again. She'd made it clear since they were twelve that he was not good enough for her. If she changed her mind now just because he had his hand on another girl's latissimus dorsi in a public shower, she could eat her heart out.

Setting his chin down on the girl's shoulder, he watched his own index finger blaze a silvery path through the droplets of water clinging to her back. His fingertip reached her spine and he traced small circles there, a taste of what he would do to other parts of her later. He wondered whether she was already too numb to feel his touch and understand the innuendo.

Eyes still half closed, she lifted her chin and parted her lips for a kiss.

Instead of kissing her, he pressed his finger into her fossae lumbales laterales, the indentations in the small of her back, and stopped. She was a beautiful girl, no doubt, and he did know her name. The situation had not quite reached that level of cliché. But he did not know what her major was, or what she planned to do for a career, or what city in Jersey she was from. His friends would make fun of him if they found out this bothered him.

The girl from home had crossed the room behind his back and settled on a lawn chair. He could hear her now, joining a conversation as if she wasn't staring a hole through him.

Maybe she wasn't.

That decided the matter. He kissed the girl in front of him. He eased her backward until she was trapped between his body and the mildewed wall. Not that he needed to trap her. She willingly opened her mouth for him.

Maybe she knew what his major was and what town he was from. He had not told her, but maybe she'd found out. Or maybe it really didn't matter.

This is what he told himself as he pressed his tongue into her oral cavity. Her upper and lower lips were erogenous zones. The harder he kissed her, the faster her sensors fired messages to the nucleus accumbens in her brain. That center in turn sent a tingling sensation to her mons pubis, awakening it to the possibility that it might be next. She and he were from different states, after all, and unlikely to be related, and sensing this through their pheromones was apparently all the motivation they or anybody else needed to start the reproductive cycle.

He was running his tongue just above her clavicle when she pressed her hands to his pectoral muscles, feigning a request that he pause. "It's awfully crowded in here," she whispered, her breath curling the steam. "Could we go to your room where it's private?"

She had made the first move. He would get what he'd come for without even feeling guilty. He sniffed deeply with satisfaction, savoring this moment—and smelled the *Stachybotrys* growing on the walls.

Before he could back out of the situation, he grabbed her hand, epidermis to epidermis, and pulled her toward the door. The crowd was thick, the mist thicker, the lights flashed and bobbed in a bankrupt approximation of a disco, and still he caught a glimpse of the girl he'd hoped was not really behind his back, watching him.

Outside the bathroom, in the frigid hallway, his companion's nipples hardened beneath her bikini top with the release of testosterone because of the alcohol, and oxytocin because of his hands on her. As he led her toward his room, she tripped. He slowed his pace and generously supported her gluteus maximus so she wouldn't fall before they reached their destination.

He closed his door behind them. She stumbled to his bed, sat down, and kicked off her flip-flops. She was a lot more ready than he was. His friends would be appalled that he hesitated. There was nothing wrong with this scenario. Nothing.

He pulled her up to standing, tossed back the blankets, and sat her back down on the sheets. Cotton, *Gossypium hirsutum,* rather than silk, a secretion of *Bombyx mori,* but he was in college and nobody lost his virginity under ideal circumstances. Otherwise he wouldn't have a story to embellish when he was fifty. Gently he drew her down on top of him. He opened his bathing suit and pushed past hers. As the nucleus accumbens in his own brain flooded with activity, he pondered what species of monster he'd become.

* * *

"A MONSTER WHO GETS SOME," KYLE murmured as we all placed Hunter's story on top of our stacks. But that comment was under the table, so to speak, not part of the official class discussion. The official discussion, starting with Manohar's opinion, was even worse: "I just want to thank Hunter for being so brave and sharing his first time with us."

The response was snorts and howls of laughter from the men in the class, and it set the tone for the discussion of Hunter's story. I expected someone, maybe even a treacherous Manohar or Brian, to point out that the narrator's "horse country" place of origin was not Long Island. The limestone fences, black tobacco barns, and green grass in winter were iconic Kentucky, Bluegrass Region, and anybody reading between the lines could have figured out that Hunter was my stable boy. But nobody mentioned this. They were too busy guffawing about sex.

The women stammered about how moving the story was, how vulnerable the narrator was, and how interesting it was to get a guy's point of view on dating. This was polite of them and hid what they really wanted to say, which was that they'd been hot for Hunter before and now they could hardly stand it. He had become a movie star.

The men snickered and said they thought the story ended too soon, which was their way of saying they realized all the women were hot for Hunter and they wished they'd thought of this ploy themselves. They tried so hard to have the right clothes, the right hair, and money for dates. None of them had ever thought to use the writing class as a pickup place.

Summer put her chin on her fist and squinted across the table at Manohar. "What do you think this story is about, Manohar?" She leaned across me and said to Gabe, "Please excuse me for speaking out of turn, but I think this is important." She turned back to Manohar. "You don't think this story is about unrequited love at all, do you? You think it's about getting laid."

"Yes!" exclaimed most of the men, while most of the women chirped, "No!" Gabe and Hunter, at opposite ends of the table, both scribbled across their papers without looking up. Hunter sat draped across his comfy chair as if the class discussed his writing every day.

"Even when it's so laboriously unsexy?" Summer asked. "There's a lot more going on here. Hunter is smarter than that."

"You're reading too much into it," Manohar said. "He's making fun of a certain other supposedly sexy story written for this class. He's showing how clinical and predictable and unsexy it really was."

I opened my mouth to tell Manohar that I'd had enough. It was one thing for him to insult my story while we discussed it in class. It was too much for him to insult my story while we discussed someone else's. He had already let me know he loathed my writing. I got it. Enough already!

As usual, Summer beat me to it. "I'm not sure whether Hunter did this on purpose or if he even realizes he did it, but there's a beautiful dichotomy between the language he uses for the two girls. The girl he's with in the shower is described in anatomical terms, like an object. He even calls her 'it' once, near the beginning. 'It does feel good.'"

The room filled with the clatter of flipping pages, then a pause as everyone searched for the passage.

"Noooo," Manohar said. "He's responding to the girl saying, 'This feels so good.' 'It' equates to 'this,' which means standing in the shower."

Summer talked over him. "The girl he's trying to make jealous is never physically described at all. He conveys only his emotions about her. He loves her so much that he can't even see her."

I had resolved not to look at Hunter while the class was discussing his story. I would not peek at him now to gauge his reaction. If Summer wanted to make more out of his relationship with me than was actually there, that was her issue, not mine. I had a vested interest in staying out of any further tangles involving this creative-writing class intersecting with my real life. To remind myself of this, I traced INTERNSHIP over and over on a scratch sheet of paper—not on my copy of Hunter's story, which I would have to pass back to him.

"Erin?" Gabe asked.

In this shocking nanosecond, I thought Gabe was asking Hunter whether I was the girl he loved so much he couldn't see.

In the next horrible nanosecond, I realized my stupid mistake. While I'd daydreamed, everyone in the class had commented on Hunter's story. Summer had forfeited her turn since she'd already responded to Manohar. Gabe was calling on me for my opinion.

I sighed as the blood rushed to my face. Blood rushed to my face every time Hunter moved his pinkie in this class. Directly across from me, Manohar must think I had rosacea.

"This was not my kind of story," I began, running my finger along the edge of the first page. I snatched my hand away, realized I'd given myself a paper cut, and sat on my wounded hand. "I can't love a story in which the characters don't get what they want—"

"Oh, I think he got what he wanted," said Kyle. Other boys chuckled.

I raised my voice. "—or don't know what they want. We've all heard the existential blues a million times. That said . . . Hunter . . ."

He looked up at me when I called his name. I would not say this to the class in general, speaking about him in the third person. This message was for him, and I wanted him to hear it.

"I thought your writing was lyrical and descriptive but completely clear. I could see this setting in the sauna."

"Almost as if you were there," Brian commented.

"Seriously." I held up my hand to shut Brian up without taking my eyes off Hunter. "It was the best story I've read for this class."

Hunter bent his head to scribble something on his story, a small smile tugging at his lips. "Better than yours?"

The class shouted with laughter.

Of course he would be an ass when I was trying to be nice. "As I said, this is not my kind of story. The other thing I would point out, though—"

Everyone quieted and leaned forward, hanging on my words. They expected another performance like my entertaining response to Manohar about my own story.

"—is that there's no dialogue," I finished.

"There's dialogue," Brian said. "The girl says, 'This feels so good'"—he couldn't resist imitating the girl's sultry voice—"and then the guy says—"

"Yeah, she says something," I broke in, "and then he says something. But the definition of *dialogue* is speaking together, trading ideas. These characters never do that. And the main character never exchanges a single word with the mystery girl who is so much more important than the shower girl."

"I thought Hunter wrote it that way on purpose," said Kyle.

"Maybe he did," I said. "That choice has some artistic merit. On the other hand, having the important characters speak to each other and interact would have been more difficult to write. Maybe Hunter took the easy way out."

This time he looked up at me without smiling. At long last, he lifted his chin, opened his blue eyes, and acknowledged me across the table as if he finally heard what I was saying.

"As long as there's no dialogue"—I spoke directly to him—"no connection between the characters, nothing really happens in this story. It's all in the character's head, and there's no action."

"Seems to me he got plenty of action." This Manohar-like comment was made by a boy who hardly ever said anything in class. If even *he* felt it was safe to take potshots at me, belaboring the issue was pointless. I looked to Gabe, my signal that I was done.

"Your turn, Hunter," he called.

The class was silent as Hunter finished writing a note on his story, or finished faking writing a note for effect. Then he grinned brilliantly at us. "Thank you for your comments. I was a little nervous about my first time"—everyone chuckled because he was so hilarious—"but it wasn't nearly as painful as I thought. Your feedback will be helpful when I revise this story for my portfolio at the end of the semester." He sounded like a human form letter.

"Did you mean to leave out dialogue?" Summer pressed him. "Was it too hard to write, like Erin said?"

He kept grinning while the smile faded from his blue eyes. "Gabe may take exception to this, but I feel that my contribution to class on the day my story is discussed is the story itself. Then you tell me what you think of the story, and I learn from that. I shouldn't have to respond to your response. That's not freshman honors creative writing anymore. That's freshman honors psychology, and I don't need any talk therapy."

"Maybe you do," said Isabelle, beside him. "Maybe you wrote something into your story that you never intended. You could learn a lot about yourself from that."

"I always do exactly what I intend," Hunter snapped.

Thirteen people stared at him. Hunter did not lose his cool. I knew this from six years in school with him. Even his new friends knew this about him by now.

He blinked, realizing what he'd done. The slow smile spread across his face again. He winked at Isabelle. "But thanks for the advice. I honestly appreciate the work all of you put into critiquing my writing."

* * *

Discussion moved on to another classmate's writing, but my mention of "my kind of story" generated another argument later in the class between Summer and Manohar about proper genres for the course. Class time ran over. I had to get up and leave before Gabe dismissed us, and even so, I was late for work at the coffee shop.

No matter. Hunter's story was all I thought about through my entire shift. I knew exactly what Summer was talking about when I walked into our room six hours later.

"I've been telling Jørdis all about it." She motioned me over to Jørdis's bed with a pair of scissors.

"My stable boy was blond," I protested, taking the scissors and the magazine Jørdis handed me and settling in the pillows beside her. "If this girl is me, why doesn't she have red hair and a face clogged with freckles? I'm not hard to describe."

"Exactly," Summer said. "He couldn't give her red hair. Everybody in class would know it was you. Nobody suspected he was the stable boy in your story because he hadn't even shown up yet when you turned your story in. But this girl is you. It's obvious. Since he was twelve, this girl has made him feel as if the earth stood still. He's still a virgin because if he couldn't have this girl in high school, he didn't want anybody else. She even has your husky voice."

I winced. "Yeah, that screams sex, doesn't it?" I had taken exception to the husky voice description. Just because I was an alto didn't mean he had to make me sound like a cougar.

"So?" Summer insisted. "How can you ignore the fact that he's talking about you?"

I wasn't ignoring it. I realized he was talking about me. I also knew he wasn't serious about any of this. If he'd really felt this strongly about me, he would not have stolen my fortune.

No use explaining this to Summer, though, because she would

find a way to twist the theft of a hundred and forty-seven horses into a romantic overture. I shook my head. "Even if the girl were me, the guy in the story isn't Hunter. The guy in the story knows all about anatomy."

"Hunter is taking anatomy," Summer said.

My scissors stopped their progress across the magazine page, and the metallic scrapings of Summer's scissors and Jørdis's filled my ears like alarm bells. I forced myself to start cutting again before they noticed I'd stopped. "No, he isn't," I told Summer. "He's a business major. Why would he take anatomy?"

"I don't know," she admitted, "but I saw his anatomy book on his bed when I went to Manohar's room yesterday."

"And why did you go to Manohar's room yesterday?" Jørdis asked with as much innuendo as her Danish accent would allow.

"Oh, it was nothing like that," Summer assured her. "I was passing in the hall outside his room—"

"Because you just happened to find yourself three flights up on a men's floor for no apparent reason," I played along.

Laughing, she put her hand over my mouth. "—and he called me inside because he was making mulligatawny and wanted me to sample it."

Jørdis and I cracked up, careful to move our sharp scissors aside before we doubled over laughing on the bed. Summer smiled ruefully at us.

Finally Jørdis managed, "You sampled his mulligatawny! Was it good?"

"It was okay," Summer said. "I would have to get used to it."

That made Jørdis and me laugh harder. Coughing through it, I asked Summer, "Are you going to sample his mulligatawny again?"

Still smiling, she shook her head. "Sometimes mulligatawny is just mulligatawny"

"Oh," Jørdis and I said together. I was disappointed that Summer hadn't made progress in her romance with Manohar. I wished I could send her on another mission, since she seemed to need an excuse to justify making a move on him, but I didn't dare. If Manohar had been as mad as Summer said about being manipulated regarding the stable-boy issue, I didn't want to push it. Gabe hadn't called me into his office for a stern talking-to by now, the third week of class. Maybe I'd dodged a bullet.

"Anyway," Summer said, "Hunter's taking anatomy. Everything that happened in the story is exactly like what really happened at the beach party. That means he's hot for you, Erin."

"That also means he slept with that blond girl," I pointed out.

"If he did, at least he wants you to watch," Summer said.

"I need to find a way to read this story," Jørdis said.

"But he didn't sleep with that girl," Summer said, dismissing the idea with a wave of her open scissors. "Remember, he left the party with you and Brian. He and Brian came back. I saw the blond girl a few more times, but never with him."

"Who left first?" I asked. "I could hear the music all the way down here. You had your argument with Manohar and left a couple of hours before the party shut down. Hunter had plenty of time to hook up with her. Looks like he did."

Deep in the night I woke. I had lain in bed for a long time without realizing I was awake. Finally something made me roll over and peer out the window nearest the head of my bed, onto the dusky street, just in time to glimpse Hunter returning to the dorm.

He was one floor down, several steps away from the front stoop, and the crisp red leaves in the trees cast him into the shadows of the streetlights. But I knew him by the way he moved. His overcoat was open to reveal jeans and a casual but expensive shirt underneath.

Overcoat? It was hardly fall, not cold enough—but glancing at the clock on my filing cabinet, I realized it must be plenty cold for him to need this extra layer in the stillness at four thirty in the morning. The wind caught the back of his coat and whipped it behind him as he grasped the stair railing with one hand. He swung himself onto the stoop, as if expending his last bit of energy would be worth the trouble because it would get him to bed that much faster. I knew the feeling.

He had disappeared under the awning now. Through floors and walls, I caught the faintest whisper of his fingers on the buttons as he punched the combination into the lock, then the groan of the door opening for him. He shut it quietly—which I wasn't expecting. I'd never noticed the way he opened and closed doors when other people were asleep, but he'd caused me so much trouble personally that I expected the door to slam. It did not. I hardly registered it closing before my ears picked up his steps on the staircase—fast at first, still excited about going to bed, slower as he reached my story.

He was as near as he would get to me now, sliding around the second-story banister on his way to the next staircase, leaning his weight into it, his exhaustion overcoming him. If I jumped out of bed and dashed through Summer and Jørdis's room and burst into the hallway, I could catch him. His sleepy blue eyes would widen in surprise, then narrow again when he saw it was me.

And then he was gone, shuffling up the first few steps of the second staircase with renewed energy, slowing as he reached the top. A pause as he circled the third-story banister.

The faintest footsteps now, slowing as they faded. A squeal as he opened his own door on the fifth floor. A thump as he shut it. Open and shut, done and over.

I closed my heart to him then. I thought I had succeeded in forgetting him ten times over. Each time I was mistaken. He managed to find his way into my heart again and sabotage it from the inside. This time was the last. In the dead of night he had gone to visit that blond girl, and now he had come home.

7

My next story was due the following day. I could have written one accusing him of sleeping with that girl. But I'd never intended to call him out in the first place, and I certainly wouldn't write another story about him now.

Trouble was, I'd lost my taste for writing romance. At least, for *these* people to read, and Hunter to smirk about, and Manohar to make fun of. My laptop and I still played Cupid on break at the coffee shop and during any luxurious hour I could spare on the weekends, writing and people-watching in the park. But that was for me, not to show.

For class I wrote a story about a girl dealing with some unnamed tragedy by closing herself in the closet of a huge, empty house, with her evil unnamed authority figure clomping around in the hallways, sending the servants to check on the girl in the closet, never venturing inside herself.

Two weeks later, my next story was about a seventh-grader obsessed with the idea that if she won the middle school spelling bee and made it to the next round, she would see her absentee father in the audience. He had finally come for her! But she never made it to that round because she spelled *desertion* with a double *s*.

Maybe I was trying to tell Hunter a little about myself with these stories, and apologize in a very roundabout way for not connecting with him in high school. Typically, I couldn't tell if he was affected by them or not, because in class his comments were blandly supportive, and on paper he wrote helpful technical comments. Sigh.

But I thought these stories moved me closer to the publishing internship, if Gabe had any sway. He seemed excited about them during class. He wrote in pencil in the margins that he saw me taking chances and growing as a writer. My classmates seemed impressed with the stories, too, and discussed them animatedly and invented deep bullshit meanings for what were essentially pages out of my middle school diary. I was surprised and disappointed that my classmates liked these stories so much, because I hated them. At this point I decided everybody in the class must be clinically depressed.

A few weeks later, the girls in class, even Summer, giggled behind their hands at how much they looked forward to Hunter's sexy stories. But it seemed to me that his fortune-teller story was just installment number two of "Anatomy Unit on the Reproductive System."

And his story was not his way of hinting that he liked me. Neither was the fact that he sat on Jørdis's bed one Friday afternoon when I cruised through wearing my belly-dancing outfit. Yes, I was a little self-conscious about walking down the street in it, and my grandmother would die, but with my jacket over the top it didn't look significantly weirder than some of the other oddities New Yorkers wore in public. I was *very* self-conscious about wearing it in front of Hunter.

"Hullo, Erin," Hunter said without looking up from his cutting.

"Hullo, Hunter," I said without slowing down. I stepped into my own little bedroom and pushed the door until it was open only a crack.

I stood there staring at the bay windows for a moment. Normally next I would close the shades on the windows. Slowly I reached for the pull on the first shade. But even after I'd closed them all, knowing Hunter was on the other side of my door while I changed, I felt as warm and exposed as if they had been wide open.

I hung my belly-dancing outfit on a hook in my room, rather than on the outside of the door where it usually stayed. That would be a painfully obvious ploy for Hunter's attention. I made myself a gourmet dinner by opening a pack of peanut butter crackers, and I settled on my bed to study.

Listened for Hunter in the outer room.

Waited for him to burst in.

Of course he didn't. It bothered me that he didn't come in to bother me, and he knew this. However, I had vowed to close my heart to him, and I meant it this time. I tried my best to throw myself into my history reading.

But come on, it was history. Versus Hunter.

After half an hour of torture, I peeked around my door. I would feel foolish if I'd focused on Hunter and wasted half an hour of precious homework time when he wasn't even there.

He was asleep.

Not quite believing what I was seeing, I tiptoed across the room for a closer look. The overhead light and the lamps on either side of Jørdis's bed shone on him like a specimen in an operating theater, but he was dead to the world. He had curled his big body on the end of Jørdis's bed. His eyelids did not flutter when I stood over him. His long blond lashes cast severe shadows down his soft cheek. His expensive T-shirt had pulled away from his waistband to reveal his tight, muscular side and the long white scar.

His late-night visits to the blonde must have worn him out.

Angry as I was, I empathized with him. If I'd been able to take a catnap in another dorm room or the library, I wouldn't have wanted to be woken. So I only slid the scissors very carefully off the ends of his fingers, away from his eye, and set them on the bedside table.

Then I went back to my room. But it wasn't long before Summer bounced onto the end of my bed, and she seemed a lot more excited than I was about Hunter's presence. "His poor scar is showing," she whispered. She stuck out her bottom lip in sympathy. "You should go rub his back or stroke his hair or something."

"He's not a puppy," I whispered back. "And I doubt he'd appreciate it. He's not here for me."

"He *is* here for you!" she insisted.

"He's cutting faces for Jørdis," I corrected her. "Everybody in the dorm has cut faces for Jørdis at one time or another."

"Yes, but most of them don't come back for more."

She had a point. And, truth be told, I did think Hunter was there for me. I just didn't know why. I huffed out a sigh and hissed, "He's already got my tuition and my inheritance and a career at my farm. He has no reason to flirt with me, sometimes, and sometimes insult me and try to make me feel awful about breaking away from my grandmother."

"He likes you," Summer whispered. "More than likes. He's interested in you romantically."

"Oh, yeah? Then why did he feel up that blonde at the party in the bathroom?"

"He was trying to make you jealous," Summer said with exaggerated patience, "just like in his story. He is giving you obvious hints, and you are choosing not to take them."

"That's so unlike him. If he wants me, why doesn't he come out and tell me?"

She shrugged. "You're so defensive. You've got a Kentucky-size chip on your shoulder, and the stable-boy story incident didn't help. I'm not saying I blame you for any of that. I'd be defensive, too. I'm saying it's an obstacle, he's trying to get around it, and you keep blocking his way."

I wanted to believe her, but it seemed too simple. "Do you know why he's asleep right now?"

She shook her head.

"He's going out at eleven thirty and coming back at four thirty, three or four nights a week." At her strange look I hurried on, "I am not spying on him. I wake up when he comes down the stairwell that late, and I watch him walk down the sidewalk. Later I watch him come back." I gestured toward my bay window.

"Maybe he has a job," she said.

"He doesn't need a job. He has my grandmother. He wouldn't jeopardize his perfect grades for extra pocket money. And there's no pattern to his days. I always work from five to eleven Monday through Thursday. The only reason my weekend schedule is irregular is that it's our busiest time and my boss wants me to make as few bad lattes as possible to reduce the damage." I felt my nostrils flare as I said, "Hunter's visiting that blonde."

Summer gave me a stern look. "You have made that up."

Had I? He'd dated a lot in high school, but the girls he went out with talked about him as if he was the perfect gentleman. They were only sad and confused that he hadn't asked them out again. He wasn't the type to sleep around. He definitely wasn't the type to sleep around and then write a tell-all story about it for a college class.

Then again, what did I really know about Hunter? I felt such a strong connection with him because our lives for the past six years had been intertwined. But we weren't friends. And this connection I felt with him . . . maybe I'd made that up, too. After all, I was a novelist.

"He's going to see that fortune-teller from his second story," I suggested. This I *really* didn't believe. I wanted Summer to reassure me.

She rolled her eyes. "Hunter Allen is not having sex with a fortune-teller. He is entertaining the men in the class, fascinating the women, and egging you on. Do you hear yourself and how you have been egged on? You are thoroughly eggy right now. You're like a freaking omelet." She bounced up from my bed and went back into her room.

A few minutes passed in which I did not get any homework done at all. I could hear her paging quietly through a book. Finally I heard the mattress creek on Jørdis's side of the room. A pillow thudded to the floor. Then I could hear Hunter and Summer talking.

Summer: "Wake up, sleepyhead."

Hunter: "Jesus. Sorry."

Summer: "You shouldn't cut out faces for Jørdis when you're so tired. You left way too thick a border around them. She's going to get you."

Hunter, after a yawn: "She needs a thicker border so she can overlap them when she glues them to the canvas. She hasn't thought this through."

Summer: "I'm just warning you."

Hunter: "Thanks for the warning."

The conversation ended, and after several moments of silence I realized I was straining my ears to hear them through the wall instead of reading history. I bent my head to my book.

"Hey," Hunter said, looming over me.

I let out some kind of strangled squeal, and my book and laptop went flying in different directions.

"Sorry, sorry," he soothed me, holding both hands up to calm me down. "I forgot how easily you startle."

"What's the matter?" Summer stuck her head through the door. "What'd you do to her?"

"She startles easily." Hunter sounded the tiniest bit miffed. "It was an accident."

Summer gave me an uneasy look, then winked at me and disappeared.

I took deep breaths and winced at my hard, fast heartbeat. Accepting the laptop Hunter retrieved from the floor for me, and then the history book, I managed, "I didn't hear you cross the room. What are you, a ninja?"

"Maybe." As he sat on the foot of my bed, his rakish smile made me suspect his next story for Gabe's class would be a ninja hook-up. But it was so hard to stay defensive when he paired the smile with sleepy blue eyes. "I didn't mean to fall asleep out there. I thought you would come out and talk to me in your belly-dancing costume." He nodded to the sad pool of green gauze that had fallen from its hook in the corner.

I thought what he meant by this was, *I put my hands all over that girl in the shower and then wrote a story about doing her. I also wrote a story about doing a fortune-teller. So I don't see why in the world you did not come into Jørdis's room and flirt with me.* This seemed to be what he was implying, but I couldn't be sure.

"I have a lot of homework," I said.

"And I have a proposition."

"'Kay," I said warily. I tried to keep my tone flat, but I was dying to know what it was.

"I promised you I wouldn't tell Gabe about the . . ." He opened his hand on his thigh. This meant *embarrassing stable-boy story.* He went on, "But I told you I couldn't vouch for Brian or Manohar."

"Oh, no," I whispered.

"Listen." He put his hand on my ankle. "Brian won't say anything. He likes you, and he likes Summer, and Summer has worked hard on him. But Manohar needs a favor."

I nodded for him to go on, hoping I would be able to hear him over the blood throbbing in my ears. Being startled had only half the effect on my pulse of Hunter's hand on my ankle.

"Manohar's rushing a fraternity," Hunter said. "Some of the older and very influential brothers have a trip to Belmont Park planned for tomorrow. It would help Manohar get in their good graces if he brought along a horse-racing insider."

I frowned at him. "You want me to handicap the races for them? Aren't you going? You could do it."

"Not like you can," he said. "I was interested in the training side, and I liked to predict which colts would train well, but during the races I wasn't watching. I was in the stable, currycombing." He squeezed my ankle hard, and I wondered whether this was unconscious. "You were the one in the stands, taking notes on the big picture."

I could have argued with him. He knew as well as I did that horse racing was unpredictable. Even though I could probably make educated guesses about winning horses better than most people, I'd never imagined using my knowledge to place bets at Belmont Park through a partner of legal age. If I'd thought I could make any money that way, I wouldn't have been working at the coffee shop.

But if I argued this point, I'd be arguing myself out of a promise of silence from Manohar. So I said, "Great!"

"One of the guys is borrowing a limo from his dad's business," Hunter said. "He'll pick us up in front of the dorm at noon." He looked at his hand on my ankle as if he hadn't realized it was there. He jerked it away and stood.

I almost forgot to ask, "Can I bring Summer?"

"Of course," he said in a tone that told me he'd been expecting this question.

Summer popped her head into the room again. "Where are we going?"

"Hunter!" Jørdis boomed from her bedroom. "What have you been doing with these borders? I told you not to cut so large a border!"

Hunter gave me a conspiratorial smile that said we both understood Jørdis and her tendency to overexcitement about cutting. I did not share the smile with him, but I didn't have to. Hunter could make me feel that camaraderie with him even when I didn't want to.

"Sweet dreams, Erin." He went out to placate Jørdis.

AT NOON THE NEXT DAY, SUMMER and I walked down the stairs in front of the dorm and into a gaggle of six boys. Several of them said, "Nice hat."

I wore a wide-brimmed velvet hat my grandmother had bought me for the fall meet at Churchill Downs last year. I needed it this cool, bright afternoon. I didn't need any more freckles. And, okay, maybe I wanted to flaunt to Hunter that I still had an iota of fashion sense. I'd dressed in a heathered green cashmere sweater and a tan suede skirt to go with the hat. I made the boys look like servants in comparison—except, of course, Hunter, who had anticipated that I would dress up for a horse race, even in New York. He wore khakis and a blazer. With his blond hair styled just so and mussed a little by the breeze, he looked like his father owned the country club.

"Thanks," I said. "Nice car." NIEWIAROWSKI & SONS FUNERAL HOME—GO OUT IN STYLE was painted on the door of the limo in careful gold cursive.

"Hey," said the guy who'd been bartending at the party in the bathroom. "You're lucky we didn't bring the hearse."

"Fuggedaboudit," I wanted to say in response to his accent. But I was playing nice and shutting Manohar up for good, so I only smiled sweetly at Summer's horrified expression as the boys opened the door of the limo and handed us inside. I slid all the way over to the opposite door. Summer huddled next to me. She must have been a little creeped out by the idea of riding in the funeral home limo. She bent over and looked under the seat.

The boys shut the door behind us. They seemed to be conferring quietly. I thought they might be cooking up something. Sure enough, when the door opened, Hunter sat on the seat facing us and slid all the way to the opposite door, directly across from me. Manohar sat next to him, across from Summer. He was glad she had come even if he was too stubborn to say so. Two more boys piled in beside us, and the other two climbed in up front.

Hunter watched me, so light and bright in front of me with his blond hair and blue eyes in the black limo, but we were spared an awkward convo because the other boys had grown loud again. They were boisterous and adorable if you had a taste for honors program nerds. The boys in the back with us shouted movie quotes through a little window to the boys in the front. Underneath the noise, Summer and Manohar had started a halting convo of their own.

I'd expected a short ride through Manhattan, but the boys were willing to go blocks out of our way to avoid the Midtown Tunnel toll. I looked out the window and watched the city go by. New York was vast, yet all I saw on a daily basis was the same college buildings and town houses. Sixth Avenue was a different world. We passed Fortieth Street. Two blocks later Manohar said we should look down the street for a glimpse of Times Square, but I was still leaning toward Hunter and looking back over my shoulder toward the Kensington Books building, wondering whether, if I worked there, I would eat my lunch and take my writing break in the big park nearby. A few minutes later Summer *oooh*ed as Manohar pointed at Rockefeller Center. I was looking in the other direction, at the strangely stark Simon & Schuster building, like something out of a Charlie Chaplin movie about people in the Depression fearing the future. At the beginning of the semester, when we visited MoMA, I'd dragged Summer with me to stare longingly at the HarperCollins building, a modern black-and-white-striped monstrosity. But I peered up at it again, picturing myself as a publishing intern walking through those glass doors. I never took my eyes off it when Summer exclaimed, "And look, there's the *LOVE* sculpture!" I was still watching the skyscraper through the back window of the limo when we hung a hard right at Central Park, throwing Summer into my lap.

In the ensuing commotion, which involved Hunter looking outraged as Manohar and another guy extricated themselves from his own lap, Summer whispered to me, "These city boys can't drive."

I nodded. "Hunter will use that."

Her eyes widened. "For what?"

"He can't stand being a passenger because he's not in charge. I guarantee you he'll find a way to drive us home."

"Drink, ladies?" The bartender, who was driving, handed a bottle of Kentucky bourbon through the little window. The boys in the back with us produced tumblers from a secret compartment in the back of the driver's seat—the limo was used for drunken wakes, apparently—and handed the bourbon around. Hunter put up his hand in an understated gesture of refusal. Just as I'd thought. After everyone else got drunk, he could drive the limo home because he would be the last one standing.

"Drink?" Hunter prompted me. One of the boys was trying to hand me a tumbler across the limo.

"No thanks," I said.

When the boys' volume escalated again, he asked me quietly, "More history homework tonight?"

"Calculus," I said. "I can't do it tomorrow. I'm working twelve hours."

I'd been careful not to use a snippy tone. Still, I hoped the words themselves would shut him up. No such luck. He said, "You're really tired."

"I'm not tired." I watched him suspiciously. "How can you tell

I'm tired?" Maybe I'd been too stingy with the remnants of my miracle cream, and I needed to use a little more under my eyes.

"When you're tired, you hold your chin up." He demonstrated, lifting his nose into the air. "You look haughtier than usual."

"Oh, nice," I said.

"I didn't mean it that way." He spread even farther in his seat, arm along the windowsill, one ankle on the other knee, taking up more than his share of space, as always. Then he gave me a cocky grin. "I like you haughty."

I did not know what to say to that. He was flirting with me again. I tried not to be flattered. He had flirted with me at the beach party right after putting his hands all over that blonde. Flirting meant nothing to him. I said noncommittally, "I think it's the hat."

"What?" Summer yelled across the car at Manohar. "I can hardly hear you." She turned to the other boys. "Simmer down! It's like freaking Boy Scout camp in here." Then she turned to Hunter. "Trade places with me."

Without protest, Hunter crouched and allowed Summer to slip past him and collapse between the door and Manohar. Hunter turned, sat down beside me, and proceeded to put his ankle on the opposite knee and his arm along the back of the seat behind me.

Summer was attempting to explain the Southern phenomenon of mud riding to Manohar, and Manohar was expressing disbelief. But between sentences and over her glass of bourbon, she took time to give me a sly smile.

I tried to ignore the tingles along my neck and shoulders where Hunter's arm accidentally touched them. I looked out the window.

At the track, the guys wanted to buy drinks—this would be a long process involving many drink stands because six people were drinking and only two of them were twenty-one—and find a place in the stands. They didn't understand that betting on horses with any aplomb took some work. While the rest of them laughed amid the crowd under autumn trees, Hunter and I grabbed tip sheets and stood at the paddock fence, watching the grooms parade the thoroughbreds that would run in the first race.

This was déjà vu, standing next to Hunter at a fence with horses on the other side. I did not want to like him or have a good time today. I wished that the stallion in front of us didn't remind me of Boo-boo, and that I wasn't itching to touch him, just to feel his warm skin and sheer power under my palm.

"Hey, it's Boo-boo," Hunter said.

He meant the horse's markings, but I chose to take him more literally. Paging through the tip sheet, I said, "No, this guy's bloodlines are from California." Then I flipped through the booklet for the next horse shaking its mane in front of us. The sire was from my farm. I'd never been too impressed with the father even though he'd won the Stephen Foster Handicap, but the dam was from a prestigious farm, and she'd won the Kentucky Oaks.

The bottom line was that horse races were never sure things. That's why people bet on them. And all the information available to me about these horses was available to everyone at the track. All I could do with my background was give it the proper weight. I muttered, "This is nothing Manohar's friends wouldn't know if they'd just done their homework."

"It's a fraternity," Hunter said. "They want the easy way out. *You* are the homework."

As he spoke, something loomed large in the corner of my vision. We both turned back to the paddock in time to see a groom lead the next thoroughbred past, an enormous bay with black points. This horse looked like strength and speed, the veins standing out in his chest as his muscles strained with the effort to keep himself from bolting over the paddock fence, through the crowd, and out into the parking lot just for kicks. He was the kind of horse I would have been afraid of back home.

"That is a beautiful horse," I murmured at the same time Hunter breathed, "That is a beautiful horse."

We glanced at each other. He smiled at me. Despite myself, I smiled back.

"You telling the boys to bet on him?" he asked.

Shaking off the chill that had washed through me when he smiled at me, I consulted the brochure again. "Not with that jockey."

"You're crazy."

"Who's supposed to be the horse prodigy here, me or you?"

"You're going to get Manohar blackballed," he said, but he wasn't looking at me. It wasn't like Hunter to let on that someone didn't have his full attention in a conversation. I followed his gaze to a blood bay colt with a white blaze. The horse looked out of his league in a race like this.

Then I realized Hunter wasn't looking at the horse. He gazed at the groom, a lanky, white-haired African-American man. I figured this out when the groom's eyes passed casually over the crowd and stopped on Hunter. His eyes widened, his jaw dropped, and then he broke into a big grin.

Hunter grinned, too. He lifted one finger from the fence in greeting.

The man realized he was still leading the horse. Down by his side, he flattened his hand, motioning for Hunter to wait.

Hunter nodded.

Then, as the man led the horse past us and made the turn in the paddock, he circled his finger at his side, asking Hunter to meet him back in the stables, I guessed.

Casually Hunter straightened and stretched his arms over his head. "I'm going to slip around back and try to talk my way into the stables. I doubt it will work, but you never know."

"Is he a friend of yours?" I asked. "Did your dad work with him when you lived here?"

Hunter glanced at me in surprise. "Yeah. I hoped I might run into him, but I never thought he'd recognize me."

I nodded. "Because you were only twelve when you left?"

"Yeah." His eyes followed the groom and colt out of the paddock. "He looks exactly the same."

"Go ahead." I nodded in the direction the groom had gone. "I'll cover for you. I won't let the others know you're human."

He gave me a look I couldn't read. He bent down, ducked under the wide brim of my hat, and kissed my cheek.

And then he was gone, sashaying through the crowd milling around the fence, holding his blazer slung over his shoulder with two fingers.

8

I watched the rest of the horses parade around the paddock, perused the tip sheet carefully, and told the boys which horse to bet on. I gave them my warning that horse racing was not an exact science and that my knowledge of the sport might give them an edge or lead them straight to the poorhouse. Nevertheless, they bet on the horse I picked, the horse won at twenty-five to one (everybody else at the track had bet on the impressive bay), and afterward the boys did not listen to my words of caution anymore.

By the lull before the last post time of the afternoon, the boys had gotten drunk and greedy. They'd insisted I pick the trifecta for them, which meant the horses that came in first, second, and third, in order. If I hit it, it would pay unbelievable odds, precisely because hitting it was nearly impossible. They were so excited that they wandered out of the stands and down to the fence where they could cheer on their horses right next to the track. I was glad. When they lost their entire winnings for the afternoon on this one race, I didn't want to be around.

But Manohar and Summer had forgotten all about betting. They had gotten drunk and fallen in love. They'd talked with their heads close together all afternoon, and from what I could overhear, none of it had anything to do with horses. Huddled close and holding hands on the armrest between their seats, they didn't seem to notice when Hunter stepped into our booth and tossed his blazer over the back of a seat, his temples shining with sweat as if he'd done some work in the stables.

"Did you see who you wanted to see?" I asked, watching the tractor tow the gate to the starting line.

"Lots of old friends." He smiled to himself.

I looked up at him, then back to the field in front of us, which was filled with warm sunlight and the slanting shadows of evening. "This track is huge. When you first came to Churchill Downs, did it seem small?"

"I never saw much of it," he said. "I was back in the stables, not out on the track." But maybe he realized that he sounded like a recording stuck on replay—we both did, reminding ourselves of what we used to be and what we'd done to each other—because he took a breath and went on, "We had our own house here on Long Island. We rented it, but it seemed like ours. And we went into the city a lot. In Louisville we lived on your grandmother's farm and that's all there was. Churchill Downs seemed tiny in comparison, yeah, but so did my whole world."

"So tell me something, stable boy," Manohar called from his seat. "I've been puzzling through this. If you stole Erin's birthright on graduation night—"

Hunter opened his mouth to protest, but Summer broke in. "Let him finish, Hunter. We've both been wondering about this."

"—how did you get admitted to college so quickly?" Manohar asked. "You've cast yourself as an innocent who happened to be handed Erin's fortune—"

I snorted. Then realized I should not have snorted while wearing an elegant autumn hat.

"Exactly." Manohar pointed at me. "To be admitted, Hunter must have applied to school ahead of time, when you did, Erin. So the corporate takeover was premeditated."

"That's not what happened," Hunter said. I couldn't see his eyes behind his sunglasses, but he sounded angry. "I'd always planned to come to school here. I'm from here, and I wanted to get back here. I got a scholarship. The same one Erin got, actually. But it wasn't enough, and if it hadn't been for Erin's grandmother, I would have been stuck in Kentucky."

"Unless you worked your way through school slaving forty hours a week in a coffee shop," I cut in. "God forbid."

"Actually," Hunter's voice rose, "Erin got the idea from me to come to school here, not the other way around."

I had kept a curious distance from this conversation, watching Hunter squirm from a few feet away. But I should have known Hunter would turn it around so he sounded blameless. I plopped down in the seat between him and Manohar, exclaiming, "That's ridiculous. My grandmother went to school here. She wanted me to go here, and when I did some research and discovered they had a great creative-writing program, I agreed. I planned on this all along. It was only when she insisted on controlling my major and my career and my life that things fell apart."

"That's not what happened," Hunter said again. "When I first met you, you swore you were going back to California."

"Back to California?" Summer broke in. "Erin, you never told me you moved to Kentucky from California."

Hunter talked right over her. "You only got interested in New York when I told you how cool it was, and I gave you a magnet with the Statue of Liberty and the Empire State Building and the other landmarks on it. My grandma gave it to me before I left Long Island, and I gave it to you, and you're going to sit there and say I stole your life from you?"

I was glad I wore sunglasses and a hat, because I could feel my face burning. Could Hunter really be the source of my treasured New York magnet? The months surrounding my mom's death were a blur to me now. I really didn't remember where the magnet had come from. I was embarrassed that I couldn't say for sure, and even more ashamed that I'd never even considered he might have a grandmother, too.

"What have you done?" Summer murmured to Manohar.

"Hey, kids," Manohar said, "I was just curious about the timing. I didn't mean to—"

Stony faced, Hunter told me, "You plagiarized my life. You're like a seventh-grader. You take notes from the internet, forget where the information came from, and copy it straight into your school paper. You plagiarized my life without even knowing it."

A bell went off in my head. After a few seconds of staring at Hunter's hardened face and thinking I was going crazy, I realized the race had started. All four of us jumped up and leaned on the rail.

"Erin, which horse did you tell them would come in first?" Summer asked.

"Number nine," I said, hoping Hunter couldn't hear over the noise of the crowd how my voice was shaking with emotion. I cleared my throat. "In the pink-and-white silks."

"He's way back in the pack," Manohar said.

"Wait for it," I muttered. "I've watched that jockey for years. On this horse, he'll come through."

"Which one did you say would come in second?" Summer asked.

"Ten, in the yellow," I told her.

"I guess that's okay," she said. "He's second now. Do the boys win anything if you're right only about that one?"

Hunter leaned toward me. "Did you tell them to box the horses?"

Hating how my pulse raced when his shirtsleeve brushed my sweater, I nodded.

"So they'll win some," Hunter told Summer. "Not nearly as much as if she hits the trifecta."

"Which one did you say would come in third?" Summer asked.

"Number seven," I said, "in blue."

"What are you doing to me, woman?" Manohar exclaimed. "That horse is dead last in a field of fourteen!"

"Wait for it," I said again. "It's a big track and a long race." I tuned them out, tuned the crowd out, focused on lucky number seven. I loved to watch horses run, extending those long muscles and battling past each other in a rush of adrenaline and mud. I would have loved to be a horse—though not a racehorse, bred and trained and prodded and controlled. I would have wanted to run wild on some plain, running because it felt good and I could.

"Erin." Summer pushed Manohar out of the way and stood between us at the rail. She squeezed my hand. "Erin, here come your horses. Oh my God! What if you were right?"

"Come on, number nine!" Manohar hollered. This was out of character for him. He stood taller on the bottom rung of the rail and pumped his fist in the air. "Number nine! Number ten!"

The pack spaced way out in the home stretch, so there was a good ten seconds at the end when number nine led, number ten ran second, and number seven ran third, and Summer bounced beside me and squeezed my hand harder and harder, and Manohar yelled louder. I expected the number four horse I'd almost put in this trifecta to come from behind, but he didn't. The crowd noise pitched higher and higher, to a climax as the horses zoomed past us. The crowd noise died off but Summer was still squealing. Manohar was shouting, "Erin Blackwell, I love you and I am sorry for every negative comment I ever made about your lascivious stories." Way below us at the fence around the field, the other four boys cheered drunkenly.

Hunter chuckled beside me. "Erin," he said, "you just won Manohar's fraternity brothers nine thousand dollars."

As I'd predicted, after the races the fraternity boys were too drunk to drive. They celebrated their victory with another beer apiece while the losing bettors milled out of the stands. They downed more shots of bourbon back in the limo. Hunter slipped effortlessly into the driver's seat. The boisterous boys piled into the back. With Manohar and Summer inseparable, that left me in the front beside Hunter.

"Where are you going?" I asked as he passed the entrance for the Cross Island Parkway.

"The bay," he said. "A little seafood joint I've missed." He glanced over at me. "My treat."

He must have guessed what I was thinking: dinner out was not in my budget. But I'd be damned if I'd accept it from him, after that business about plagiarizing his life. "No thanks," I said. "I don't need your charity, or my grandmother's, either."

Shouts of laughter came through the window from the backseat. "The guys owe you dinner out of their nine thousand dollars," Hunter said.

"Maybe, but they're too drunk to realize it."

"Well, you're not sitting in the limo while we go in and eat." His voice grew tight. "Somebody will buy your dinner and you will eat it, or I will tell Gabe I am the stable boy."

I huffed out an exasperated sigh. "I've just solved this problem with Manohar. I've paid my dues. You can't hold the stable boy over my head and make me do anything you want."

He pulled the limo to a stop at a light. "Yes, I can."

We eyed each other for a few heartbeats. I glared angrily at him. I was mad at him for manipulating me, and madder at myself for letting him see I was angry. He half-smiled back at me, eyebrows raised in question. Then he glanced at his Rolex, a gesture strategically planned to look casual. I knew it was staged and the message was clear: *I have your grandmother's credit card, and you don't.*

Then he cocked his head to one side. The smile fell away, and he lowered his voice to an offended growl. "It's only dinner." Horns honked behind us, but he held my gaze for a few more seconds before pulling the limo forward. Then he asked, "How much weight have you lost since you've been here? The freshman fifteen refers to gaining fifteen pounds, not losing it."

Normally Hunter was the politest person I knew—on the surface, anyway. He'd only made this rude comment about my weight because he was already angry with himself for rudely forcing me to go to dinner. I waited for him to hear himself and feel even guiltier. My most effective response to Hunter was to say nothing at all—if I could stand it. He expected a retort from me. He didn't expect silence.

"You look great," he said quickly. "You always look great. I just mean . . ." His voice trailed off.

I watched him from under the brim of my hat.

He scowled at the road, swinging the limo into as tight a turn as he could manage at an intersection crowded with restaurants and hungry Long Islanders. "You've told me before that you're not spending every cent you make on the dorm. You're still going to plays and movies, right? You could spend some of that money on food. Restaurants are a huge part of the New York experience."

"Peanut butter and crackers are fine," I said breezily. "I see what you mean, but I have to draw the line somewhere."

Manohar turned around and spoke to us through the window. "Why don't you move out of the dorm?" he asked.

"No," Hunter said quietly. Somewhere in the backseat, Summer squealed, "No!"

Manohar went on, "Wouldn't it be cheaper to live in an apartment with a lot of roommates? Not as nice, maybe, but at least you could afford it."

"No," Hunter said again. This time Manohar craned his neck to look at him.

"Yes," I told Manohar, "it would be cheaper. I did that last summer."

"And she had a bad experience that spooked her," Hunter said.

"It didn't spook me," I said. "It only made me very angry and got me fired."

"It *should* have spooked you," Hunter said. "Manohar, she hasn't lived here long enough to know who she can trust. She needs to be in the dorm with a sign-in desk and security. Don't bring it up again."

"That doesn't make sense," Manohar insisted. "How do you know she can trust her randomly assigned dorm roommates? Jørdis with a slash, for God's sake!"

"She seems less dangerous as you get to know her," I said.

"And Summer could be a serial killer," Manohar said.

Summer's giggle reached us from the backseat.

"It's my life, Hunter," I said, "and you're going to have to trust my judgment. Sorry."

Without taking his eyes off the road, Hunter reached behind him and slid the window shut with a bang. "You are so stubborn!" he burst out, loud enough that the boys in the back quieted, listening through the window for what dark path our conversation had taken.

"You're just doing all of this to get back at your grandmother," he said. "How can you keep insisting you don't belong on that farm? Don't you take the trifecta as a sign?"

"You know as well as I do that hitting the trifecta was pure luck. I nearly picked the number four horse to show."

"But you didn't. This business is in your blood."

The sun was setting now. As Hunter laboriously pulled the limo into a congested parking lot, orange light shone directly into his blue eyes, making him squint.

He looked like a kid then, the twelve-year-old kid I'd met so long ago in a rolling green field in the summertime, bright sunlight glinting in his blond hair.

We should still be friends. We were made to be friends, not enemies. Maybe he recognized the insanity of our situation, too, and that's why he was trying to persuade me to steal back the birthright he'd stolen.

"It's not in my blood." I lowered my voice because I had no wish to share this with the limo. "Romance novelists write that about their heroines all the time. It makes no sense, that the horse farm was in the heroine's blood. Or the city was in her blood, or the wild Pacific coastline, or the oil-drilling rig on her parents' vast Texas estate. The place was not in the heroine's blood, Hunter. The simple fact is that she grew up there, and her overbearing grandmother insisted that she move back there, and the heroine finally gave in—"

"She did?" Hunter asked, blond brows up.

"In romance novels, Hunter, not in real life, and then everybody unanimously agreed it was in her blood, to make her feel better about moving back to the horse farm when she didn't want to. But she didn't feel better. She felt the same as she always had, that she wanted to be a writer and she did not want to do it on a horse farm in Kentucky."

"Not yet." Hunter stopped the limo along the edge of the crowded parking lot and turned off the engine. "But you will, because you'll get tired of being poor. I know because I've been poor, and it sucks. If you weren't rich, you would never, ever walk away from an opportunity like running your grandmother's farm. You would not want to be a writer. It would never occur to you to give up your family's support so you could see how the other half lives. And that's all it is for you. You are not living the life of a starving artist. You're only visiting. You can string yourself along on scholarships and tips from the coffee shop, but if you ever lose your job, or get thrown in jail for possession of someone else's pot, or get hurt, your grandmother will be right there to catch you when you fall. You know it, and she knows it. Face it. You will never be poor, no matter how hard you try. And eventually you're going to realize that."

"Leave 'er alone!" came a shout from the backseat. Then, "Box your weight, Allen!"

Hunter blinked but didn't otherwise acknowledge the frat boys yelling at him. "Erin, you waltz through life with grace and confidence that only come from old money. You will never bow to anybody like a person would who'd grown up poor. Even if you desperately needed a morsel of food to keep from starving, you might think you were begging, but the people with the food would give you some because they would think you were in charge. You couldn't beg if you tried." He got out of the car and closed the door.

While he'd been talking, the boys and Summer had bailed out of the backseat. I found myself alone in the silence, looking out over ancient brick buildings beaten by the Atlantic winds, a stranger in a strange land. The boys were from here. Even Summer seemed to blend in better now, but me? I had a wide-brimmed Derby hat perched primly on my knees.

I jumped as Hunter opened my door.

"Sorry. Didn't mean to startle you." He held out a hand to help me from the car.

* * *

A COUPLE OF HOURS, A HUGE shrimp dinner, and a very long limo ride later, Hunter dropped us in front of the dorm. As the bartender collapsed into the passenger side so he could direct Hunter in driving the limo back to the funeral home, he offered me a thousand dollars for my advice that had made him and his friends nine thousand. I calculated in my head how many hours away from the coffee shop that money would buy me. And I could feel Hunter's eyes on me, judging the poor little rich girl. I said no.

Manohar and Summer had seemed so tight all evening that I was surprised when she followed me up to our room. But as she peeled off her skirt and stood unsteadily staring into our open closet, head on the door frame, I realized she was exchanging her cute afternoon-on-the-town outfit for a comfy, subtly sexy night-in-with-new-boyfriend outfit. Brian must be away from the room on a date.

I wondered what Hunter was doing tonight.

She nearly fell over pulling on tight jeans. She'd hardly said a word since we came in. I could tell she wanted to talk to me about where she was going, but she didn't know how to say it. I didn't say it for fear of embarrassing her and scaring her off the project altogether. Two strangers, meeting by fortunate chance, falling in love—there was nothing more romantic, and nothing for her to be embarrassed about.

She was embarrassed anyway. She sat beside me on her bed, where I was carefully polishing the pricey and oh-so-comfortable boots I'd worn to Belmont. "If I don't come in tonight . . . ," she began.

"Mm-hm?" I prompted her, spreading extra polish on the worn toe of one boot.

"Don't worry about me. I'll just be upstairs. Manohar has the private room like you."

"That sounds nice." I looked up at her and smiled. "Maybe stop drinking? Because it's such a big night."

"Potentially." She nodded. "I'm through drinking for the night. I'm sober. Er. Not sober but soberer."

"Okay."

"I'm worried about you, though." She pulled off her sweater and stood at the closet door again, waiting for a better one to appear. "You and Hunter really went at it a couple of times. I never understood what went wrong."

I gave my attention to the toe of my boot, piling even more polish into a deep scrape in the leather. "I guess being around horses reminded us of why we never got along in the first place." Not since the seventh grade, anyway. "Is he planning one of his late-night treks tonight?"

"That was my impression." She pulled a sweater over her head and then looked at me with her hands on her hips. The off-the-shoulder black sweater made her look even sexier and more sophisticated than she realized. The effect would have been just what Manohar was looking for if she hadn't been swaying slightly. Or maybe that would help.

Then she said, "I don't want to abandon you."

"You're not abandoning me." I waved my rag dismissively, releasing the odor of polish. "The second we start passing up nookie just to support each other's neuroses, we need to talk about an adjustment in our relationship. But while you're up there . . ."

I hated to ask her for another favor, since the first time I'd asked her to pump Manohar for information, they'd argued and she'd slumped into a funk for three weeks. But if all went well, she and Manohar were about to share his very small bedroom. I decided it was okay to ask. "Could you find out from Manohar where Hunter is going late at night?"

"I already asked. Manohar doesn't know. Hunter says he can't tell Manohar now that security has been breached. Which means me." She threw back her shoulders and proudly poked out her chest. "Which also means he's going somewhere he doesn't want you to know about."

I agreed. But to me it seemed likely that *somewhere* was the velvet-draped couch of the fortune-teller's shop. Or, ouch, the blonde's dorm room.

Summer cocked her head at me. "You love those boots, don't you?"

I cackled, realizing how hard I'd been polishing the toe. "I do love these boots. Moreover, my grandmother paid a lot of money for these boots when I was in high school. I probably will never be able to afford a pair of boots like this again. Gone are the days when I would come home and kick them off and throw them in the closet because if they got beat up, I could just buy another pair. I am trying to make them last by cleaning them and polishing them and putting them away carefully." I gave the heel one last rueful wipe. "It's all very *Little House on the Prairie*."

She stepped closer and peered at them. "If it were *Little House on the Prairie*, you would wrap them in paper and put them on a high shelf."

"Or I'd dig a pit for them in the ground and fill the pit with hay to keep them fresh and cold."

"Or you'd pack them in a barrel with salt."

"Jesus Christ," I said, "they're boots, not herring."

"You should have taken that thousand dollars," she said. "You earned it."

I waited until she left for her quiet night with Manohar. Then I raked all my clothes off her closet rod and plopped them on my bed. I pulled my underwear out of the bottom drawer of my dresser and even stacked my textbooks on the pillow.

Every item I owned fit on the bed. I divided the items into two piles: items that my grandmother had bought and items that I had bought with money I'd earned since I moved to New York. I looked very, very carefully at my grandmother's pile and considered throwing it away. I could toss some of it, but there was one thing I simply couldn't part with. My laptop. I might as well throw my writing career away. And if I couldn't throw out absolutely everything she'd given me, the exercise was pointless.

The more I thought about it, the more I realized there was no way to get around Hunter's argument. Only a rich girl would consider throwing out a prized possession just because it was a gift from someone she was angry with. It was a gesture of the very privileged.

I stood looking at all my stuff. Enough of this. I was wasting time. I had homework to do, and a job to go to at six in the morning. I cleared all my textbooks off the pillow except calculus.

Footfalls sounded in the stairwell. I looked up as if I could see through the wall. These could be Hunter's quick steps. This was the wrong time of night. But it was the weekend, and Summer had said she thought he was leaving.

Sure enough, as the heavy front door of the building closed and I peeked out the bay window, it was Hunter's tall frame I saw mingling in the evening crowd on the sidewalk with his overcoat slung over his shoulder, ready for his trek back in the wee hours when the air would be frigid and black.

The following Thursday, the creative-writing class discussed yet another of his stories. Add the back room of a cocktail waitress's bar to the list of possible *somewheres*. The only way to find out where Hunter was going at night was for him to stop teasing and just tell me.

The story I composed over the next week was designed to make him do just that.

9

But on the day it was due, I couldn't let it go.

Students whose stories were discussed on Monday had to turn in the stories the previous Friday by noon. It was eleven fifty-five on Friday. I sat across from the front desk in the five-story lobby of the library in a mod chair of red fur that would have looked funky and adorable except that it was matted with wear and mysterious stains. I gripped "Anything Is Possible" in both hands, bending it in the middle, sullying it with my sweat, ruining the pristine condition I preferred for my stories because I thought they looked professional and made readers less likely to tear them in two during class discussion.

On the large digital clock behind the front desk, eleven fifty-five blinked to eleven fifty-six. I needed to turn this story in, but I could not. I had written it for a specific purpose, to shake Hunter out of his pattern of seeking me out, shutting me down, and writing a sexy story about somebody else. If this story didn't motivate him to tell me how he really felt, nothing would.

The problem was that in prodding Hunter to lower his defenses, I'd lowered my own too far. The other stories I'd written for class had been fictionalizations of my life. This one wasn't fiction at all.

At eleven fifty-seven I was second-guessing myself. Why had I written this story anyway? What had possessed me to do this to myself? I could quickly write another story as a replacement. It would suck, but at least I could protect my soul from the prying eyes of the class.

I couldn't risk it. Gabe might have some system of knowing when a story had been turned in late. At the very least, some of my classmates might come into the library and ask for the reserve folder in the next few minutes so they could read the stories before starting their weekend. I would be busted, my grade would suffer, my dreams of the internship would be gone. It wasn't worth the risk.

At eleven fifty-nine I wiped both wet hands on the matted red chair, crossed the lobby, and asked the kid behind the counter to add my story to the reserve folder for my class.

Before I could change my mind, I ran away, back across the lobby, past the group of chairs, and up the stairs.

My money from the summer was running out faster than I'd expected, and I'd signed up for extra shifts at the coffee shop the whole weekend. I had an early American literature survey (bleh!) paper to finish in the two-hour window before my belly-dancing class, and no time to lose. I settled at a table on a second-story balcony with a glass wall below the rail so I could see the lobby floor. This was one of my favorite places to study. The white noise of five stories of library was the perfect background music since I was sans music player and earbuds.

Nothing changed about the white noise, I was pretty sure. The scanners at the checkout desk below me blooped softly, the elevator slid up and down, and behind me girls were having too loud a conversation for a library. But something changed. Something made me look up from my laptop toward the front desk on the first floor.

Hunter was checking out the stories.

He took the folder and handed over his student ID in exchange, then headed for the group of chairs where I'd just been sitting. Nothing unusual about that. It was a convenient place to read if you'd popped into the library only to read the stories for class. He didn't choose my fuzzy red chair. He sat in the larger carved chair upholstered in golden velvet, a stylized throne.

But he didn't seem like a king, for once. The huge chair made him smaller in comparison. He looked young, curled up with the stories, one leg folded under him. I hadn't seen him sit that way since middle school, happening upon him reading under a tree in my grandmother's pasture. He would not sit that way if he knew people were looking at him. Strange what a gaze did to Hunter.

I watched him. I knew he was reading my story rather than one of the others because my paper was a higher-quality bright white, one of the few luxuries I sprung for anymore. He stared at one page for a long time, leafed back to the page before it, read the whole passage again. He winced. I tried to figure out which of the many wince-inducing sections he was reading, judging from how many sheets he seemed to have left. I couldn't tell.

Reaching the end, he held the story up and stared at it for a few minutes. He stretched and popped his neck, then settled back down to read the other two stories. But the bright white story came out again. He read it through, slipped it back into the folder, turned in the folder at the desk, and left the library. He'd scratched a lot of comments in his notebook about the other two stories, but after reading mine, the first time and the second, he hadn't scrawled word one.

Maybe he was saving his comments to tell me in person. All weekend I half-expected him to confront me as I worked at the coffee shop, or read on a blanket with Summer in the park, or wrote in my room and listened for him in the stairwell. He did not confront me. I did not see him. My story hadn't affected him the way I'd hoped. He'd gotten the last laugh after all.

That's what I thought until class on Monday.

Anything Is Possible

by Erin Blackwell

She knocked on the closet door, then opened it slowly. Her daughter probably had her earbuds in as usual and wouldn't hear the knock anyway, but she tried to warn her daughter as best she could. Her daughter had an exaggerated startle response; doctors had said witnessing domestic abuse might have caused this.

Her daughter looked up easily from her pillow nest in the closet and smiled. "Hey."

"Hey." She sank down into the fluffy softness in front of her daughter. "What are you reading?"

Her daughter showed her the cover: *Pride and Prejudice.*

"Haven't you read that before?"

"Like four times. But it gets better every time."

She didn't doubt her daughter. She wasn't much of a reader herself, but she'd seen quite a few movie and TV versions, and the more recent ones were definitely better. "Well, I'm turning in," she lied. "Don't stay up too late reading, okay?"

"I won't," her daughter promised. Her daughter had bent her head to the book again before she had even closed the closet door. She suspected her daughter was lying, too.

Free of this responsibility, she hurried down the grand staircase, careful not to look as if she were hurrying. She waltzed right past the office where her mother still slaved over the books for the business, anxious to find a way to make it leaner smarter better richer and exceedingly more boring. If her mother burst out of the office at this moment, she could say she was headed to the kitchen for a snack. But her mother, like her daughter, stayed put behind a closed door.

As she sneaked oh so quietly out the side door, careful of the squeak that sounded when it was opened too far, she began to feel foolish. She was thirty-two years old, way too old to be sneaking around behind her mother's back, and her daughter's.

But thirty-two was way too young to have a twelve-year-old. At eighteen she had run away to Hollywood to escape the iron fist of her mother and prove her worth by making it on her own as an actress. At twenty she'd had a baby. Now she'd run away back home to escape the iron fist of the father of her child.

She would not stay here, she told herself as she leaped from the porch stair, over the corner of the crunchy gravel path, to the dewy grass where she wouldn't be heard. Moving through the wet night toward the barn was like drawing closer to her destination in life after a long and fruitless detour. Her new man made her feel like anything was possible. They would take his son and her daughter, strike out on their own, and make a new life for themselves. They had not discussed this but she knew it would work out.

"Just like your career as a Hollywood actress worked out," said a voice in her head. But if she had listened to the voice in her head, she never would have pursued her dreams. Granted, her dreams had not worked out, either, but better to pursue them than to have stayed here when she was eighteen, and to have hung her dreams in a black barn alongside stalks of tobacco to cure and age and dry.

Her mother's huge house was surrounded by large grassy hills, like a ship rocking in thirty-foot seas. At the bottom of one hill she could see nothing but stars above her in the black sky. Climbing this hill, gradually she saw more and more of the long, low horse barn. No features of the ancient building were visible in the night. It was only a black block obliterating the starlight, one open doorway filled with brilliant light, and the smell of cigarette smoke.

He was waiting for her.

She was shocked by the intense wave of desire that swept through her. She had felt this way a hundred times in high school, a thousand times during that shining year in Hollywood when she'd still thought the world was hers. So seldom had she felt this way since—perhaps a few times with the father of her child. Every time he struck her, and apologized the next day, calling up that desire became harder. She picked up speed through the dewy grass until she ran toward that feeling.

The man had seen her coming and had ground his cigarette under his riding boot. Now he laughed and caught her in his arms and swung her in a circle outside the barn. He had not grown up here like she had. He had grown up somewhere far away but similar, and she felt as if she had known him longer than a month.

"You haven't changed your mind." He set his forehead against hers and chuckled these words to her. He was a tall, strong man with a lightness about him, always laughing as he spoke. He did not judge her for wanting him.

"I haven't changed my mind." She took his rough hand and led him through the labyrinth she knew so well: past the barn office, down the dark main corridor with horse stalls on either side, to the bunk room in back.

She'd had men here before, when she was a teenager with no business here. She hadn't regretted her actions then. Now, looking back, perhaps those wild transgressions and her mother's reaction when she found out had been the hottest fire lit under her feet and had sent her two thousand miles away. She dreaded her mother's reaction still. But with any luck her mother would not find out until her relationship with this man, exactly her age, was stable and happy.

"You are a beautiful woman." He smiled down at her, running his rough fingers through her curls. "Here I thought I'd found a job in paradise, and then from out of nowhere comes an angel."

"Not from out of nowhere," she teased him. "Out of the two thirty Greyhound from Glendale."

She bit her bottom lip, wishing she hadn't made this silly joke. As a teen she would have made dozens of jokes like this in quick succession, daring a boy to keep up with her. The father of her child had taken these jokes to mean she thought she was smarter than he was, and twice this had been the reason he punched her. Exactly twice. She kept score.

But her new man grinned and lightly touched his fingertip to her nose. Gently he eased her backward onto the sagging mattress covered with a clean quilt faded to pastels. With surprising force he took her mouth with his. She tasted cigarette and mint and comfort.

Later they dressed. "Put it on," he joked from the mattress, and she donned her clothes while pretending to move in reverse. She stepped outside the barn with him while he smoked a cigarette. She didn't smoke, and any other time the smell and the habit would have annoyed her, but they seemed a part of this man, an imperfect but honest part.

He offered her a cigarette and she should have taken it, and one more. Then they would have remained outside with room to run when the father of her child stormed through the front door of her mother's grand house and out the side door.

But she declined, and in the few more minutes she thought she could spare before her mother finally turned in for the night and perhaps looked in on her to make sure she hadn't escaped again, she asked this kind man to show her the horses. She had seen them all when she'd first arrived home. She had run her hands over them to meet them and had exercised a few of them, but she wanted to see them through his eyes.

They went into a stall with a massive brown stallion. They moved one stall down to discuss a white colt, then a black filly. The man said he'd heard the filly's dam had looked exactly like this filly and had been at the farm when the woman left fourteen years before. The woman thought he must be mistaken. She did not want him to be mistaken, but she did not recognize this horse.

She removed her hand from the filly's withers and placed it on the man's chest—with measured speed, so the filly would not be startled. "Did you hear something?"

The man eyed her in disbelief, then looked in the direction of the barn door. There was a crash, a curse, the woman's name called gruffly by the father of her child, and more faintly by her mother, in the distance. And then his silhouette filled the open doorway of the stall.

There was no time to explain to her lover that the interloper was the father of her child, who must have suspected she would run back to her mother and had finally tracked her down.

There was no time to explain to the father of her child that one should never, ever shout around a horse.

The filly reared. The woman tried to duck, but her lover was close behind her. The filly's horseshoe with a thousand pounds behind it struck her in the temple.

She died instantly, or so they told me. Perhaps they told me that to comfort me, and her painless death was the biggest lie of all. I will never know for sure. I was in the closet with my earbuds in, reading *Pride and Prejudice* for the fifth time.

But if she remained conscious for a little while, I know what she was thinking. When you're starting over and anything is possible, "anything" includes an early death.

10

"It's your first story's troubled older sister, on crack and in rehab," Manohar said.

I was accustomed to the class bursting into laughter when Manohar commented on my stories. This burst was more of an explosion, as if all my classmates had been holding their breath for two weeks, waiting for my next turn to write a story, and Manohar's next turn to unwrite it.

"I guess it's better than your first one," he said after the titters died down, "but it's still so unbelievable."

Now I understood. Hunter had read my story in the library, run straight to Manohar, and told him what I'd written. Wouldn't it be hilarious if they teased me in class by saying my story was unbelievable, when it was the truest thing I'd written yet? At the beginning of class, I had thought Hunter looked ill at his end of the table, and I had wondered again whether I'd affected him with my story. Now I knew I hadn't, and I hated him.

"Why do you always go first?" I hollered before Manohar could say anything else.

He looked around. "Because I'm in the chair of being first."

I turned to Gabe. "Why does Manohar always go first? It's not fair."

Gabe put his hand over mine and said, so quietly I wasn't sure he meant the rest of the class to hear, "It's not a game."

He had no idea.

"Here's my concern," I said, and I did mean the whole class to hear. "Manohar announces that my story is unrealistic. He's put that idea into everybody's head, and now the rest of the comments will follow along those lines. I wonder if anybody else honestly thought my story wasn't realistic, or if it's just Manohar being Manohar."

"I thought that, too," said a guy on the other side of the table, half raising his hand.

"Me, too," said Wolf-boy.

"But this story is set in the same place as my first story," I pointed out. "Everybody's comment about the first story was how realistic it was." Or maybe only Hunter said that.

"This one is realistic as far as setting," Manohar explained. "What's so unrealistic is the over-the-top drama. In your first story you had a young couple going behind the bushes to do the nasty."

Summer threw her pen across the table at him. "Pig."

Manohar ducked. "At least the first story wasn't far-fetched. But this time you've got a love triangle, and a midnight tryst, and a tragic death. It's like a made-for-TV movie."

"What's wrong with made-for-TV movies?" I asked, bracing myself on this slippery slope. "They employ a lot of people—a lot of actors, and a lot of writers." I was so worked up now I didn't have the wherewithal to write INTERNSHIP on my notebook.

"I just think you can do better than that," Manohar said.

"How?" I demanded.

"I think you can write a story more realistic than that."

"How do you know this didn't happen?" I thought I heard my voice ringing around the ceiling, which meant it was way too loud, but the challenge from Manohar had gotten personal.

"This couldn't have happened," he said.

"How do you know?"

Hunter cut both of us off. "Manohar, did you ever think the story might be real?" He laid his hands flat on the table.

"And how do you know?" Manohar asked Hunter. But he slowed as he said this, and I could see on his face that he was registering the fact that Hunter and I had known each other before, Hunter knew my story, and Hunter knew this story.

"I can see she's upset." Hunter gestured to me, then turned back to Manohar. "I put two and two together. I have more highly developed social skills than you. Look at her!"

Now the remnants of Hunter's voice rang around the ceiling. The silence that followed was heavy and dark, like the skies outside the window. Tension sped underneath like the traffic zooming by on the street below.

Whoever spoke next and broke the silence could change the mood of the class and take the floor. I should do this. I should claim agency in the discussion of my own story. This would show Gabe how serious I was about my craft.

I could not. I kept my eyes on "Anything Is Possible" in front of me, my stomach tied in slipknots.

"I'm sorry," Hunter burst out. "Manohar, what I said was out of line. Gabe, I'm sorry for speaking out of turn. And Erin . . ."

He paused, waiting for me to look up. He would not go on. The silence would descend again until I acknowledged him.

I peeked out at him from beneath my bangs.

"I'm sorry, Erin." He flashed a confident smile at me, and angry blue eyes. "I know you can defend your own story."

"Are you okay?" Isabelle put her hand on his wrist, comforting, as if they were dating.

"No," he mumbled. "Tired." He looked down at the table. "Now I've lost my pen."

Isabelle and the three other people nearest him ducked their heads under the table to look for it.

"Brian?" Gabe said suddenly.

"Me?" Brian blinked at Gabe. "Oh, my turn! I loved this story. It's a cross between Danielle Steele and *National Velvet*."

The class tittered uneasily and never fully recovered from Hunter's outburst. Now that he'd planted the seed of the story as real, they tiptoed around my feelings and didn't say much. I wasn't listening anyway. I gripped the edge of the table with white fingers and tried to slow my breathing, staring down at my story but hyperaware of Hunter's presence just beyond my peripheral view.

I JUMPED UP WHEN GABE DISMISSED the class. "Erin!" Summer called.

"Can't stay," I threw over my shoulder. "I'll get fired. My boss says seven strikes and I'm out."

Gabe opened his mouth as if to speak to me. I hurried past him, out of the classroom building and onto the sidewalk.

Sharp, cold wind scented with diesel blew into my face. I paused to juggle my book bag and shrug on my coat. Then I hurried toward the coffee shop, past two mounted police officers at the edge of the park, the horses nickering to each other. I tried to shake off my story and the sick feeling I got when I thought of Hunter at the foot of the table. I was making us both sick. We were in New York, starting new lives. There was no reason for us to circle each other slowly, throwing Kentucky in each other's faces. As I stepped through the employee door, I vowed to bring a smile to customers' faces for the next few hours, and think of nothing but serving a damn great cup of coffee. There was a first time for everything.

But when I stood behind the counter to take orders, the table next to the window where Hunter and I had sat was directly in my line of sight. Each time I served a customer and waited for the next one to step up, I stared out at that table, those empty chairs.

Finally, when there was a lull, I pretended to need chocolate syrup from the storeroom, and I brought my copies of "Anything Is Possible" up front with me. Held my breath while I thumbed through the stack and found Hunter's copy. Infuriatingly, he'd scrawled his name across the title page without making another single mark.

Gabe wrote in pencil at the end of his copy,

Erin,

I think you are going in the wrong direction.

Don't you?

And then Manohar, Brian, and Summer stepped up to the counter.

"A latte, please," Summer said, loudly enough for my boss to hear in the back room, "and draw a little heart in the foam. You're so good at that." Under her breath she asked, "It wasn't really a true story, was it?"

I nodded, glancing sideways at Manohar and Brian, who were crowding the counter and listening in.

"But not about you, obviously," Summer said, "with you being alive and all. Your mother?"

I nodded.

All their eyes widened. Summer asked, "Is she—"

The look on my face stopped her.

It did not stop Brian. "But . . . your dad is her husband in the story?"

"Not husband," Summer said under her breath. "Father of her child."

"Whatever," Brian said. "What happened to him?"

I opened my mouth and nothing came out. My mom was dead. Why did their questions about my dad hurt even more?

"Where is he?" Brian persisted.

I swallowed. "Vancouver, last I heard."

"When was that?" Summer asked.

"Six years ago." Six years, three months, two weeks, and three days.

"And her lover in the story . . . what happened to him?" Manohar asked. He seemed genuinely curious about this drama in real life.

"He still works at my grandmother's horse farm," I said. Summer looked the question and I confirmed, "Hunter's dad."

"No way!" Brian exclaimed. All three of them gaped at me.

I glanced toward the door to the back room, expecting my boss to appear with his hands on his hips. I glared at Brian. "Sir, can I take your order?"

"Does Hunter look like his dad?" Summer wanted to know.

"Yeah." If they were not going to tell me what they wanted, I was going to serve them black coffee. I slipped a cup under the tap. "This is to go, right?"

"Do you look like your mom?" Brian asked.

"No," I said. "Red hair skips a generation. I look like my grandmother."

"But if your mom and Hunter's dad hooked up," Brian persisted, "does that make you and Hunter brother and sister?"

"No!" Summer and Manohar and I all shouted at him at the same time.

I glanced toward the back room again. "Look, you're going to get me in trouble. When I wrote that story, I thought I was getting it off my chest so I could face Hunter head-on. Instead, I feel a million times worse, and I don't want to talk about it, okay?"

"When do you have a break?" Manohar asked.

"Nine," I said warily.

"I'll come back," Manohar said. Clearly he had his own interpretation of *I don't want to talk about it.*

They took their to-go cups and wandered out of the coffee shop, leaving me to serve strangers and stew in my own juices. And like clockwork, at nine o'clock, Manohar reappeared alone. He gave me a small wave and sat at Hunter's table by the window.

I sat down across from him and slid him a latte with a butt drawn in the foam.

He didn't even look at it. He focused his dark gaze on me. "Summer didn't put me up to this."

"Did Hunter?"

"Hunter!" he exclaimed. "Hunter's been nuts all weekend. Nuts for Hunter, that is. Quiet and antisocial. I thought he had the flu. Now I realize he must have read your story on Friday." He leaned forward. "I had no idea your story had a grain of truth to it, Erin. I wouldn't have said those things in class if I'd known."

I blinked at him, not believing at first what I was hearing: an apology, sort of, from Manohar. After all the anxiety he'd caused me over the past six weeks, I wasn't ready to kiss and make up, but I did manage to shrug and say slowly, "Don't worry about it."

"I am worried about it. I tried to apologize to Hunter after class, and he told me to fuck off!" He collapsed against the back of his chair in exasperation. "I decided to work your end of the equation. Ironically, you seem to be the more reasonable party."

I sighed and put my chin in my hand. "Can we get back to the part where you were sorry?"

He waved his hands in the air. "I don't want to take it too far, mind you. Knowing that your story is based in reality doesn't elevate it in my mind."

"Thanks."

He held up his hands to silence me. "Our instinct is that if we're taking a story from reality, automatically it will be realistic. But that's not true. For instance, my father plays bluegrass banjo. He loves country music. He's a stockbroker but he thinks he missed his calling. And in just about every story I write, I think about putting in an Indian father who plays bluegrass banjo. It's something familiar to me. I could write the hell out of it. The banjo would make a great symbol. Of something. But people would say my writing wasn't realistic."

I opened my mouth to tell him that this was the most interesting thing I'd ever learned about him, and the most believable. For the first time he seemed like a real person with an embarrassing family in his background, not just a dapper Indian boy with a bad attitude. I would much rather have read a story about his banjo-pickin' daddy than the dystopian pablum he usually turned in for class.

But he went on, "Besides, every time you write anything remotely like reality, it involves Hunter somehow. Hunter is calm and cavalier about everything but you and your writing. So if you don't mind, to keep the peace, stick to your romantic fantasies from now on. But leave Hunter out of it."

WHEN I WALKED HOME FROM THE coffee shop a little after eleven that night, I found Summer sitting on her bed, reading. I had expected her to be up in Manohar's room. I knew she was headed there now because she still wore makeup. She was waiting for me.

She patted her bed. I set my book bag down carefully, to preserve it, and sat beside her, then kept sitting down and down until I lay flat in her pillows and stared at the cracked ceiling.

"You love him so much," I heard her say.

"No, I don't."

"I just can't understand how things have gone so wrong between you two for so long."

I didn't want to talk about this, but looking at the ceiling made it easier. My stomach twisted into knots and I sucked in a breath against the pain, then blurted this out: "After my mom died I couldn't look at him because his dad had been there with her when she died. Anytime I looked at Hunter, the whole thing replayed in my head. I couldn't look at his dad, either. That didn't last long because my grandmother told his dad to get me back on a horse right away so I wouldn't be scared. But by that time, school had started and Hunter was the new kid and people were calling him my stable boy and I hadn't done anything to stop it."

"Oh," she said, as if that were the end of it and she was sorry she had asked.

I kept going, now that I had started. "Then he got hurt. You know, the scar? And it was like my mother was dying all over again. I wanted to see him. I walked down to his house to ask his dad to take me to the hospital with him to see Hunter. But I just stood in the driveway for a while and couldn't knock on the door.

"When Hunter came back to school, he seemed to resent that, too, and we went through the rest of high school that way. People would tease him about being my employee and they would tease me about going after the stable boy, and girls would tell me he was perfect for me. They didn't understand how much he hated me or why. Then we were seniors and competing against each other for a scholarship to the same college."

"Oh," she said again. This time she reached over and stroked my hair on the pillow. That made my eyes fill with tears.

"The night of the Derby he did something nice for me," I choked out. "I hoped we were starting over. And then he stole my farm."

She stayed quiet for a few minutes. Finally she said, "You are a phenomenally bad communicator. I'm surprised you want to be a novelist. Or maybe that's *why* you want to be a novelist."

I sat up, wiping the hair away from my wet face. "I love you," I said.

She snorted. "I'm easy to love."

"No . . ." I leaned forward and hugged her, just like that. My stomach twisted again as I did it, but I hugged her. Squeezed her hard.

She rubbed my back soothingly and said into my shoulder, "I love you, too." Then she held me at arm's length. "Let's go to a midnight movie. You never get out."

I shook my head. "I have to read for history." Then I looked toward the ceiling again. "You go on upstairs. Manohar is waiting."

It took me a while to convince her, but she did eventually go. I moved to my room and unloaded my textbooks from my bag. But the loneliness of the empty room was overwhelming tonight, and the very thought of wandering alone across the ancient battlefields of my history chapters made my head throb. I took a quick trip down the hall to the bathroom to remove my makeup and cleanse myself of the coffee smell. I was so sick of spending long evenings standing up and serving lattes in the coffee shop that I would have preferred the odor of Thai garbage. I stretched out in bed, half asleep already.

Hunter's footsteps echoed in the stairwell and through the wall at the head of my bed. Suddenly wide awake, I flipped over and stared at the wall, ready to defend myself if Hunter burst through it. I leaned forward on my fists, head down as the noise descended. The front door of the dorm squealed open and thudded shut. I hopped to the other side of my bed and peeked out my window as Hunter walked away down the sidewalk, open overcoat blowing behind him.

Enough was enough. I had to know.

I jerked on the clothes I'd worn that day, slipped on my shoes, and shrugged into my own overcoat. Running out the door, I grabbed a scarf from my bedpost. Scarves were in fashion and I hadn't yet needed it for warmth. Tonight it was functional. As I dashed down the stairwell, I tied it around my red hair.

When I shoved open the front door, he was still visible one block up on the almost empty sidewalk. I hurried after him, as fast as I could go without running and drawing attention if he happened to glance around. I did run when he turned a corner, and I half-expected him to be waiting to startle me when I rounded the corner myself. Instead, I glimpsed his blond hair as he jogged down the steps to the subway.

I'd ridden the subway a lot when I first arrived in New York—why not, when a monthly card bought unlimited rides? I was amazed that it would take me anywhere in the city. Then it had broken down on me a couple of times. There had been a period when construction was awful and I kept getting on the wrong line and it would always spit me out in TriBeCa. Lately I'd hardly ridden it at all. When class had started in September, my Manhattan had shrunk to a tight circle of dorm, class, coffee shop, library, dorm.

Now I stepped onto the escalator and descended into the bowels of the city. From this angle, the staircase seemed to smooth out into a conveyor belt. That's what my life had become, and, judging from the dark circles under Hunter's eyes lately, maybe his life, too—a relentless machine, chewing us to pieces.

At the bottom of the escalator, he walked forward into the light of the subway platform and disappeared from my view beneath the edge of the curved ceiling. He would have to look behind him while I was following in order to spot me. If he did, he would see me. There was no way around this. I had made myself as unobtrusive as possible, but he would still see me unless I was actively hiding behind a pillar, which would arouse the suspicions of the other passengers and the police. I didn't know where he was going, so I didn't know what would be there and why I might want to go there alone late at night. I would be busted. And when I was busted, I would have no excuse, only the truth: "I am going to die unless I find out about your secret love."

I stepped off the escalator just as the northbound train was pulling alongside the platform. I watched him board, and I ducked onto the same car through the rear door. The subway carried enough passengers for me to blend into the mass of dark overcoats, but not so many that Hunter had to stand and give his seat to an elderly lady. He sat and opened a book. From half a car back, I watched him read.

As a stop approached, he pocketed his book, stood, and reached for the bar overhead. I lowered my chin, bracing myself for discovery. He didn't look toward me. He closed his eyes, gripping the bar hard to keep his balance in the swaying car.

Doors slid open. He filed out with the crowd. I stayed twenty paces behind, my heart throbbing harder and harder as we climbed the stairs up to the street. If the trek ended at a cocktail lounge, I would know as he slipped inside that his most recent story for class was not fiction after all. If he entered a fortune-teller's storefront, I would stand in the cloud of incense smoke that wafted outside and know I should let him go.

What worried me was ambiguity. As I hurried up the dark sidewalk after him, I hoped he would duck into a drugstore so I could spy on him as he made out with the blonde from the beach party who worked as a sales chick behind the counter. At least then I would know. But if he used a key to an apartment building and the door locked behind him, I would stand in the street rebuffed and thwarted, never to know whether he was picking up a clandestine game of poker or buying Ecstasy or carrying on an affair with his forty-something anatomy professor.

Ahead of me he stopped at a busy intersection. I hung back, advancing to the corner only when the light changed and he crossed. The thought occurred to me that his destination might be the building directly in front of me. It could not be, I decided. I waited for him to veer to the side and continue down the sidewalk beside the building, toward his real destination.

A hospital loomed ten glassy stories over the intersection, its bright emergency room carved out of the corner, ambulances blinking ominously, blue and red in the driveway. The lights danced through Hunter's blond hair as his silhouette crossed the driveway, edged between ambulances, and disappeared into the brilliant lobby.

My eyes stung with tears for the second time that night. My heart knocked against my breastbone. My mind ran frantically through the possibilities, each more awful than the one before. Hunter was dating a beautiful brain surgeon with a taste for younger men. Hunter was devotedly visiting his blond girlfriend from the shower, who had fallen ill. Hunter was ill himself. He was dying slowly. He wanted the rest of his short life to be as normal as possible. That's why he couldn't let me know where he was going. He didn't want my grandmother to snatch his college education away now that he couldn't fulfill his obligation as her heir.

I had to find out. I stepped into the street.

Out of the corner of my eye I saw the taxi coming. I knew what I'd done wrong but it was too late to jump back. A jolt in my hip, and then I was skidding across the asphalt on my back.

Everything stopped. I was staring up between the tops of buildings at the orange glow of the overcast night sky, and the street around me seemed strangely quiet, but in my head I heard the echo of the tires screeching. I should get out of the street. The next car would kill me.

I put my hands behind me to push up to standing. My back stung like fire. The pain in my hip took my breath away. The taxi idled in front of me, a small dent in the hood. The door opened, releasing Middle Eastern rock music. The driver stood up behind the door, pointed at me, and cursed me in Arabic.

On the far corner, in front of the hospital, four people in green scrubs stood beside a stretcher, waiting for the light to turn before crossing the street. I rolled off the unbearable pain in my hip. Facedown I examined the asphalt, tiny white rocks showing through where the blue petroleum base had worn away. The people in scrubs eventually reached me with their stretcher. When they asked me who they should call for me, I gave them the only phone number I could remember.

11

Hunter filled the opening in the privacy curtains. He wore green scrubs like the doctors and nurses who had scraped me off the pavement. For a split second I mistook him for an adorable doctor who looked a lot like Hunter. I knew it was Hunter when he gaped at me with a mixture of outrage and horror, his face pale, and demanded, "What did you do?"

"Crossed the street," I said. "Badly." Wincing, I eased up from the gurney, putting my weight on my hand and my good hip. Only a few minutes had passed since they had brought me in, ascertained I wasn't dying, and dumped me here. I still felt very shaky from the shock of being hit. But I didn't want to face Hunter lying down.

In two steps he bent over me and wrapped his arms around me. He was careful not to press on my hospital gown low against my back where the road rash was, but his touch on my shoulders radiated pain to the raw parts. I winced again.

"Oh, God, I'm sorry." He let me go but hovered over me, placing his big hands on my shoulder blades. He was so close that the air felt hot between us. "What did you hurt?"

"This is just where I skidded across the road." I gestured behind my back and then flinched at the sting in my skin as I moved my arm.

"How far down does it go?" My back felt cold as he lifted one flap of my paper gown and looked.

I kept my head down, my red cheeks hidden. He was peering

at my back where my skin was missing. What could be sexier? Even if the circumstances had been happier, I was wearing no makeup and I was sure my hair was matted from my scarf. There was no reason for my blood to heat as if we were on a date instead of a gurney.

But my body did not listen to logic when it came to Hunter. He was not examining my wound. He was captivated by the sight of my lovely and unblemished bottom. I was a novelist. I could dream, couldn't I?

Lightly I asked, "Are you asking whether I have gravel embedded in my ass? By the grace of God, no."

Hunter let my gown go and stood up. "The doc said the car hit your hip," he insisted. "Is it broken?"

I rolled on my side to face him. "It really hurts," I said. "If it were broken, I think it would hurt worse."

He nodded. "When I broke my ribs, I couldn't breathe."

"That's because your ribs punctured your lung."

He pointed at me. "True." Then he cocked his head to one side, blond hair falling into his eyes. "I'm surprised you remember that."

I winced again, not from physical pain this time. It had hurt so badly to care about Hunter but to hear about his accident third-hand. And that had been my fault. I should have nurtured our nascent friendship before everything had gone awkward. I had my excuses, but I was the one who had retreated into the closet and shut the door.

And now we were so far apart that neither of us had any idea why the other was at this hospital. "You work here as a clerk?" I asked.

He shook his head. "I volunteer here as an orderly."

"Why are they letting you see patients, then?"

"I was going to see you whether they wanted me to or not, because it's you." His eyes seemed to darken as I watched. "But the doc on rotation lets me sit in on examinations, sometimes. She knows I want to go to med school."

Now something different passed behind his eyes. He was realizing what he'd accidentally told me.

"You want to go to med school?" I asked in disbelief.

He opened his lips. His broad chest expanded with a deep breath underneath the green scrubs. "Yes," he said on a sigh.

"Which is why you're taking anatomy, and calculus instead of business math. You're a pre-med major."

He smiled tightly. "Yes."

I had always viewed Hunter as a suave opportunist. Looking back, I wasn't sure why I'd assumed he was doing right by my grandmother. "You have no intention of majoring in business and running my grandmother's farm after graduation."

"No."

Not without admiration I said, "You're just milking her for everything she's worth."

Now that he knew he was caught, he charmed me with a big grin. "Basically."

I was glad we'd faced off and I'd finally pried the truth out of him while I was propped up. But my hip ached like nothing I'd ever experienced, and I simply couldn't balance on my tender bones any longer. "Any swindler of my grandmother is a friend of mine" came out a groan as I eased forward to lie down on my stomach on the table, one hand on my ass to make sure the paper gown didn't ride up to reveal even more of my broken body to Hunter.

His arm shot across my chest to support me as I lay down. I wondered whether he knew exactly what he was touching underneath my paper gown—but surely that was the farthest thing from his mind. Most people did not think dirty thoughts at a time like this. Only me.

He sat on a stool and rolled it up to me. "That explains what

I'm doing here." He put his chin down on the edge of the gurney, watching me like a big friendly dog. "What are *you* doing here?"

He was so dreamily handsome, looking at me with concern in his eyes, and his tone was so gentle, that I almost answered him.

"You followed me," he said.

I shifted on the gurney, trying in vain to find a more comfortable position. My hip sure did hurt.

"You wanted to know where I was going so late at night," he said. "I've seen you watching me through your window."

Note to self: when boys look back at you watching them in the darkness outside your well-lit window, but their expressions do not change, you relax, assuming they can't really see you watching them, when they can totally see you.

There was no way around it now. "I was afraid your stories in Gabe's class were real," I muttered.

Hunter's eyebrows shot up. "That I was having sex with a bar waitress? And you followed me to find out? For somebody who hates me, you sure are interested in my sex life."

"I don't hate you, Hunter." I felt my eyes filling with tears yet again. I was in pain of various degrees and types, but what brought me to tears was a hurt from six years before and eight hundred miles away.

His fingers touched mine. At first I thought he would tug at my gown again. Then his fingers slipped past my palm and intertwined with my fingers. I had known his hands would be calloused from farmwork even now, an adaptation to an old life that took a while to wear off. Even so, I was surprised by the rough feel of his skin against mine.

His hand moved up to stroke my hair. It felt so good, and the tingles racing down my arms were so delicious, that I fought the urge to close my eyes and purr. It was weird, but now that I knew he wasn't having the sexy adventures I'd suspected him of, he seemed sexier. We had arrived at some adult place where people had actual relationships with each other and they worked out, if we were very lucky.

At a sudden thought I jerked awake. "What about the blonde?"

"What blonde?" he asked, surprised. His rough fingers moved across my hairline.

"You act like I'm so silly to think your stories were real, but you were *with* the blonde in the bathroom."

"Oh! Right. I forget her name. I haven't seen her since then. I told her I wanted to make you mad and asked her to let me paw her for a few minutes."

I found it difficult to be angry with him when his fingers were in my hair, stroking lightly. I did my best. "Then you acted shocked that I was mad."

"I *was* shocked that you were mad. Before then, I'd thought you didn't like me very much."

"Even after the stable-boy story?"

"You said it was fiction." He sighed and put his chin in his hand, setting his elbow on the gurney close to me, stroking my hair with the other hand. "Everything you do surprises me. That's how you keep my attention."

I looked up at him, stared deep into his blue eyes that reflected the fluorescent lights in the ceiling. I kept his attention. I licked my dry lips and took a breath to ask him what that meant.

Before I could speak he said, "I'm supposed to take you to X-ray in a few minutes."

"Wrong." I shook my head, and my hair hissed back and forth on the gurney's paper covering. "I'm going to refuse it, and I'd appreciate some help in speeding that up."

His hand stopped in my hair. He said darkly, "You can't refuse it."

"It's my right, and I have to. My grandmother kicked me off

her health insurance. I'm on the university's cheapo student insurance, which means I get emergency care but I have to go to student health first or they might not pay. I can't afford an X-ray and my dorm room, too."

"What if your hip's broken?"

"We agreed it probably isn't. Anyway, I'll find out tomorrow morning when the student health office opens." I didn't look forward to spending the rest of the night in this much pain and afraid to put my foot down, but there was no other way.

"You are not leaving," he ordered me. A nurse swished by outside the curtain. Hunter looked over his shoulder at her, then sidled closer to me and lowered his voice, but his tone was as intense as before. "I will not let you leave until you see the doctor."

"You can't stop me." I met his gaze and tried to look as determined as he did, which was difficult with my hip aching in a new way. Some of my muscles had been so surprised by the hit that they forgot to hurt at first. Slowly, they were remembering.

Suddenly he sat up, face clear and friendly. "I'll fix it. Back in a sec." He kicked off from the bed, propelling the rolling stool all the way through the opening in the curtain.

I turned my head to one side and closed my eyes against the white light, trying to get comfortable, melding my body with the hard gurney. I was so sleepy. It was after midnight. I could not imagine Hunter staying awake and alert here night after night.

"Hey," he coaxed in a low voice.

I opened my eyes, squinting against the light. His hand was in my hair again, and he leaned over me.

"I'll help you up," he said. "We're going to X-ray. I took care of it for you."

"What do you mean, you took care of it?" I slurred. I didn't want to go, but his arms were underneath me, easing me toward the edge of the gurney and a waiting wheelchair padded with pillows. I was afraid any resistance would result in another game of hospital gown peekaboo.

He settled me so gently in the soft wheelchair that my hip and my back hardly hurt. Pushing me past the curtain and into the bustling emergency room, he leaned close, over me, to say, "I fixed it. They're going to lose the records of your visit, so you'll never get billed. But you're my girlfriend."

"What do you mean, I'm your girlfriend?" What delicious blackmail was this? And was it worth the price? Perhaps I could stand it.

"I had to make them think I have a vested interest in you," he whispered. "They never would have agreed to lose your records if I told them you were my friend at twelve years old but not so much at eighteen and I had pretty much walked in and stolen the birthright to your family farm. See? Shhh. Hey, Brody." He slapped hands with another man in scrubs wheeling an empty gurney in the opposite direction. The man eyed me, waggled his eyebrows at Hunter, and kept going.

"Couldn't you have said we're friends and left it at that?" I needed to keep up the facade that I did not like the idea at all. At the same time, I was a little afraid Hunter would call the charade off.

"I have a lot of friends," he explained, wheeling me into a waiting room marked X-RAY. He rounded the wheelchair and knelt in front of me. Behind him, a door stood ajar. A contraption I assumed to be an X-ray machine was visible through the crack. He glanced over his shoulder at the door, then turned back to me. "Sorry about this," he murmured as he slid both hands into my hair and kissed me.

All I could do at first was feel. His lips were on mine. His hands held me steady, so I couldn't have shrugged away if I'd tried, but I would not try. Bright tingles spread from my lips across my face and down my neck to my chest. I longed to pull him closer for more. I reminded myself that we were faking this for a reason. I didn't want to make the kiss deeper than necessary in case it turned him off.

Hunter deepened it. His tongue pressed past my teeth and swept inside my mouth. One of his hands released my hair and caressed my shoulder, traveling down. The farther his hand went, the higher I felt. My hip hardly hurt and my back pain was gone. I wondered how low his hand would go.

I never found out. A shadow stood in the doorway and cleared its throat.

I stopped kissing Hunter back and braced for him to jump away. He did back off, but very slowly. He sat back on his haunches and glared at the X-ray tech as if she had a lot of nerve. His cheeks were bright red.

"So, Hunter," she said mischievously. "This is your girlfriend."

"Hullo." I gave her a small wave.

"And you got hit by a taxi while you were crossing the street to visit Hunter? That is so romantic! Have you seen *Sleepless in Seattle?*"

"Not romantic," I said flatly. "I hate that movie. They don't meet until the last scene. They don't kiss at all." Too late I realized I sounded like I was begging Hunter for more.

"But in that movie," the tech said, "they talk about *An Affair to Remember*. Have you seen *that?* Deborah Kerr is crossing the street to meet Cary Grant and gets hit by a car. Years later he comes back to her and she's paralyzed from the waist down."

"You call that romantic?" I heard myself yelling. "That is repulsive!"

Hunter stood and put a heavy hand on my shoulder as he pushed my wheelchair past the tech and through the doorway to the X-ray machine. "Erin is in a lot of pain," he murmured to the tech, "and she doesn't want to think about being paralyzed from the waist down."

After that the tech was a lot nicer, because Hunter had a way with people. Hunter lifted me onto the table and left the room so he wouldn't be irradiated or see my bony ass. The tech rolled me around as gently as she could.

Then Hunter wheeled me back behind the curtain. A nurse finally gave me some pills for the pain, and that's when the night began to fade. I remember a tech cleaned and bandaged my back. That was intense. I had been kidding about the gravel embedded in my back, but he found some small rocks, sure enough, and plopped them into a metal pan and showed them to me, and Hunter yelled at him.

I remember that a doctor told me my hip wasn't broken but I would have a bruise the size of a grapefruit or, since citrus fruits were out of season, an acorn squash. I laughed at this but Hunter did not. He stood there with his arms folded. Some trick of the fluorescent lights overhead formed deep shadows under his eyes.

We began to talk of leaving. I mentioned the subway and he got angry, I thought, so I didn't press it. My overcoat was retrieved, thank God, because I couldn't afford another, but they'd cut my clothes off me when they brought me in. Hunter went to change out of his scrubs and stole some for me.

Toward morning I was too sleepy to protest as he stood between flashing ambulances in the driveway, hailed us a taxi, scooped me from the wheelchair, and placed me inside the car. I lay along the seat on my good hip with my head on Hunter's hard thigh and his callused finger stroking soft patterns on my neck where my hair fell away. In a burst of adrenaline I might have run screaming into the street again if Middle Eastern rock had played on the radio, but this cabdriver had a taste for disco.

Under the throbbing beat I asked, "Why are you volunteering as an orderly in the middle of the night?"

"I'm a white male, so I need all the help I can get for admission to med school. The assumption is that if you're a white male, you've had every advantage." He yawned.

"Why do you want to go to med school?" I asked. "Were your broken ribs a turning point for you, and you've been driven to become a doctor and help other people like you ever since?"

"No." I thought he laughed a little, but I couldn't quite hear over the music.

I glanced up at him and saw only the lights of late-night clubs flashing pink and green across his face. Looking up at him caused me to shift my weight, which hurt, so I settled back and closed my eyes again. Talking to him this way was easier, especially considering my next question. "Are you sick?"

Suddenly I felt the same fear that had propelled me into the street at the hospital without looking both ways. He would be taken from me before we even knew what game we were playing.

"No," he said.

I sighed my relief very slowly and carefully against his thigh so he wouldn't notice. "Is your mother sick?"

He paused long enough that I thought I'd hit on the horrible explanation. But his finger never stopped stroking my neck. Finally he said, "No. She lives in New Jersey. She's never taken much of an interest in me. My dad does not have good luck with women. Why do you ask?"

"I'm trying to figure out why you're not majoring in business at the University of Louisville. I know you wanted to come back to New York, but you could have taken six or seven years and worked your way through Louisville. Swindling my grandmother out of a college education, volunteering at night—you're going to a lot of trouble here."

"That's true."

I waited for his explanation. When he didn't give me one, I guessed. "Did you mention medical school to a high school teacher who told you that you couldn't do it?"

This time his finger stopped on my neck.

"That's it," I declared. "They knew you weren't well off and your mother wasn't around. They assumed you weren't med school material. Therefore you became med school material. You're Gatsby. You're working your way up. You probably have a journal where you keep track of your calisthenics."

"You need to learn not to say everything that pops into your head." His sharp tone cut across the disco beat.

"You're right," I said immediately. I had finally reached a friendly place with Hunter—very friendly, if you counted fake dating for the purpose of cheating the medical system—and then ruined it. "Hunter, I'm sor—"

"In the guidance counselor's office in high school," he interrupted me, "what they say to *you* is, 'We can get you into a great college where you can learn to be a better millionaire.' What they say to *me* is, 'We can get you an entry-level job at UPS. You can work your way up. If you wanted to take a few college classes to make yourself feel like you're going places, that's fine as long as they don't interfere with work. Someday maybe you will even get to drive the truck.'"

"I'm really sorry." I had seen Hunter angry, but I had never heard him bitter, and I desperately needed to fix what I'd broken. I pushed up through the pain so I could sit upright and face him across the taxi.

He held me down with one heavy arm. "No, *I'm* sorry. I just . . ." He looked down at me and stroked his finger across my neck again, more deliberately now, as if forcing himself. "It's not strange that I'm fooling your grandmother into paying for my education. It's strange that you're not. You could have lied to her about majoring in business and taken English classes on the side. You could still do it. Why is it so important that she doesn't help you, and that both of you *understand* she's not helping you?"

"Because." I shouted the word. The taxi driver half-turned in his seat. I watched him to make sure he put his eyes on the road again and didn't hit any love-starved novelists.

"My mother wanted to be an actress and my grandmother told her she was cutting her off, surprise. So my mom booked for L.A. when she was eighteen. Maybe she would have made it if she hadn't gotten pregs when she was twenty."

"With you," Hunter said.

I nodded on his thigh. "Even after I was born she got a few bit parts, but mostly she would work as a secretary, and then she got training as a paralegal. My dad mostly didn't work. That was a big thing they fought about. He always had some reason for why he wasn't working. He was always saying she was the one with the rich family, why didn't she ask her mother for money, and she always said she wasn't asking that bitch for shit, not after what her mother had said to her when she left. But she wouldn't marry my dad, either, and I never knew why, but now I wonder if it was because she didn't want him officially part of her family, with access to the family money that he talked so much about and seemed so eager for."

"So you're a bastard," Hunter said.

The question caught me off guard. "You mean—was I born out of wedlock? Yes."

"Then I've got one up on you after all."

"What do you mean, you've got one up on me after all? Are we in some sort of contest? A birthright contest?" I watched the colored lights from the shops we passed reflecting on the vinyl seat. "Never mind. Don't answer that. I guess we are." After six years we'd finally admitted we liked each other. It had taken us all of an hour and a half to hate each other again.

Or did we? His hand had moved to my face, brushing my bangs lightly away from my forehead with his calloused fingers. "So, you have to win this battle with your grandmother because that will prove she was wrong all along. If you win, your mother wins."

I adjusted my head on his thigh, unable to find a comfortable position. He was way too muscular to be a pillow. And I murmured, "My mother is dead."

12

Deep in the night he laid me on my bed. Summer and Jørdis whispered questions. I got lost in sleep and painkillers but at some point during the next day or the next, Summer brought me a walking cane and a huge breakfast and said Hunter had dropped them off. When I limped back to class, he started sitting next to me in calculus—not flirting with me or hovering over me but acting routinely pleasant and torturing me with wonder at whether he'd really wanted to kiss me that night in the hospital. Summer was all aflutter at the whole incident. She agreed with the X-ray tech that getting hit by a taxi while crossing the street to see Hunter was romantic, until I showed her the black bruise on my hip and the slowly healing gouges in my back.

But a week and a half after my accident, when I'd already come back from the coffee shop and delivered a cup to Hunter for his long trek to volunteer at the hospital, Summer peeked her head into my room and asked me with wide eyes whether I'd read his new story. I had gotten wise by then. I did not get my hopes up. I could have rushed to the library and read it when he was scheduled to put it there for us, but then I would have obsessed about it until class time.

I knew better. I waited until the last minute, Thursday, after a lunch of peanut-butter crackers, to limp to the library and read all the stories for class. Hunter's last.

That way I was furious for only ten minutes, the space of the walk between the library and the honors classroom building, before I faced him.

The Space Between

by Hunter Allen

His eighth-grade science teacher tried to explain how big space was. Space was so big, it seemed, that there was hardly anything in it, thus its name. Space.

He did not get it, and he wanted to. He hated the rare times when he didn't understand something in class. So that night after he had fed the horses and eaten the dinner he heated for himself in the microwave, and his dad was ensconced in front of the television with a pack of cigarettes and a cooler of beer at his feet to save trips to the refrigerator, he sat at the kitchen table with a pad and a calculator and worked out the relationship between the scale of the planets and the scale of the space between them. He started by making Mercury the size of a baseball, but that made the sun sixty-six feet wide. He shrank everything again. Mercury was now the size of a pencil eraser, and the sun was six feet wide. Mercury was eighty-five yards from the sun.

He still didn't get it. Could space truly be that big? He decided to walk out the model. Then he would understand. He crossed his father's line of sight and opened the front door. Standing on the porch, he could see the orange ball of the sun just disappearing behind the grassy hill on which the boss's house sat. The black silhouettes of trees slashed across the bright pink sky.

He leaned back through the door and called to his dad, "I'm going for a walk."

"Stay away from that girl," his father said.

He didn't respond to this. He didn't have to, because his father was watching TV, not him. He simply closed the door and walked out into the twilight, face burning, chest tight with embarrassment and anger and dread and longing.

He stepped off the wooden porch, onto the walkway of stone pavers a hundred years old. They led down a grassy bank to the gravel road that wound through the enormous farm. In New York, where he had come from not too long before, in early springtime the grass still would have been brown. Here in Kentucky it was already long and green and juicy for the horses.

He retrieved a measuring tape from the truck. Standing in the gravel road in front of his small house, he looked to the right. The road disappeared over the hill, but he knew it bumped from grassy hill to grassy hill until it finally met the two-lane highway a mile off. That was the direction his father wanted him to go.

He looked to the left. The road disappeared over that hill, too, but he knew it pitched higher and higher with more and more hills until it reached the high point of the farm, where the boss's house perched. That was the direction his father forbade him to go.

He loosened a large limestone rock from the century-old wall next to his house—fuck this farm, anyway—and set it on the end of the tape measure to keep it secure in the middle of the road. Then he started walking up the hill. The tape measure was only a hundred feet long, so he kept having to mark his place in the road and start over in order to make progress. After eighty-five yards, he stopped and looked around. He was standing beside an enormous old oak. If the sun was six feet wide and sat directly in front of his house, this was where Mercury would be to scale, a barely visible pencil eraser. He wasn't sure his classmates would understand this analogy, but he did, and he appreciated for the first time the vastness of space, the emptiness, the vacuum.

He walked another sixty-four yards up the road, gravel crunching under his work boots. The sky had deepened to rose now, and he might have been worried about a car creaming him without ever seeing him in the dark, except that there was nobody out here to run him down—only the boss, and the people who worked on the farm, most of whom had gone home for the night already, or lived here like his dad in an ancient house built back when it was acceptable for workers to live on their employers' land.

He stopped and looked around. He was standing next to a large mossy boulder that jutted from the grass, maybe a marker of something long gone, maybe a tombstone, maybe just a boulder. He had wondered about it since he'd arrived here at the farm. Now he set his tape measure down on the road and walked over to the boulder. The moss was soft, with creepy-looking white flowers that glowed like an alien species in the disappearing light. He looked back toward his house. It was a football field and a half away now, and if the sun were six feet wide in front of his door, Venus would be here, the size of his thumbnail.

He slid a piece of paper out of the pocket of his jeans and consulted his calculations.

He tugged the tape measure so the end of it escaped the last rock he'd placed in the road. The tape measure zipped back into the case. He made a mental note to pick up all his rocks when he was finished. If a farm truck was damaged running over one, his father would kill him.

He set the end of the tape measure down in the road again and secured it with a new piece of the heirloom fence. From Venus, he walked another sixty-four yards, down the other side of the hill and halfway up the next one, and stopped. If the sun was six feet wide in front of his front door, which he couldn't see anymore because the hill was in the way, but he knew how far away it was, Earth would be here, also the size of his thumbnail. He looked around. Now he could see the boss's house on top of the highest hill of all, looming regally in white-painted brick over the wild and verdant rolling hills, like a Victorian lady in a hunting party.

He considered his calculations again. He thought the experiment was working out well. Of course, if he performed this demonstration at school, he would lay it out starting in the science classroom. He would take the whole class on a walk out of the classroom (Mercury), down the hall (Venus), outside the building (Earth). They would have to walk a third of a mile to get to Neptune. That was the only drawback. But Neptune needed to be a third of a mile away, or he would have to reduce the planets so much that nobody could see them, which was not good for the purposes of demonstration. He thought his teacher might balk at the class taking fifteen minutes to walk two-thirds of a mile just to see where Pluto would be at the darkest reach of its orbit, because it would seem to her that they were goofing off and were not on task when nothing could have been further from the truth.

But as he shivered in the twilight, he realized that she might have a point. He himself had no desire to walk the entire two-thirds of a mile to Pluto over another eight hills and up a grade to the stables. Three planets had been enough for him and he got the gist. Pluto had been downgraded to a dwarf planet anyway.

Satisfied—really wanting to finish what he'd started and walk the rest of the solar system, but cold and satisfied enough—he pocketed his calculations, zipped the tape measure up, and started back toward his house, remembering again that he needed to pick up the rocks and put them back in the fence where they belonged.

Out of the corner of his eye, he caught a movement in the grassy valley below the white mansion. It was the girl, urging a black filly into a gallop, hair streaming behind her. He had thought he might run into her, but he'd assumed that if he did, he would be looking up at her. Now she was in the hollow, and he was on the crest of a hill, looking down.

I COULD HARDLY SPEAK WHEN GABE asked me what I thought of Hunter's story. I definitely couldn't think. I said something about his penchant for scientific jargon that distracted the reader from the emotion of the story, and I wondered, along with Summer, whether he was writing that way on purpose.

I did not wonder out loud whether he'd moved the setting of his story to Kentucky in order to hint to Gabe that we knew each other and had been toying with each other in our stories. I did not tell him what I thought of his story:

After living the life of a self-made chick for the last five months, and having Hunter psychoanalyze that experience for me, I realized that maybe there was an advantage after all to growing up with money. Maybe I did think better of myself because my grandmother owned a Kentucky horse farm. I didn't worry as much as someone else would when I was down to my last pack of ramen noodles, or when I got hit by a taxi. I knew that if I ever did deign to call her for help, she would send me money.

But if I did have those feelings of superiority, they did not survive Hunter writing a beautiful story in which he gazed down on me as if I were someone to be pitied. I saw myself exactly as he saw me.

And that made me angry.

The interminable class finally did end. Gabe gave me a look I didn't really see, hefted himself out of his chair, and left. The rest of the class got up giggling, as usual. Their chatter about Hunter unexpectedly turning out to be a space nerd had already changed to chatter about heading to the dining hall together as they passed over the threshold to the hallway.

Hunter stood with his back against the open door, blond head cocked at me in question.

"Coming?" Summer asked me.

I shook my head, never taking my eyes off Hunter. She stood beside me a moment more, hand poised on the table. I could tell she was looking from him to me, sensing the electricity, knowing we had communicated something awful to each other through a story. Again.

"I'll wait for you." She walked through the door. I listened for her voice and Manohar's and Brian's to recede down the hall, but they didn't.

"Everything okay?" Hunter called to me.

He sounded like a noncommittal friend asking after my health. I looked like a crazy person sitting at the table after everyone else had left, staring at "The Space Between." I was going to sound like a crazy person no matter what I said to him next.

It had to be said. I stood with my book bag, swept up "The Space Between" without a single mark on it, and crumpled it in one fist. Rounding the table, I shoved his story at his chest.

He took the wad of paper. "What's the matter?" he asked innocently.

I thought of Summer, Manohar, and Brian just outside the door, listening. I did not want them to hear this. But if I asked Hunter to step away from the door and close it so we could have a private conversation, I would be showing him how much I cared. I was through with that.

I moved even closer to him and met his gaze. "I'm below you?"

"I don't know what you're talking about," he said evenly, looking me straight in the eye, obviously waiting at the door for exactly this altercation, which proved he did in fact know what I was talking about, and I had had enough.

"I'll tell you what I'm talking about." I touched the thumb of my opposite hand. "I wrote a story about how much I liked you. I never meant for you to read it." I touched my pointer finger. "You wrote a story about how much you hated me."

Hunter's grin melted from his face. He took a breath to say something.

"No, you're right," I interrupted him. "Not one story. You wrote three stories like that." I touched my third finger. "I wrote a story about my mother, hoping we could talk about it." I touched my fourth finger. "In response, you wrote a story about looking down on me." I touched my pinkie, really banged on it with my other finger, until I bent it backward and hurt it. "Don't write any more stories about me, Hunter. And I won't write any more stories about you. Deal?" I whirled toward the door.

"Wait," he said.

Whatever. I'd reached the threshold. The light was brighter in the hallway, and Summer, talking to Manohar and Brian, looked up at me with concern in her eyes.

"Erin." His hot hand was on my shoulder. He pulled me back into the room, against the door, out of their line of sight.

He leaned close. This must have been because he didn't want the others to hear, but I could almost have pretended that he wanted to be near me as he growled against my cheek, "If that's all you got from my story, that I hate you, you're not a careful reader."

Even though my heart raced with his closeness, I tilted my head and stared at him blankly. "I don't know what you're talking about." Two could play that game. I rolled away from him and stepped around the door frame.

He caught me and pulled me back again.

Pinned me against the door.

Crushed my lips beneath his.

I let him sweep his tongue inside my mouth and take over my body there in the rich room for one long, taut minute. Then I realized what I was doing, and what he was doing. I pushed his shoulders. Hunter did not push easily. I shoved him away hard and nearly toppled over myself, bouncing my sore hip against the door and sliding off.

Hunter grabbed my forearm before I fell. "What's the matter?" he asked, eyes glassy.

I started to speak and realized I'd pressed my fingers to my tingling lips. I put my hand down. "What's *always* the matter? You'll be nice for the next two weeks, and I'll agonize over what we mean to each other. Then you'll write another story for class. You're experimenting with me like you play with the women in your stories. All my stories are about you. And I can't do this anymore."

I jerked my arm out of his grasp and stalked out of the room, past my wide-eyed friends.

As I descended the stairs, holding on to the rail to keep from wrenching my hip, I heard Summer stage-whisper to Hunter, "What did you do to her now?"

The coffee shop was slammed and just got busier as the night dragged on. A new off-off-Broadway play in the theater next door had gotten great reviews—I'd wanted desperately to see it but hadn't had a spare second—and when it ended each night, it dumped the patrons into the shop, thirsty for lattes.

Somehow I managed to write my story for next Monday's class anyway. I scribbled sentences on discarded receipts and a hundred napkins when my boss wasn't looking and stuffed them in the pockets of my apron. Late in the night when I got off work, I wondered whether Hunter expected me to bring him coffee again for his trek to the hospital. I trudged in the other direction, to the library, where I typed every receipt and napkin into my laptop, printed off the file in the computer lab, and turned in my story to the front desk before I could chicken out. I constructed my sentences of the strongest steel, honed them to fine points, and hurled them straight at Hunter's heart.

13

Way too early the next morning, he knelt on the tiny space of floor between my bed and the door, packing my suitcase.

I propped myself up on one elbow and gazed at him to make sure I was seeing what I thought I was seeing, his muscular shoulders working underneath a thin cashmere sweater as he neatly folded my clothes, the morning sunlight filtering through the shades and gleaming in his blond hair. I mumbled, "Hunter, what the hell."

"Rude. You're grumpy because you're not getting enough sleep." He glanced up at me. I caught a glimpse of dark circles under his own eyes before he turned his attention back to the suitcase. "There's nothing wrong with this dress, but I want you to wear it with these shoes, okay? Do not wear a feather boa with it, or a swan around your neck, promise me. You looked great when we went to Belmont, but your style gets eclectic on occasion."

"Where am I going?" I asked.

"We," he said.

I huffed my impatience. "Where are we going?"

"Home. Your grandmother requests your presence at the Breeders' Cup."

The story I'd just turned in for Gabe's class was set in Louisville. For a moment I thought Hunter had read it and was taunting me, daring me to go back there and prove the story wasn't fiction. But he couldn't have read it. Not unless he'd gone to the library between two and eight in the morning.

No, this was heavier, weighty with reality. If he'd told me two months ago that my grandmother requested my presence, I would have asked that he convey to my grandmother where she could stuff it. Eight weeks had crammed much more into my mouth than I could chew. Hunter had to be very careful that he fulfilled her wishes, lest she ask too many questions about the business degree he was not earning. I wanted to help him make a fool of her. I didn't want to cause him trouble by refusing to go with him.

Or . . . maybe I did, now that I knew he looked down on me. He was looking down on me now. I heard his quick steps across the hardwood floor and felt the heat of his body in the cold room as he knelt beside my bed. He put his hand on my arm. "Erin."

He was not going to leave me alone. He would not even let me hide my tears. Giving up, I rolled onto my back, arching it to keep from pressing my newly healed scrapes against the New York City T-shirt I'd been sleeping in, and sniffled. "I don't want to go anywhere with you, especially Louisville."

This was not true, and I knew it as soon as I said it. He had stolen my birthright and cheated my grandmother and looked down on me and I still wanted to be wherever he was, on the off chance we might make that connection I'd wanted with him for so long.

He sensed this. His thumb moved on my arm, seductive as ever, but he watched me somberly, as if he took me seriously for once.

"I have to work all weekend," I said.

"No, you don't. You're not scheduled on weekends to make bad lattes with foam spleens. You only fill in for people on weekends, and they haven't called you yet. I checked with Summer before she left for class."

"But they could still call," I murmured. And after three days out of work with a bruised hip last week, I desperately needed the money. Which reminded me: "I don't have the money for a plane ticket."

He released my arm, reached into his coat pocket, and showed me my boarding pass: Blackwell Erin Elizabeth.

"I'll miss my belly-dancing class this afternoon."

He rolled his eyes. "How many times have you skipped it before?"

"Never. I'm sure as hell not sabotaging my chances at a publishing internship with a D in belly dancing."

He watched me, waiting for me to admit how lame my excuses were getting.

"I have a history paper due on Monday," I protested. "And a huge calculus test. You know that. You have the same test. Going out of town this weekend would be academic suicide."

"I have an anatomy test, too. We'll study on the airplane on the way down," he said in a soothing voice. "We'll study on the way back, and anyway, we're coming back Sunday morning. It's only a Saturday of studying you'll miss." He raised his blond brows at me.

Suddenly I was aware of the fact that he stood over me, and I was in bed, wearing a T-shirt and panties and no bra. He might not know that because I was half covered with a sheet, but I knew it. And I wondered how Hunter Allen's sex life fit into this complicated puzzle. He had taken the college tuition my grandmother had planned to give to me. In return he was obligated to do her bidding and bring me down to see her. There was no room in this equation for a relationship between him and me, yet he stood over me and my body tingled.

"Your dad will be there," he said.

I lay paralyzed for a moment, staring into his clear blue eyes. Hunter touched me and Hunter coaxed me and I sifted through my reactions to each, but my reaction to the idea of seeing my dad made no sense at all. I jumped up, forgetting I was embarrassed to have Hunter see me in my T-shirt and panties, and snatched my boarding pass from him to examine it more closely. "My God, are we even going to make this flight? Why didn't you wake me sooner?" I handed it back to him and watched to make sure he pocketed it.

I shoved my toes into my flip-flops and snagged my bucket of toiletries. Brushing past him on my way out the door because the room was so small, I threw at him, "I'm going to grab a shower. Don't forget to pack my hat."

We were quiet in the car to the airport, and at the gate. Hunter alternated between reading a textbook with a skinless torso on the cover, liver and lungs and heart exposed, and frowning at a stack of note cards covered in his illegible scrawl.

I pretended to read history. I tried, but my mind was on another sort of history. My brain spiraled through my first twelve years in California, my dad yelling at my mother because we didn't have any money, my mother yelling back at my dad that we might have a little more if he would get off his ass, culminating in the showdown in my grandmother's stable that I hadn't even seen. There had to be some explanation for my dad's behavior then and his disappearance afterward. There was a perfectly good reason for why he had left me with my grandmother after my mother died, and why he had never contacted me again. He was coming to Kentucky to see me and he would clarify everything.

Hunter had bought the tickets too late for us to have seats together, and that made things worse for me. Nobody I knew watched me, so pretending to read history was a moot point. I looked out the window, wondered about my dad, and willed the plane to fly faster. I wanted to see him so badly. I would forgive six years of abandonment just to sit at his feet and gaze moonily up at him like a Dalmatian kept in a pen.

By the time we touched down in Louisville, I had worked myself into a frenzy of questions. "How did my dad know I would be here?" I asked, hurrying after Hunter in the terminal.

He kept glancing up at the signs pointing us toward baggage claim. Neither of us was very good at airports, we'd found. When he and his dad had moved to Louisville, and when my mom and I had escaped to Louisville, we had all ridden the bus.

"I don't know," Hunter said.

"Maybe he thought my grandmother and I are getting along," I mused, running after Hunter as he turned a corner, "and of course I would come home to see her for the Breeders' Cup."

"Maybe," Hunter said, stopping in front of the carousel that would spit out our suitcases.

"That doesn't make sense," I said. "I doubt he'd think of the Breeders' Cup. He doesn't know anything about horses."

We stood in silence until the carousel ground to life. Hunter snagged his bag. He put one hand on my arm to stay me when I recognized mine, and he lifted it off the carousel for me. He started across the wide room toward passenger pickup with both suitcases in tow, but I took mine back from him, saying, "Maybe the Breeders' Cup is coincidental. He assumed I would be living at my grandmother's house, still in high school, because he's forgotten how old I am."

"I don't know," Hunter said again.

Suspicious this time, I looked him in the eye as we walked along. When he met my gaze, then fussed with his suitcase handle again, I knew he wasn't telling me everything he knew. "What is it?" I insisted.

"My dad," he said, nodding toward the sliding glass doors and slipping his sunglasses on.

Tommy had parked the Blackwell Farms king-cab pickup truck

at the curb. As the airport doors slid open for us, I let the weight of my suitcase on wheels slow me like an anchor. Hunter reached the pickup first. Tommy bear-hugged him and they slapped each other on the back. They were both blond and had similar features, but Tommy's face was weathered from the sun, and he wore a Blackwell Farms baseball cap and windbreaker that made him look strange embracing Hunter in his cashmere sweater and expensive sunglasses, obviously the heir to a horse fortune.

Tommy held Hunter at arm's length and beamed at him. Tommy had all Hunter's friendliness without any of Hunter's what's-in-it-for-me calculation. It was hard to picture him as the distant father from the story Hunter had written for Gabe's class, but certain elements of it rang true. Tommy was a drinker, I knew. He had been a smoker, but Hunter had badgered him into quitting. Tommy had complained about this at the stable every day for a year. Now he rolled a toothpick in the corner of his mouth, chuckling at something Hunter had said.

Then Tommy turned to me with his arms stretched wide. "Erin! How's the princess?"

"Hey, Tommy," I said, going in for a hug. My grandmother had always discouraged me from hugging the help. She embarrassed me. I embraced Tommy and let him pick me up and set me back down.

"Hunter said you'd lost weight." Tommy patted my tummy underneath my clothes. "Good thing you're wearing that overcoat or you might blow away."

On cue, icy wind gusted across the terminal driveway. I hadn't known much about Kentucky when I moved here from California, and I'd been surprised by the tenuous winter that started in November: an overcast sky that spit tiny particles of ice instead of snow.

I wiped the wetness from my face. "Has my dad gotten here yet?"

"Your dad?" Tommy repeated, rolling the toothpick to the other side of his mouth.

"Or do you two have to stay away from each other? I shouldn't have asked." Tears stung my eyes. I could hardly see.

That's why I was slow to understand the questioning look Tommy was giving Hunter, and the stony expression Hunter returned.

I think I might have gasped, "No!" and slapped both hands over my mouth. I wasn't really aware of what I was doing besides staring at the sign beside the sliding glass doors, greeting visitors unfamiliar with the area with the various pronunciations of the city's name: LOOAVULL. LUHVUL. LEWISVILLE. LOOAVILLE. LOOEYVILLE.

"Son—" Tommy began.

"I don't want to hear it," Hunter interrupted him. "Mrs. Blackwell wanted to see her and I didn't know how else to get her on the airplane. Around here I could have slung her over my shoulder, but they frown on that in New York. Erin, come back."

As I walked down the terminal sidewalk, I held up one finger to let them know—or at least to let Tommy know—that I needed a minute. Hunter couldn't care less what I needed. I stomped down the sidewalk, tears mixing with the icy wind in my face. I would let the cold wind dry me out and then I would turn back. Except more tears kept coming as I thought about my dad. He had not done anything. Not anything new. Hunter had only scratched the scab off that wound. Hunter, whom I kept trusting for some reason. Why would I think he was on my side? He was swindling my grandmother. He could screw me over, too.

A shadow beside me made me turn my head. The Blackwell

Farms truck crept backward along the curb, keeping pace with me. The window slid down and Tommy hollered, "Erin, get in the truck before Homeland Security crawls up my ass."

I stomped a couple of steps more, but I was running out of sidewalk. UPS made Louisville one of the world's busiest airports, but the passenger side of the airport was small, to match the city, and the terminal ended just ahead. I had no desire to wander through the industrial wasteland to the Ford plant.

I stepped over to the truck, jerked open the door, and tumbled into the backseat, shouting into the front, "Why did you tell me that, Hunter? What is the matter with you?"

Hunter leaned between the front seats to face me, sunglasses still obscuring his blue eyes on a cloudy afternoon. "It was the only way I could think of to get you here. Even the threat of going to Gabe with the stable-boy story wouldn't get you to come back to Kentucky to see your grandmother, and she really wanted to see you. She was hysterical when I told her you'd gotten hit by a car. I didn't have a lot of choice."

He didn't say he was sorry. He didn't even *look* particularly sorry behind his sunglasses. He admitted his transgression with no apology.

A lot like my dad.

"You mean, you didn't have a choice if you wanted to stay in college on my inheritance," I corrected Hunter. "I hope nothing this important comes up again, because the stable boy is all you have to coerce me with now. Baiting me with my dad only works once per lifetime."

"Stable boy," Tommy muttered, shaking his head.

Luckily the farm wasn't far, so I wouldn't have to sit in the truck with Hunter for long. Of course, I'd spend the afternoon, all day Saturday, and Sunday morning stuck at my grandmother's house. I had sworn to her that she would never see me again and here I was, only five months later. Broke, too, or I would have told Tommy to drop me off at a motel.

Instead, he drove the truck off the interstate, turned onto the narrow blacktop winding through the hills to the farm, then pulled onto the grassy shoulder underneath a huge, fire red maple. "Get out, both of you," he barked.

Tommy did not bark often. The ice shower had stopped, so I couldn't use the weather as an excuse. I slid across the seat and onto the ground, drained of emotion and shivering in my coat, looking down at the feet of Tommy and Hunter, standing in front of me. I had nothing to be ashamed of—Hunter was the one who should be ashamed—but I was afraid I looked like hell after crying and I didn't want him to see me like this. I was an idiot, which made me want to cry again.

"I'm not spending the whole weekend with you two sniping at each other," Tommy said. "Erin, we're going to solve this the way we settle things at the stable when your grandmother isn't looking." He nodded at Hunter. "Hit him."

"Don't make her do that," Hunter told Tommy. "She'll break her hand."

"Ha! You think awfully well of your chiseled chin," I said, but Tommy drowned me out, yelling, "Let her hit you or I will hit you myself."

"This is excellent parenting." Hunter emphasized his words with an okay sign of his thick fingers. His Rolex flashed in the sunlight before he put his hand down. "Here, Erin." He closed his eyes and lifted his chin.

I edged toward him, balling my fist, feeling better already. "Open your eyes," I said. "I want you to see it coming."

"If I open my eyes, I'll dodge you," he said matter-of-factly, as if he was used to settling his differences this way with the other stable hands. He closed his eyes again.

I struck while I had the opportunity. Didn't pause to think about technique or the proper position for my fist, thumb in or thumb out, just hauled back and hit him.

But in the split second before my hand connected with his face, I saw a flash of one of my family's apartments in Los Angeles, an early one, because I glimpsed the ocean through the window across the room, and as the years went on we'd had less and less money and we'd moved farther and farther from the sea. I saw my dad hitting my mom.

I redirected my fist, only grazing Hunter's chin, and stumbled into the side of the truck. A strong arm hooked in mine and kept me from falling. Hunter drew me to him, chuckling. "Are you okay?"

I shoved him away from me, slid back into the truck, and slammed the door. He wasn't even sorry and I couldn't even get revenge. There was no good in this. With a final sniffle I opened my history book, wishing I hadn't come.

I don't know what argument Hunter used outside the truck, but predictably he hopped into the driver's seat, and Tommy took the passenger side for the short drive up to the farm.

A few minutes passed wherein the truck hummed, country music twanged on the radio, and I read the same paragraph in my history book four times.

Then Tommy asked, "So, did you two hook up yet?"

"Tommy!" I squealed. "What a question!"

"What?" He half-turned toward me. "I'm just asking."

"If we hadn't hooked up," I said, "that question would be awkward and embarrassing. And if we had hooked up, it would be—"

"—awkward and embarrassing," Hunter said.

Tommy watched Hunter driving for a moment. Tommy's expression was inscrutable, and I could see in the rearview mirror that Hunter's was, too. "So you *have* hooked up," Tommy concluded.

"Of course not," I said. "Hunter met his girlfriend in the bathroom. He has a fortune-teller and a bar waitress on the side."

"Never say I didn't raise class." Tommy turned all the way around to face me. "And how do you know this?"

"We live in the same dorm."

Tommy grinned. "Uh-huh. You're from the same town, the same farm even, you live in the same dorm, you know all about each other's business, but you haven't hooked up."

When he put it that way, why hadn't we? He made it sound as if the prerequisites for hooking up were familiarity, proximity . . . and he must sense the desire, at least on my end. He didn't understand the complications, the humiliations, the hundred reasons why not that hummed underneath us like the never-ending sound of New York traffic, or the drone of the Kentucky interstate behind the autumn trees.

"It's none of your business, Dad." Maybe it was because I could hardly hear Hunter over the motor and the radio, but I was surprised by how embarrassed he sounded, and wistful.

We rounded the last bend. The trees parted to reveal my grandmother's towering mansion. It perched on the highest hill in all of the rolling pastureland that formed the farm. Like many of the historic buildings in and around Louisville, it was built in the Italianate style of the 1870s. If a photo of a classic Southern mansion was stretched on a computer until the ceilings and windows were ridiculously high—that was this overstated style of architecture, so elegant and imposing it was threatening.

"Here we are, princess." Tommy opened his door, presumably to haul my suitcase out of the payload.

"I'm not staying here," I said quickly. "Hunter can stay in my room, where he belongs. I'm staying with you, Tommy."

Tommy and Hunter both looked over the seat at me in surprise. Tommy said, "That's not proper. Your grandmother will have a cow."

"No way," Hunter said.

"You owe me that much." I caught Hunter's eye and drove home my meaning. I had no intention of telling my grandmother that he was taking her for a ride, but Hunter didn't know that. At least I hoped he didn't.

Hunter's blue eyes drilled into me just long enough to trigger my heart palpitations. Then he uttered an obscenity and left the truck, dragging his own suitcase through the giant front door of my grandmother's house.

"Your grandmother will march down to my house and get you herself," Tommy said as he drove back down the lane.

"She knows she can push me only so far," I said. "The apple doesn't fall far from the tree, unfortunately." He parked beside his little house, and I jumped out of the truck before he could change his mind.

This house could have sat in a Louisville neighborhood with other bungalows like it, and it wouldn't have drawn attention. But here on the farm it drew my attention. It was white timber above and local limestone below, with a slate roof, like all the outbuildings. It matched the gatehouse, and the historic kitchen with a vast brick oven, and the barn. I would not have chosen to live in a servant's house that matched the barn. I knew from Hunter's latest story for Gabe's class that he felt the same way.

I crossed the wooden porch and waited for Tommy to unlock the front door. Hunter had been in my grandmother's house plenty of times. He'd even been in my room, during that childhood moment so long ago when we were friends. I had never been in his house. I followed Tommy through the narrow hallways, past a kitchen remodeled in the 1970s, to a tiny bedroom with a huge window that looked on the lane out front.

"Here you go, son. I kept everything just like you left it," Tommy joked, depositing my suitcase inside. "I'll give you a few minutes to freshen up, but I need to get back to Churchill Downs. Then your grandmother wanted me to make sure you and Hunter got to the party at the Farrells' tonight."

A party at the house Whitfield Farrell still shared with his parents? This trip was seeming more and more like everyone in my old life had pored over my new story for Gabe's class—the one Hunter hadn't read yet—and re-created it. "I'm not going," I said quickly. I had no desire to live out that antifantasy.

"Suit yourself," Tommy said, "but you'll have a hard time avoiding the party tomorrow night. It's here."

He backed down the hallway. I heard the door close and watched the truck pass in front of the house, toward the mansion. In a few minutes the truck passed again, headed for the interstate. Tommy was in the passenger seat and Hunter was driving.

Now that they were gone, I looked around. I was sitting on Hunter Allen's bed. Eat your hearts out, girls in Gabe's class! And I saw why Hunter had looked so horrified at the idea of me staying in his house. The walls were covered in glossy posters of fast cars and movie starlets wearing thongs. This shouldn't have surprised me. He'd probably tacked them up when he was fourteen. It surprised me anyway to discover that Hunter was a teenage boy after all, and that he was—what was the word he'd used in his comment on my first story?—gauche.

I crawled to the head of the bed, taking way more pleasure than I should have from the sensation of his rough bedspread rubbing my skin, and got a closer look at his walls. Taped between the posters were certificates for his academic awards. First place, seventh-grade math tournament. First place, tenth-grade science fair. Senior-class valedictorian. He'd won everything but the writing contests. Those were mine.

I sat back against his headboard, as he must have sat up reading every night, and surveyed the whole wallpaper of white diploma-like rectangles superimposed on the larger images of trashy pop culture. That's when I saw the cardboard sun, six feet across, behind his dresser where a mirror should have been, with the tiny planets floating in front of it, Earth the size of his thumbnail.

14

Bundled against the cold wind, I walked up the lane, past my grandmother's mansion, and over the hill to the stables, built a hundred years before of solid wood and limestone and covered in ivy, picturesque to a tourist who didn't know better.

Most of the staff had gone to Churchill Downs. Only a skeleton crew was left to care for the horses that weren't racing. I slipped easily into the office and changed into the riding clothes I'd left in the closet, and my helmet. Very important: always wear a helmet. I could feel that my clothes were looser than they'd been when I left, but luckily the office didn't have a mirror. I transferred the apple I'd snagged from Tommy's refrigerator from the pocket of my overcoat to the pocket of my riding coat.

I walked through the rest of the front stable where we kept the money-making horses we liked visitors to see, the race winners and their parents and offspring, through the large gravel courtyard empty but for a few pies that kept their smell to themselves in the cold air, into the back stable and around the corner.

Blinked at the white horse in the corner stable. Either I'd forgotten the layout of the barn in five months away, or Boo-boo was missing.

Digging my fingernails into the apple in my pocket, I walked quickly through the cold barn, glancing at the horses that peeked out of their stalls, searching for a stable hand. When I found a new guy grooming a brown gelding, I tried to keep my voice calm but it came out a croak. "Where's Boo-boo?"

He looked around at me, startled. I watched the realizations march across his face: this was a stranger, this stranger had red hair like Mrs. Blackwell, this was the prodigal granddaughter everybody had been talking about, the one dragged back from college by Tommy Allen's boy. Then a touch of fear that the stables had sold off the girl's favorite horse and she would have a fit. This man looked like he'd been slapped by a spoiled brat before.

"Boo-boo," I said impatiently. "High and Mighty. By Rocky Mountain High out of Might Is Right."

"Oh!" As he realized he was not in trouble, his shoulders relaxed. He pointed with his grooming brush toward the other end of the back stable. "Rock Star has taken a shine to her. We moved her next to him because she calms him down. Want me to saddle her up for you?"

"No thanks," I said, hurrying toward my horse. The new guy had not gotten the memo that nobody saddled horses for the old lady's granddaughter. Tommy had seen to that. He'd taught me that if I wanted something done right, I had to do it myself.

Relief flooded me as Boo-boo poked her head out of her stall to see who was coming, ears pricked up. When she saw me, her ears moved forward. If I'd been twelve, I would have sworn to anyone who would listen that Boo-boo recognized me and loved me. However, I was eighteen. I knew better. I was holding the apple out in front of me.

The time in the stall was always the hardest for me. My body tensed, waiting for the horse to rear, and my brain kept replaying the accident I hadn't seen.

Boo-boo was a thoroughbred, looming and nervous like all of them. But she was relatively sweet tempered. Tommy had picked her for me when my grandmother insisted that he put me back on a horse a week after my mother died. Boo-boo's soft, surprisingly nimble lips plucked the apple out of my palm. As she chomped, I stroked the side of her head firmly, as Tommy had taught me. Cooing "Boo-boo-boo-boo-boo" to her, I squeezed the terror out of my brain. The way to stay safe was never to let a horse know I was afraid. I wiped the apple juice on my jeans and put up my hand to make sure I was wearing my helmet before I ventured farther into the dark stall to find the tack.

Riding was dangerous, with the constant threat of being thrown and trampled, but ironically, once I was up in the saddle and away from Boo-boo's legs, I felt safe. I directed her out of the stable—she was in great spirits today, kicking up her heels and shaking her head as if bragging to the other horses that she was going for a run and they were not, ha ha, so there—and I trotted her across the paddock to the back pasture. Then I loosened the reins and let her go. She loved to run.

Normally I loved it, too, the green grass flashing past, the bright fall trees, the cold wind in my face, the always foreign feel of a huge animal galloping underneath me. Today I was sore. Every step of the horse jarred my hip and sent a ripple through my back. Even my fist gripping the reins was sore after grazing Hunter's hard jawbone. After a few minutes of riding I grew used to the pain and settled in for a long ride. Usually Boo-boo and I dashed out for a gallop after school, and then I had friends or homework or reading to occupy me. Today I decided we would explore every corner of the farm. I had nothing else to do besides study history and calculus, and I might never be back.

Something inside me died that long afternoon while Hunter was at the races. I finally lost all hope in my dad. He was not coming for me. He did not harbor a secret wish to become reacquainted with me. He was not dying to complete our family but was prevented from doing so by foreign spies. He had left me to bury my mother and my grandmother to raise me, and he had moved on with his life. If he had anything to do with it, I would never hear from him again.

But more likely, he would die before me, and I would receive the news just when I was about to get married or give birth or embark on my national tour for my best-selling novel. I had looked forward to my dad's return as the climax of my story. Now I knew he would ruin my happiest day for me, an unexpected plot twist.

Boo-boo chomped through the reins as I pulled her up short out of a canter. We had reached a far pasture, many rolling hills away from the house and the barn. Standing on a limestone boulder under the golden canopy of an oak was the horse that had killed my mother.

She'd been two at the time and there had been talk of trying her in the Derby the following spring. After the accident, my grandmother never raced her, though she potentially lost millions of dollars with that inaction. She just put the filly out to pasture. If the decision had been mine, I would have shot her myself. But as Tommy had explained, horses bore no malice. They were skittish herd animals escaping danger.

They were not, however, mountain goats. Boo-boo danced impatiently as I gazed toward the black horse on the gray rock under the yellow tree. How had she gotten up there? The back of the boulder sloped more gently, I remembered. That was the explanation. But my heart did not slow down.

In Hunter's most recent story, the girl he looked down on rode a black filly. I wondered again what his story had meant.

I WOKE TO THE SOUND OF dishes clanking in the kitchen and the scent of bacon. Untangling myself from Hunter's bedclothes and sliding my history book off my face, I squinted at the dark window. Dawn had not broken. In the dimmest light glowing from under the bedroom door, I could just make out the planets stuck to the sun above Hunter's dresser.

"Tommy!" I exclaimed at the overflowing kitchen table. "You didn't have to cook all this. I hardly eat anything in the morning. I'll just have some coffee."

"Coffee," he repeated in exactly the Long Island accent Hunter used when he said *coffee*. Turning with a skillet of eggs, Tommy jabbed the spatula toward an empty chair at the table. "Eat. Hunter told me you're living on peanut-butter crackers. Eat or you're walking to Churchill Downs." He flopped eggs onto my plate. "Or are you hiding here all day?" He sat down at his own place and handed me a platter of biscuits.

Hiding sounded like an excellent idea, but it wasn't what I'd had in mind. "I need money," I said.

He stopped eating and eyed me from across the table. The look he was giving me . . . I had never seen this look from him before. I wondered if, for the first time, I was seeing that father from Hunter's story. I had thought Tommy was a happy-go-lucky old soul who would give me the shirt off his back, but perhaps I'd gotten that impression only because I'd never asked him for anything.

Quickly I clarified, "I want to work for you today. Could you use an extra stable hand? Pay me what you used to pay Hunter."

He raised his eyebrows, chewed and swallowed before he responded. "It's your grandmother's money, you know."

"At least I will have earned it."

In his grunt I heard acquiescence but also impatience at humoring the poor little rich girl. I might have told him never mind, he didn't have to satisfy my whim. But I did want to spend the day at

Churchill Downs. And I did not want to spend it in the owner's box with Hunter and my grandmother.

In the darkness I helped Tommy load a brown stallion and a dun filly into the trailer. We drove back up the empty interstate and through the neighborhood of nineteenth-century houses in the style of my grandmother's. At the orange stain of sunrise across the gray sky, we pulled slowly through the gate at Churchill Downs, all white-painted wood with twin spires towering over the grandstands.

Then we started work. I fed horses, watered horses, groomed horses. I didn't exercise them because this close to their races, the trainer wanted specific experienced people riding them, sensing problems. I did, however, lead horses to and fro, and when a stallion reared up and kicked in protest at going back into the Blackwell Farms trailer, I was the one who leaped forward to grab the reins and talk him down. I acted automatically. It was only fifteen minutes later, when the truck leading the trailer pulled away and Tommy squeezed my shoulder, that my heart pounded at the danger I'd been in. An hour after that I realized I hadn't been wearing a helmet.

Groups of agents and buyers and my grandmother's assistants wandered into our farm's section of the stables and out again, talking business over bourbon in clear plastic cups, lighting cigars after they'd walked away from the hay. I used to be part of these groups. I would hang at the periphery with other tipsy teenage heirs to horse farms, often Whitfield Farrell. I expected to see my grandmother in one of these groups. Repeatedly I peeked under a horse's belly to look for her without looking like I was looking. I never saw her. Around noon I did, however, see Hunter.

He grinned with a middle-aged agent and my grandmother's elderly lawyer, both powerful men, handy to know if you were pretending to take over a venerable business that had been in someone else's family for five generations. They stood in the warm sunlight that had finally burned through the clouds. He took a sip of bourbon and watched me over the rim of his cup.

And then he was laughing at something the lawyer had said. He'd joined the boys' club with a great personality, good looks, and no effort at all. I wasn't sure anymore that he'd been watching me over his cup. He was in the sunlight, after all, and I was in the darkness. He couldn't see me.

Staying on my feet and taking care of horses all day would have hurt enough, but my bruised hip started to throb, and my shoulders ached from holding the spooked horse steady. I noticed other stable hands sipping sodas and smoking cigarettes beside the vast parking lot, but I never asked for a break, and Tommy never suggested I take one. I suspected he was giving the princess exactly what he thought she wanted.

Just before the last race of the day, after we'd sent our best horse to the paddock to be shown off, Tommy jerked his head toward the track, telling me to follow him. In the sunshine I shed my Blackwell Farms jacket and tied it around my waist. We found a space at the white fence where we could see the track—nowhere near the finish line, which was in front of the grandstands, but with a great view of the fourth turn. He bought us both a hot dog at a cart. I bit into mine immediately, giving him my thanks with my mouth full. I hadn't eaten since he'd fed me that morning.

As I ate, I watched him down huge bites. The whole hot dog took him four. Hunter did not eat like this. Hunter could eat a hot dog with a knife and fork and make you think everybody ate it like that on Long Island.

"What is it?" Tommy asked me. A dab of mustard clung to the corner of his mouth.

I handed him my napkin as a hint. "Were you in love with my mother?"

The half smile stayed in place on his lips. He and Hunter were both good at smiling through anything. But I saw his reaction in his eyes. He winced a little, crow's-feet deepening and then relaxing in a split second.

"I didn't have time," he said, wiping his mouth.

"So it was lust," I said.

He squinted at me. "Nnnnnn . . . Maybe. She was beautiful. She was also very funny. Like you. And your daddy didn't treat her right. Like he doesn't treat you right."

It was my turn to wince. I hadn't forgiven Hunter for dragging me down here on that pretense.

"That was a lot of it," Tommy said. "She needed me. She said she needed me. The drive to rescue the damsel from the dragon is real strong, and real hard for a man to resist. That story never ends well, and I knew that going into it."

I looked out over the track. We faced the back of the starting gate. Grooms were leading horses into it one by one. Our farm's horse did not want to go. Nose inside, he braced his back feet outside the gate so they couldn't close him in. Two of our grooms put their shoulders against his ass and pushed. I asked Tommy, "Why didn't my grandmother fire you?"

Tommy watched the show at the gate, too, or seemed to. "Why didn't she ship that filly off for dog food?"

"Because the filly meant no harm." I recited what Tommy had explained to me when I was older and ready to listen.

The grooms managed to shove our horse inside the gate and snap the doors in place behind him before he could kick their heads off. They walked away mopping their brows with their sleeves as other grooms approached the gate with the next horse in the line-up.

"Honestly," Tommy said, "I think she kept me on because of Hunter. She knew this was a good place for him. She's always liked Hunter."

"She sees herself in him," I said. "They're both manipulative and crazy like a fox."

"There's that," he said flatly, staring out over the track, as if my grandmother and Hunter did not bother him at all. Or as if they bothered him very much. Both emotions looked the same on Tommy.

I asked, "When Hunter and I lived here, did you tell him to stay away from me?"

Tommy turned quickly toward me. By the time I looked over at him, surprise was gone from his face, but I'd seen that sudden movement.

He said carefully, "I did. Your grandmother would not have wanted to see the two of you together."

"But you said she likes Hunter," I pointed out. "She's giving him her freaking farm." At least, that's what she thought.

Tommy nodded. "Hunter has brains like I've never seen. He's smart, like his mother. He'll do right by this farm, since you don't want to. But it's one thing if he gets your grandmother's business. It's something entirely different if he gets you. He's not—"

Good enough is what Tommy didn't say. The unspoken words hung in the air between us. I wondered whether he thought this was what my grandmother believed, or if he believed it himself.

"Why are you pushing Hunter and me together, then?" I asked in exasperation. "You sat there in the truck yesterday and asked us if we were hooking up."

"I wasn't pushing you together," Tommy said calmly. "I was commenting on what I saw, which is that you've already been together. I could see it all over his face." Tommy fished a toothpick out of his pocket and put it in his mouth.

"Really?" I asked, wishing it were true, hoping against all logic and good sense that Hunter had fallen for me and his dad had sensed this. "I've always found Hunter's face unreadable."

Tommy rolled the toothpick to one side of his mouth and talked around it. "He's got my face."

"Right," I said as the starting bell clanged and the doors on the gate banged open.

15

Several hours later, Tommy and I unloaded a couple of horses at the farm, unhitched the trailer, and drove down the hill to his house. He headed right back out to a celebration with the other stable hands. My grandmother's horse had won the last race at the Breeders' Cup. Whenever she received a five-million-dollar purse, it was her custom to send a case of fine bourbon to the stable hands. You're welcome.

I was done with being a stable hand, I decided, and I did not want any bourbon. My muscles ached to the point that I could feel the individual fibers scraping against each other every time I moved. All I wanted was for this horrible trip to be over. I stumbled into Hunter's bedroom and tossed the bills Tommy had given me for my work onto the bed. They landed beside Hunter's anatomy note cards, stacked neatly and secured with a rubber band.

I picked them up and turned them over curiously, as if I had never before seen such an exotic prize. He definitely had not left them for me to find for some reason. He might do that with his dorm room key or his wallet, but he would not play fast and loose with his homework. He must have stepped in to look for something—surely he'd left something he'd meant to take to college with him, even if I hadn't—and he'd forgotten them.

He needed them back.

Slipping the stack into the pocket of my farm jacket, I shut the door of Tommy's house behind me and trudged up the lane toward my grandmother's house, taking care to stay in the long green grass, well off the road. Everybody coming to and from her party was driving drunk.

I slowed as I approached the mansion towering over me, three white stories pointing straight for a full moon in the starry sky. The driveway was full of expensive cars. I would be recognized even in my stable-boy clothes if I went through the front door, dragged from group to group of ecstatic old people, until I was forced in front of my grandmother. I waded through the cold grass around the house, across the patio, and tiptoed through the side door.

Hunter stood in the hallway, with both hands on a marble-topped eighteenth-century console table, taking a hard look at himself in the enormous mirror. I stopped. I knew he hadn't heard me come in because he hadn't moved. I could present him with the note cards and then . . . I wasn't sure what.

I didn't dare. He stared at himself, leaning forward as if inordinately concerned with the dark circles under his eyes.

But he stayed that way for so long that I finally took a few steps toward him. I passed the back entrance to the kitchen, which leaked dance music from the live band in the ballroom, and kept walking until I saw him from a new angle.

His eyes were closed. He was not staring at himself. He was steeling himself, and as I watched he took a final deep breath and pushed off from the console.

I skittered into the kitchen before he saw me. I walked backward until I bumped against the island—ouch, granite countertop gouging my barely healed skin—and spun around at a clinking behind me. A dark-haired figure straightened with his hands around a bowl of potato salad. Whitfield Farrell was going through my grandmother's refrigerator like he lived here.

"Erin!" he exclaimed. "Guess what I heard."

Whitfield and I had not parted on good terms. The last time I'd seen him was the Derby party, when Hunter had told him to get his hands off my ass—the inspiration for my unfortunate stable-boy story. But if Whitfield had been sober, we would have pretended to forget all about that. For the sake of our families getting along and doing business, we would have embraced, backed off, and conversed politely, as we'd both been trained.

Whitfield was not sober. "I heard that you told your grandmother you didn't want her fucking farm," he slurred. "You ran off to New York City"—*ran* was a jerk of the potato salad bowl hard enough to send the plastic wrap flying off the top and sailing down to the granite top of the island—"and she gave her farm to Hunter Allen."

"You're kidding," I said.

"And . . ." He held up his finger for silence, nearly dropping the bowl.

I rushed around the island and caught the bowl before it dropped, then set it on the counter.

This was a mistake, because now I was only a foot from Whitfield. He took off my cap and tossed it to the high ceiling. It rang a huge pot hanging from the rack over the island. "I heard you were playing stable hand today. I don't understand you at all."

"You don't have to. I'll see you around, okay?" I had thought I'd rather die than set foot in my grandmother's party, but now the dance music and the crowded foyer leading to the front door were the lesser of the evils. I took a step in that direction.

He stopped me with a hand on my bruised hip. "Why are you making it so hard on yourself? Look at me."

I should have pulled away from him. He would have been right on my heels as I entered the foyer, but then I could have escaped him in the jovial drunken crowd.

His tone and his words stopped me. "Look at me." He spoke

tenderly, the way I'd longed to be spoken to by a hero with an important message just for me.

I looked up into his eyes, which were green like the winter grass. I had talked closely with him a hundred times before. I'd never noticed what color his eyes were. And as my life veered closer and closer to the story I'd just turned in for Gabe's class, I made a mental note of this detail to add to my story when I revised it for my end-of-semester portfolio.

"You don't have to make it so hard on yourself," Whitfield crooned. "It's not a crime to inherit millions of dollars."

"I don't think it's a crime," I protested. "I just—"

He nodded. "Want to live your life without being told what to do." His face inched closer to mine, and my urge to back away dissolved as I watched his lips. He understood exactly where I was coming from. Hunter did not.

"Just do what they tell you, Erin," Whitfield whispered. "You'll have the last laugh in the end because you will be the millionaire, and they will be dead."

"Whitfield," Hunter called sharply from the doorway to the back hall. "Get your hands off her."

I tried to step away from Whitfield, but his fingers dug into my bruise.

Whitfield shook his head at Hunter. "Just because you say it doesn't mean people are going to do it, Allen. You may have a hold on the old bitch, but nobody will ever forget where you came from."

"You know what?" I interjected, trying again to pull away as Whitfield held me firmly where it hurt. "I'm just going to—"

"We talked about this last May," Hunter boomed. "Get your hands off her or I will knock your teeth in."

Whitfield gaped at Hunter.

I held my breath.

Hunter took a step forward.

"Okay!" Whitfield exclaimed, holding up his hands. "I don't want you to cause a scene at *your* house, Hunter." He turned to me. "Remember what I said."

Hunter took another step toward him.

Eyeing Hunter, Whitfield grabbed the bowl of potato salad and escaped through the doorway to the foyer.

"Well!" I exclaimed. "That was tense."

Hunter watched me, brows down, blue eyes dark. "I'm not cut out for this." He rounded the island, sidestepped me, and followed Whitfield into the foyer. At first I thought he would try to catch Whitfield, but then above the crowd I saw the massive front door open and close, and I knew Hunter had left.

I pushed through the party after him. Old people stopped me and hugged me and told the roaming waiters to bring me drinks and asked me if it was true my grandmother was grooming Tommy Allen's son to take over the farm instead of me. These were exactly the conversations that I'd dreaded, that I'd braved in coming back here to see my father.

My heart raced at the idea that Hunter was walking away from me. If my grandmother caught me here, she would insist on having a long discussion with me. By the time I got away, Hunter would be gone. I couldn't let him go—not when he'd played hero to my damsel in distress for a second time. Not again.

Finally I extricated myself from the party and dragged open the front door. Outside in the cold moonlight, the green grass shone in long waves, but no tall blond boy waded through it or trudged along the lane. He really was gone.

Then I heard shouts and man laughter way over at the stables. My grandmother had sent the stable hands bourbon. They would be playing basketball.

Sure enough, I rounded the stone corner of the stable, out of breath and sick with worry, just in time to see Hunter, stripped to the waist, wearing only the khakis and lace-up shoes from his horse-farm-heir uniform, sail through the air in a perfect layup. His white skin gleamed spookily in the strange light. He was breaking a sweat already in the cold air, and the scar on his side stood out like a marker from some ancient magic. He dunked the ball through the netless hoop and landed flat on his feet on the asphalt parking lot.

Half the men moaned a triumphant "Oooooh!" and the other half a defeated "Aaaaaw." Then another shirtless man pointed in my direction. "Erin!" The game stopped as I slid onto a white wooden bench against the stone wall. Several more stable hands called out to me.

"Good work today, Erin!" Tommy shouted above them. Drunk now, he was a lot happier with the job I'd done than he had been sober. "As good work as Hunter ever did, and she doesn't complain like Hunter."

Several of the men shoved Hunter in different directions. He didn't seem to mind. He grinned at me, looking—proud, dared I say?

"You want to play with us, Erin?" another man asked. I don't think he meant anything by it, but the others read innuendo into it and groaned.

"I haven't had nearly enough bourbon for that," I called back. "I'll just sit here and watch, and I'll call 911 when someone tears an ACL."

Most of them turned away, resuming their positions for the game. Only Hunter continued to stare at me with his blond head cocked to one side, bare muscular chest shining, basketball on his hip. He sounded genuinely puzzled as he said, "You don't have a phone."

I opened my hands and shrugged. I recognized this uncharacteristically slow-on-the-uptake Hunter from our conversation in the coffee shop two months before. He was drunk.

"Ball!" the other men called. Hunter turned and tossed the ball into the crowd.

The game began again. I watched the men dodge each other, throw over each other, lose their balance and stumble drunkenly out of the area of play, then jog back again. I watched Hunter's muscles work underneath his skin, his body retaining surprising grace even though bourbon had slowed his brain. Sweat darkened the blond hair at his temples. He grew hotter as I got colder, shrinking in my Blackwell Farms jacket on the hard wooden bench.

When two men leaped for the ball at once and tumbled in a tangle on the asphalt, Tommy shouted, "We gotta call this. Come inside. Next round's on me." The bare-chested men slapped each other high-fives and moved through a doorway golden with light, into the stable office.

Only Hunter stayed behind. He tugged his shirt out of a nearby tree. As he buttoned it he said, "Hullo, Miss O'Carey."

"Hullo, David." I tried to keep my voice from shaking with cold and anticipation.

He pulled his cashmere sweater over his head. "Did you remember to bring me the anatomy note cards I hadn't forgotten?"

So he'd left the note cards in his bedroom on purpose after all, to give me an excuse to find him at the party. With tingling fingers I reached into my jacket and handed him the cards. He pocketed them, a sly grin pulling at one corner of his mouth.

"What's with the British accent?" I asked. "They wouldn't have talked like that in America by 1875. They might have had a lingering Scotch-Irish inflection because so many of them were recent immigrants and they didn't have television to flatten the brogue."

He stared at me. In my usual wonky way, I'd blathered too much information. He had started the conversation from "Almost a Lady." I wasn't sure what he meant by this, but I was excited about finding out. So I began the conversation again. "Hullo, David. Would you like to walk behind the stables?"

"I would soil my slippers," he said, "and the maid would notice in the morning."

He was reciting my story, but he was also rejecting me. I stood and pasted a smile on my face to show him it was all in fun. "Okey-doke. Tommy said he can't take us to the airport tomorrow because he's leaving for Churchill Downs too early, but one of the other guys will take us. I'll see you in the—"

Before I could take a step away, he reached out and grabbed my elbow. "I was making a joke."

"About our positions being switched, with you owning the farm and me working as a stable boy? You're hilarious. You know what you should do with that kind of talent? You should go to college in New York and study creative writing."

He laughed too heartily at this, tugging at my elbow. "Come on."

I tried to slow my breathing. It formed white clouds in the frigid air, and Hunter could see how excited I was. "Where are we going?" I asked.

"Behind the stable!" he said in exasperation. He pulled me until I walked with him along the stone wall and past the last corner. As we turned and kicked through the gravel against the back wall, he stated the obvious. "I have never been this drunk in my life."

I chuckled. "It's part of the job description."

His eyes widened. "It is! It really is. And it's not the volume so much as the longevity. I think I had my first mint julep at ten o'clock this morning."

He slid onto the lone bench against the back wall of the stable, where potential buyers could watch horses trot around the paddock. I sat next to him, but not too close, still unsure about what we were doing here. Beyond the paddock fence, the green hills rolled and rolled under the stars, gently descending to the tree line. We sat there in the silence and the cold for a few moments. I tried to memorize this: vast farm below, the depthless sky above, and Hunter beside me. Not touching me. Just there for me.

He broke the silence with a sigh. "This is so crazy. *You* should be schmoozing your way through blue-blood Kentucky, not me."

I shrugged. "I won't lie. I'm sore right now. But I had a lot of fun being a stable boy today. In New York I never long for the horse parties or the horse people, but I do miss the horses."

"Yeah. Dad said you took Boo-boo out for a long ride yesterday. I was glad to hear that. I'll bet she was so happy to see you."

"Why? I'm sure she didn't recognize me."

"What are you talking about?" Hunter demanded. "Boo-boo loves you. She always has."

"She would love any random person holding an apple."

His lips parted and his blond brows went down in a concerned expression. Suddenly he jerked his head away from me and sneezed. I didn't remember ever seeing him sneeze before, even with all the hay and dust constantly hanging in the air in the barns. But Hunter *did* sneeze, and what I'd thought was his concern for me had actually been a presneeze expression.

Then he turned back to me. "Erin," he said gravely, "that is the saddest thing I ever heard. That story you wrote for Gabe's class. About the girl alone in the mansion, with nobody to talk to?"

I nodded.

"I wasn't there in your house with you, obviously, so I don't know," he said. "But from watching you with your grandmother at the stables right after your mother died, it seemed like the two of you didn't really talk. You remember your grandmother made my dad get you back on a horse the next week?"

I laughed shortly. "I will never forget that."

"He told me you did not seem okay. He thought your grandmother wasn't talking to you about what happened and you had no way to deal with it. After this went on for a few weeks, he wanted me to try to talk to you."

I blinked at him in the darkness. "You didn't, though."

"We were already in school by then. Your friends had made fun of me. I was twelve. My higher brain functions weren't fully developed. I was so in love with you."

The cold had woven its way into the fabric of my jeans and settled like a coating of ice in the folds of my jacket. Now I warmed again, puzzling through Hunter's words. I didn't know whether to take him seriously. "Your love for me was a symptom that your brain hadn't developed, or—"

"Shut up." He turned to face me. "I am drunk and I am trying to confess, so just let me do it, okay? I had fallen in love with you over the summer. Then this horrible thing happened to you and you stopped talking to me. I thought you blamed me, or my dad. Which he deserved."

"No," I protested. "It was an acc—"

"I took it as a rejection." He put his hand on my knee and looked me straight in the eyes. "It's taken me all this time to figure that out. But I regretted it every day. And I'm truly sorry." He sat back against the bench and faced the stars. The place where his hand had rested on my knee felt colder than ever.

"I'm sorry, too," I said, "so we're even. I didn't visit you in the hospital when you got crushed by a horse. For much the same reasons regarding love and rejection and being young." *And being a cold bitch, born and bred,* I thought to myself, because he was trying to make a connection with me, and I couldn't even meet him halfway.

"That went on for six years," he said. "You didn't talk to me. I didn't talk to you. You didn't talk to your grandmother. And now she's disinherited you. So in all that time, you never told her how you feel?"

"How do I feel?" I leaned forward, honestly curious about what he would tell me.

"You love horses. You love the farm. But everything about it reminds you of your mother dying and your dad leaving. You never dealt with it back then. You're trying to deal with it now. You've gone far away to a place with no horses and very little grass, and you're studying how to write a story with a happy ending. If you can write that ending for yourself, maybe you can come back."

Listening to this was like watching a colorful origami box unfold. Only it was Hunter showing me the contents. That made me very uncomfortable. I sat back and folded my arms across my chest, hugging myself against the cold.

"When I brought you here," he said, "I thought your grandmother would summon you. She must be waiting for you to come to her instead. Now I see that you and I may fly back to New York tomorrow without either of you giving in."

"Hm," I agreed.

"But if you do stumble upon each other and have a talk"—he turned to me and took my hand this time, warming it between both of his—"can't you please tell her how you feel?"

I shook my head. "No."

He dropped my hand and slouched against the bench. "I wish you would, because I'm not sure how long I can put up with this."

"I'll bet you can put up with it a little longer," I said brightly, desperate to get out from under the heavy subject. "How much do you love college in New York?"

He grinned. "I love college in New York. I love just being in the city. I love my classes. I love the hospital. I wish I weren't there at two in the morning because I also love sleep, but I do love the hospital. I love Manohar and Brian. In a manly love kind of way, of course."

"Of course," I said, the corners of my mouth stretched tight, trying not to laugh. "You get along great with everybody. Because that's what you do."

"Because that's what I do," he agreed. "Do you love college in New York?"

I sighed, a big puff of white air. "I do love college in New York. Lately I've been so busy with work and homework that I might as well be in Iowa, but I remember loving college in New York a month ago. I'm afraid it may be coming to a close, though."

He leaned nearer. "Seriously?"

"If I got that internship," I said, "I could hold on. Otherwise I'm in trouble. I wanted so badly to start my publishing career in the publishing mecca. But maybe that's not possible for me now. I can write anywhere, I guess." I laughed.

He didn't laugh. "What will you do, then?"

"I might try California," I said. "It's almost as expensive as New York, though. And it's tainted in my mind because my mother tried it with the worst of luck."

Hunter's movement toward me was so sudden that I instinctively shrank back. Then I realized he was reaching for my hand. He took it in his warm hand again, rubbing my palm with his calloused thumb. His voice was smooth like a song as he said, "I would not love college in New York if you weren't there."

Suddenly I was flushing hot in the freezing night. "You wouldn't?" I whispered.

"No. When I said I love it, I listed all these things I love about it. I left you out." He let my hand go and touched his finger to my lips. "I love *you*."

I stared stupidly at him. Was he joking again, reciting another line from my story? I didn't remember writing this.

He leaned in and kissed me. I didn't respond for a few seconds. My mind lagged behind what my body was feeling.

"Say it," he whispered against my lips. "I know this is hard for you. Tell me."

"I love you." Hearing my own words, I gasped at the rush of emotion.

He put his hands on either side of my jaw and took my mouth with his.

My mind still chattered that something was wrong with this picture. My body stopped caring. I grabbed fistfuls of his sweater and pulled him closer.

He moved his lips to my cheek, to my ear, back to my mouth. I had never been kissed like this in my life. Each time I thought I should protest because there were so many unsettled matters between us, Hunter kissed me harder, forcing those concerns out of my mind. The cold air heated up around us.

He unsnapped the top of my jacket and slipped his hand inside. His warm palm cupped my breast beneath my shirt.

Then he straightened, blinking at me, and pulled his hand away.

"What is it?" I asked.

"Okay," he panted. "I'm going to kick myself for this in the morning, but I don't want to do this while I'm drunk. And I don't want to do it behind the stable. I want everything to be perfect between you and me." He stroked my hair away from my face. "Are you mad?"

"Mad?" I squeaked. "No. Horny? Yes. Frustrated?"

"Yes." He set his forehead against mine.

"Yes," I agreed. "Mad? No."

He watched me with serious eyes. His gaze fell to my chest. He fastened the snaps he'd unfastened a few moments before, then put his hands on my shoulders. "I'm just so thankful we're finally together."

"Me, too," I whispered. I felt uncomfortable saying this. I wished I had a cell phone so I could call Summer for verification that I was not making a terrible mistake. But she would yell at me and tell me to stop being stupid. I did not need her permission to fall in love.

He kissed me on the forehead, then stood, holding out his hand to me. "I'll walk you home."

I took his hand and swung it as we rounded the stable again, back the way we'd come. "*I'll* walk *you* home," I said.

"No," he said with exaggerated patience, "*I'll* walk *you* home." With his other hand he gestured toward the top of my grandmother's mansion, just visible over the rise. "I'm not leaving you wandering around in the night with all these drunk people and, my God, Whitfield Farrell and his fucking bowl."

I giggled. It made me insanely happy that he was jealous of Whitfield Farrell. "You're drunk, though. You might stumble into the road and get hit by a car."

"They will be sorry," he said. "I will dent their car. I am strong like an ox."

I burst into laughter, and he laughed with me. He was so handsome in the gentle starlight, and he looked so happy. I couldn't remember ever being this happy myself. I was still nearly broke and my grandmother hated me and I had a history paper due Monday that I hadn't started writing, but I could handle all of this with Hunter laughing beside me. I squeezed his warm hand.

"I'll cross back through the pasture if it makes you feel better." Dropping my hand, he draped his arm around me and pulled me close for another kiss on the forehead. He walked me all the way down to his house, backed me against the front door, and thoroughly kissed me good night.

16

I sprang out of bed. Sunlight streamed through the window. I hadn't intended to sleep so late. I needed to get started on my history paper. I wanted to see Hunter.

I showered and dressed in record time. My stomach rumbled when I saw that Tommy had left me a big breakfast in the kitchen, but I could come back for that later. I shrugged on my overcoat and dashed up the lane.

Outside my grandmother's mansion, I stood at the foot of the hickory tree, looking through the yellow leaves at my window, two elongated stories above. When I'd lived here I'd never had occasion to sneak out of my room. That part of my stable-boy story had been wishful thinking. But I'd made sure that I could sneak out if I needed to. I had been planning my escape from this place for a long time. Now I could sneak in.

My hip ached as I took massive steps up the hickory branches, careful not to let twigs scrape my face before my first time with Hunter. I snagged my overcoat a few times and panicked all over again at the idea of tearing it and freezing to death in New York City because I couldn't afford another, but eventually I reached my windowsill. The ancient window, huge panes rippled with age, was unlocked, just as I had left it last June. I lifted it open and dropped inside my room, which looked huge to me now. It was four times the size of Hunter's room, and sixteen times the size of my mini-bedroom in the dorm. I turned toward my bed.

It was neatly made. Hunter's suitcase was open on the coverlet. He was up already.

After a disappointing peek around the empty bathroom, I tiptoed out into the hall. He was here somewhere. If I could find him without encountering my grandmother first, I could lure him back to my bedroom, and we could finish what we'd started last night. He had wanted perfection for our first time. This would be it.

After cursory glances into the upstairs parlor and the movie theater and the library, I sneaked down the wide, curving staircase, fingers tracing the banister rubbed silky smooth by a history of trailing hands. When I reached the bottom, I stopped short and sat on the last stair. I could hear Hunter and my grandmother through the arched doorway to the kitchen, saying my name.

"Erin found out I'm majoring in pre-med instead of business," Hunter said.

"Hunter Allen," my grandmother scolded him. I could picture the angry line forming between her exquisitely arched brows. "How could you let that happen?"

"I'm in the honors program with her," Hunter explained in his most persuasive, reasonable, in-control voice, the one that made women fall in love with him. "You asked me to get into a couple of her classes so I could keep tabs on her. But it works both ways. If I'm close enough to find out things about her, she'll find out things about me."

My grandmother protested, "But what are we going to—"

"I took care of it," Hunter interrupted her. Nobody interrupted my grandmother, or so I had thought. "I told her I'm just fooling you into paying for my college, and you have no idea I'm in pre-med."

My grandmother cackled. "That's rich."

"Well, it worked," Hunter said. "For now. But I don't know how long—"

"Just fix it, Hunter," my grandmother said. "You can fix anything with your charm. All you have to do is convince her to major in business and run the farm. And make certain she's not fooling me like you're fooling her! Surely that won't take so long? You said she's starving. Let's see if she can spend a Christmas without my pralines!"

"I'll step in before she starves," Hunter said, and I thought I detected a disapproving tone toward my grandmother. Amazing what this boy could get away with. "But you're right. I'm getting closer to convincing her. Bringing her here was a good idea. It reminded her of how much she loves this place. One of the guys at the stable told my dad she was out for hours on Boo-boo yesterday afternoon."

"On whom?"

"Boo-boo. Her horse. You know, High and Mighty. By Rocky Mountain High out of Might Is Right." The breakfast dishes clinked. "Congratulations on your win yesterday, by the way."

"That horse certainly earned back the cost of the trip to Dubai to buy him," my grandmother said, and the conversation turned easily enough from manipulating me to buying horses.

I sat on the stair and listened to them for a few minutes more. I could sit here until they finished breakfast and came out of the kitchen to discover me, and I could confront them. Or I could go storming into the kitchen now.

Or I could creep back up the sweeping staircase the way I'd come, because it didn't matter that they knew that I knew. All that mattered was that both of them had betrayed me even more deeply and blatantly than I had imagined, and that the love I'd thought had grown between Hunter and me was the worst kind of lie.

Every step he'd taken toward me—acting like my stable-boy story had affected him, writing his own sexy stories, taking me to Belmont, kissing me in the hospital, dragging me home—he'd taken to make me fall in love with him so he could advise me to follow in my grandmother's footsteps. If I did as he said, she gave him a free ride.

As I crossed my room, stepped into the tree, and closed the window behind me, I struggled to pound my feelings for Hunter into a small box, like squeezing my grief into a box when my mother died. I said to myself, *Hunter never liked me. I should not want him anyway because he is in cahoots with my grandmother. He has no interest in me romantically. I am still okay, I am okay, I am okay.*

It wasn't working. The further we'd gone, the more I'd realized I wanted and needed him, needed desperately to connect with him, even if it was only physical. I needed his touch, was starved for it.

I was concentrating so hard that I missed my last foothold in the tree and fell on the ground, directly on my sore hip. Pain jabbed through me. Tears stung my eyes.

I limped back down the lane. Just as I reached the path to Tommy's house, I heard a car topping the hill. My grandmother rode in the backseat of the limo she took to races. She watched me through the tinted window as she passed, eyes hidden by big designer sunglasses, mouth pulled into a disapproving frown.

An hour later I answered a knock on Tommy's front door. Hunter gestured to the farm truck waiting in the lane. "Your chariot awaits." Then he pushed me inside, where the driver couldn't see us, and kissed me hard on the mouth. "Good morning."

AFTER THE TAXI DROPPED US OFF in front of our dorm, Hunter walked me up to my room and pressed me against the hall wall. "Just because we're here in New York doesn't mean we're going back to the way we were," he said, nuzzling my cheek. "We have a hard day tomorrow and we need time to work through this, but things will be different between us now. Promise me."

"Promise." My voice sounded too bright to my own ears, my delivery ironic. But Hunter had played the devoted new boyfriend all morning in the airport. He didn't seem to notice that I regarded him with lust and stony silence.

Ten hours later I was hunched over my laptop at my desk, struggling with the last paragraph of my history paper, when I heard a commotion in the outer bedroom. I rolled my desk chair back and peeked around the door frame. Summer was there with Manohar, Kyle, Isabelle, Brian, and Brian's new boyfriend, all of them leaning on the others, tipsy. Bringing up the rear, standing at the threshold to the hallway, was Hunter.

"Erin!" Summer called when she saw me. "We came to find you. Aren't you done with your paper yet? We're going to the club, baby!"

My heart leapt. Summer, Jørdis, and I had had a great time at the club the week before classes started. I hadn't had time to go since.

"I have a test tomorrow," I said. "I've almost finished my paper, and then I'm going to bed." That is, I might be going to bed. Despite my best instincts, that depended on what Hunter was doing. Angry as I was with him, I could not let him go to that club with Isabelle.

"You don't need all that sleep just to pass a test," Brian said. "You need to relax and get your mind off studying for a while, and you can do that at the club."

"Oooh, what's this?" Brian's boyfriend exclaimed, peering at one of Jørdis's works in progress. She'd started to glue the faces onto a board. All at once, everyone else tried to explain Jørdis's art, and Jørdis.

Hunter walked over and leaned through my doorway. His shadow blended with my shadow on the wall behind him until I couldn't tell one from the other. "Are you going?" he asked me quietly.

I was about to burst with anger. I should tell him I knew everything about his deal with my grandmother. But then our relationship, even our friendship, would be over. I wanted to get him out of my system, didn't I? Otherwise I would wonder for the rest of my life what he would have been like. I would dream about him.

"I'm going if you're going," I said, looking him straight in the eye.

He disappeared into the larger room. I heard him say, "She's going."

"Hooray!" Now Summer poked her head into my room and whispered hoarsely, "Do you want a drink before we go? Or drinks? Manohar has a flask of—I don't know what it is, honestly."

"Oh, God, no," I said. Just what my calculus test needed.

"Suit yourself." Now she disappeared from the doorway. She said more loudly, "Hunter, Manohar has a mystery flask!"

"Oh, God, no," Hunter said.

My fingers paused over my laptop keyboard. He couldn't have overheard my whispered convo with Summer. Yet we were saying the same thing, feeling the same thing at the same moment, worried about school and frankly somewhat exasperated with our friends and sooooo bone tired and yet desperate to be with each other. I had always viewed Hunter as different from me—the opposite of me, really—and now I hated him thoroughly, yet tonight he was the person most like me in the universe.

"Come on, Erin!" Summer called.

I rolled backward in my chair and leaned through the doorway myself. "Go on without me. I'll be right there. I've lost my train of thought for this paper. I can't finish with you guys standing here."

"Come on," Hunter reprimanded them. "Leave her alone. She'll show up in a while." They groaned begrudgingly and shuffled out. The last one to leave, Hunter looked back over his shoulder and asked me, "Won't you?"

I nodded. I didn't see how, honestly. I had lost my bead on this paper. I didn't see how I could miss this night with Hunter, either.

But thirty minutes later I did finish, then changed into club clothes and stared at myself in the mirror. I definitely was no classic blond beauty. But I had always done the best I could with what I had. On this particular night, worn-out looking from days of worry and hard work and little sleep, I supposed I could have been a model in a gritty heroin-chic fashion-magazine spread.

Yes, I would do for Hunter.

I heard the music from the club a block away. I couldn't see the lights—the windows were blocked out, as if something delicious and secret was going down inside—and in the shadows near the door, Hunter leaned against the brick wall, waiting for me.

He met me halfway down the block and walked with me. "I shouldn't have let you come by yourself," he grumbled, "but by the time I realized that, I was afraid that if I went back for you, you'd come a different way and I'd pass you. Why are you a young woman in New York without a cell phone, again?"

"Are you kidding? A cell phone costs two hundred packages of ramen noodles every month."

Before I realized what he was doing, he had paid my way into the club. I tried to protest, but he couldn't hear me over the music. We wound through the writhing crowd, Hunter leading me by the hand. Summer and Manohar danced at the edge of the floor—Manohar, dancing! courtesy of the flask—and Summer pointed us toward an empty booth, the table scattered with glasses and a pitcher of soda.

Hunter slid onto the red velvet bench against the wall. I could sit on the bench across the table from him. Or I could sit on the bench beside him. I didn't have to sit right next to him. He'd acted all day like we were together and he couldn't wait to seal the deal. If I sat close to him, I'd be making my first move toward seducing him in return, though I knew full well I would dump him before he had the chance to dump me.

Decision made, I plopped down beside him on the bench without looking at him.

He said something. I couldn't hear him.

"What?" I asked, turning to look at him.

He watched me intensely, strobe lights flashing across his long nose and sparkling in his blond hair. He crooked his finger at me, beckoning me closer.

Only so I could hear what he'd said, right? I leaned toward him.

At the same time, he stopped crooking his finger at me and laid that hand back where it had been, across the top of the seat.

So as I leaned my head toward his mouth, his arm was sort of around me.

"Are you as tired as I am?" he asked.

I still could hardly hear him over the music, but I knew he was talking loudly because his breath in my ear made my skin dance.

"I'm stone-cold sober," he said, "and I feel more drunk than I did last night."

What he said rang so true, so unexpectedly and absolutely true to my life in that moment, that I laughed, and I smiled at him as if he were my friend, and I couldn't stop laughing.

He laughed, too—chuckling at first, watching me, unsure as to whether I was putting him on. Then laughing with me, a full-body laugh that had us both leaning forward across the bench, toward each other.

Finally the giddiness passed, mostly because my mouth hurt from smiling. Also because a few girls passing by the table had glanced in our direction and I was afraid we'd get kicked out for doing Ecstasy. But the lovely feeling remained, the warmth of laughing, the nearness of Hunter, smiling at me.

The smile stayed on his lips, but his eyes looked worried as he leaned toward me again and said in my ear, "I'm not sure I can handle pre-med."

I backed away from him enough so that I could look into his eyes. He was dead serious, and again, what he said rang true. I nodded. "I know exactly what you mean. But you will feel better tomorrow. You'll hardly remember feeling like this tonight."

He watched me, eyes serious. "Why will I feel better tomorrow?"

I shrugged. "Because your tests will be over, and you will have gotten some rest tonight." I'd thought what I meant was obvious. Weird that I understood him perfectly, and he didn't understand me at all.

"I will?" He leaned forward to talk into my ear again—but this time his cheek touched mine, and his stubble combed across it, dragging a tingling sensation behind. If our friends on the dance floor glanced in our direction, they would not be able to tell we were touching each other. They would think we were still leaning close to hear each other, like before. They would have no idea that every nerve in my body sparked to life and burned as he growled in my ear, "Would you like to dance?"

I gave him a small nod. He stood and held out his hand to me. I put my hand in his. He led me onto the dance floor, in a clear space in a dark corner where the strobe light did not quite reach and the pink searchlight never swept.

Pulling me close, he wrapped one arm around my waist and put his other palm to my cheek. "I've done this all wrong," he whispered in my ear. "I want to start over."

At the feel of his breath on my earlobe, my heart shivered, sending tingles across my chest. My lips parted. I moved my cheek against his hand so he stroked me softly.

"This is a slow country song," he whispered, his voice audible over the throbbing techno beat only because his lips moved against my ear. "And we are alone."

Then he kissed me. His lips were on mine, pressing hard and hungrily. His hands were on the back of my neck, his fingers weaving into my hair, holding me in place as he opened my mouth with his tongue. His hands moved from my neck down my back and around to my front—not far enough to cup my breasts, but far enough to tell me what he wanted. I could not see whether anyone was watching us. He did not look. His eyes were closed, fists gripping my slinky blouse, lips on mine, like he would never let me go.

My heart was beating out of my chest. I did not want to do this with Hunter when I knew he was only toying with me. I did not want to do this in front of my friends. Eventually they would find out that he was toying with me, and that I had known this and had let him.

But there was no way I would break that kiss. His warm tongue was in my mouth, tangling with my tongue, sweeping over my teeth, claiming me as his. My blood raced through my veins and seemed to throb toward him like the ocean tide pointing toward the moon. It was one of those things in life a writer needed to experience: feeling smitten, rendered helpless, being taken.

"We have to go back to the dorm," he mumbled against my lips.

I nodded just a little, gently enough that I didn't remove my mouth from his.

This time I was the one who led him by the hand through the crowd. I was shocked that he put up with this all the way across the flashing dance floor. He must have reasoned that if he could keep me happy long enough to bed me, I would listen to reason about my career choice, he could talk me into running back to my grandmother, and a college education would be his. He let himself be led.

Summer glanced up from her dancelike tangle with Manohar. Her eyes widened. I'd told her in the afternoon that I would fill her in on my weekend with Hunter after I finished my history paper, but I hadn't implied—or thought—that I would be leading him by the hand out of a club later. She spoke to Manohar. He jerked his head up wearing her astonished expression. So Hunter hadn't told Manohar about us, either. Not that there was any "us" to tell.

We hurried through the cold night scented with Italian garbage, holding hands, hardly speaking.

The dorm was Sunday-night quiet as he backed me against the outer door to my room and kissed me hard. His hands reached around my waist, found their way up to my breasts and touched them through my blouse and bra this time. I put my hands behind his head to mash him closer, but by then he'd fumbled through my purse and stuck my key in the lock. The door opened behind me.

We crossed the larger room quickly and closed ourselves in my tiny bedroom. As we embraced again, I began to understand the mistake I was making. He was in my bed, and I would never be able to sleep again without thinking of him here. He kissed me, and if I opened my eyes a sliver, I could see my makeshift bedside table, actually my filing cabinet, sporting the New York City magnet. He lay down on top of me, and past his shoulders I could see my laptop glowing. I smelled him and tasted him and now when I came here every night, I would think of him, which was exactly what I never, ever intended to happen.

17

Half asleep, I opened my eyes and puzzled through what I was seeing. Hunter Allen lay beside me. His bare muscular arm crossed me. He reached to my filing cabinet and touched the New York City magnet.

In the blue glow from the streetlights outside, he slipped out of bed. I watched him pull on his jeans and move toward the door. He didn't fasten his belt. Maybe he didn't fasten the jeans, either, because they sat very low on his hips, so low that I would have turned around to watch him go if I'd passed him in the hall like that.

With his hand on the doorknob, he glanced back at me and saw me staring.

He came back and knelt on the side of the bed, leaned forward, and kissed the tip of my nose. "Go back to sleep," he whispered.

Then he was gone, carefully opening the door without a squeak and shutting it most of the way behind him.

The outer door to the hallway closed softly. I felt this more than heard it, a little bump through the building.

Footfalls sounded in the stairwell, higher and higher in the walls.

Then silence.

I took a long breath, enjoying the last of his warmth lingering in the sheets around me. As my chest moved, the warm sheets slid against my skin as if he were still here. But it was over and he was gone.

Eventually the breath had to come out again as a sigh, and I was sobbing, coughing. I rolled over and coughed into my pillow so I wouldn't wake Summer and Jørdis. The pillowcase smelled like him.

I was lucky I'd found out in Kentucky that I'd been fooled all this time. I'd slept with him to get him out of my system, and that plan had backfired. He had jumped up and beat a trail out the door and up to his own floor as soon as he came to his senses and realized where he was. If I had expected anything different, I was still the fool I'd been trying so hard not to be.

Footfalls sounded in the stairwell again. Descending.

It wasn't Hunter. It couldn't be him coming back to me. Or if it was, he simply realized he'd left his coat in my room, and his shirt . . . and his underwear.

The hall door bumped shut.

I held my breath.

My door opened. He would gather his things and make a hasty exit.

He closed the door softly behind him. He shed his jeans in the soft light and slid into bed beside me. Because I'd rolled over to sob into the pillow, there was less room for him now. He pressed against me until I scooted over with my back to him.

Soft clicks sounded behind my head, and then the tiniest beep. He must have retrieved his Rolex from his room. He was setting his alarm.

"You never take that thing off," I whispered, hoping my voice didn't sound shaky from crying. "Why didn't you wear it tonight?"

"I didn't want to know what time it was," he whispered back. "I still don't, but I'm paranoid about missing that anatomy test. I'd rather stay here with you forever."

He said it so casually. His watch beeped a few more times. But heat spread across my chest—adrenaline from excitement, and horror. Was he saying what I thought he was saying?

To double-check, I whispered, "I thought this room made you claustrophobic."

"Not with you in it." He set his Rolex on my filing cabinet, a hollow metallic sound. Then he spooned hot against me, draping his arm over my waist.

He kissed my hair.

My bed was a soft nest surrounded by windows onto the cold city, but I felt my arms prick with chill bumps when he kissed me. He was not acting like he had seduced me for money. He acted as if he was happy to be with me and loath to leave. If I was right this time, he was not going to like the story I'd written in anger on Thursday night, which we would be discussing in Gabe's class tomorrow.

He woke me by kissing my mouth in the gray morning light.

"My anatomy test is at eight," he whispered between kisses. "My books are upstairs." He kissed me more deeply, sighed as if I'd tempted him and he'd finally given in. He collapsed on top of my bare body. "I don't want to go, but I've got to."

He raised himself off me and looked for his clothes on the floor.

I gazed warily at him, but I supposed it was still early enough that he mistook my misgivings for sleepiness.

"I'll see you in calculus, okay? And creative writing." My body tingled as he leaned in and gave me one last, lingering kiss. Then he opened the door. He murmured something in the larger room. Summer giggled. The outer door closed.

I pulled on sweats and poked my head into the larger room. Jørdis, in her pajamas and thick, heavy-rimmed glasses, made dissatisfied noises in Danish as she peeled faces off her collage and flicked the curled paper into the trash. Summer stood at the mirror over her dresser, evening out her hair with a pick.

"I'm really sorry, guys," I said as I walked in. "I should have asked your permission for Hunter to sleep over. It just sort of happened."

"What bull." Summer grinned.

Jørdis nodded. "Why do you think he cuts heads for me? I do not think he enjoys cutting heads."

I was still trying to digest the fact that she thought of her art as "cutting heads," which was disconcerting, when she went on, "I don't mind what you do with him as long as I am not the one who has to sleep in the wee chamber."

"Well, you don't have to worry about that," I said. "It won't happen again."

"It won't?" Summer squealed, setting the pick down. "What do you mean?"

"Have you read my story for Gabe's class?" I asked her.

She nodded. "It was different. Brutal. I meant to ask you about it. It seems like you were depressed when you wrote it, or tired."

"Angry," I corrected her. "It's about the guy Hunter helped me get away from last May."

Her eyes widened. "Has Hunter read it yet?"

"Obviously not," I said.

"What is the matter with this story?" Jørdis asked.

"It's incredibly dirty," Summer said. She and Jørdis turned to me, outrage on their faces at the thought that I would treat a gentleman such as Hunter in this manner.

"Honestly, guys," I said, "a lot has gone on between Hunter and me and our families over the years. More even than you know about. I thought he was using me last night. I was mad and I used him back. But now that it's happened, I think there may be more between us than using each other. And if that's true on his end, I just screwed up everything with this story."

"Why do you keep doing that?" Summer squealed again.

"I'm writing what I know," I murmured.

"You don't know shit," Jørdis said. "This boy clearly loves you. He sits here on the bed and cuts out my photos in the hope that you will walk by."

"What do I do?" I whispered.

"Call him!" Summer forced her cell phone into my hand.

Feeling weak, I sank onto Jørdis's bed and punched in the number I knew by heart. "Busy." Who was he calling this early in the morning?

"Text him," Jørdis said.

I dropped the phone into my lap. "I can't bother him with this right now. He's headed into a huge anatomy test." Shaking my head, I handed the phone back to Summer. "I'll try to talk to him in calculus class."

But he came into calculus just as the TA was passing out the test—probably because he'd taken extra time with his anatomy test. He sat beside me and gave me the most brilliant smile. But we couldn't talk. And while I was still struggling with imaginary numbers, he turned in his test and left. He had to be headed to the library to read my story. I couldn't follow him because I had to go to history to turn in my paper.

That's why I sat in the creative-writing class in the afternoon, poring over my story, reading it as Hunter would read it. The other students eyed me and whispered as they came in and sat down in their upholstered chairs. I put my hand over my mouth, anticipating the worst.

Obedience

by Erin Blackwell

"You will do as you're told," her grandmother said. "Your college tuition is a gift, and I am not obligated to give it to you. If you choose not to follow in my footsteps—study business, and run the family farm—I choose not to help you."

The girl looked around her grandmother's office, at the crystal chandelier, the silk Persian carpet, the rich leather-bound books on the walnut shelves, and considered her grandmother's words. If she took her grandmother's offer, she would give up her dream of becoming an artist. But how could she support herself out in the world? She would be destitute and so . . . low.

The girl made her decision. "You're right," she said, "and I'm sure I'll thank you for this tough love when I'm older."

"That's the way." Her grandmother smiled, a perfect bow of blood red lipstick. She reached out with one perfectly manicured hand and stroked the girl's hair away from her eyes for the first time since this argument had begun several weeks before. "Now that we have that settled, you know what would make me even happier?"

The party started soon after their talk. BMWs and Mercedes and rare collector cars pulled into her grandmother's driveway in place of the fine coaches and spirited horses of yesteryear. The girl stood at the tall front window, pulling back the silk drape, watching for her target. His family owned the neighboring farm, and her grandmother had suggested that the two of them would make an excellent couple.

And why not? The girl called a roaming waiter to her side and took her third glass of wine from his tray. He flared his nostrils in disapproval. She did not care. She was high and he was low. Right?

"Right," said the boy, securing his own glass and taking her hand. As he pulled her toward a dark corner of the party, he whispered, "I love to see you like this."

"Like what?" she asked. "Wasted?"

"Heirs to a fortune do not get wasted," he corrected her. "We simply socialize. Do you want to socialize with me?" He slipped his hand inside her cardigan, unbuttoned the silk blouse underneath, and forced his fingers past her lacy bra to her breast. Gently he pinched her nipple. Electricity shot straight to her crotch.

Was this what her grandmother had in mind? She was sure her grandmother would heap praise on her for befriending the heir to the farm next door, as instructed. She was not so sure her grandmother would approve of the boy pinching her nipple in public. So she asked, "Did you bring your own car?"

"Did I ever." He took her by the hand again. This time he led her winding among the dark bodies drinking and laughing. The light had begun to blur, but she thought she saw grins flashing at her and the boy. She and the boy were so sweet and such a perfect match! As they passed between the wall and a massive buffet table that shielded them from view, the boy put his hand up her skirt and into her panties.

The heavy front door of her grandmother's mansion seemed to open for them like the sets moving and changing in front of the characters in a Broadway play or a romantic Depression-era movie production. As she stumbled after the boy, out of the mansion and into the vast yard, she realized she was about to lose her virginity in a sleek black Porsche, which definitely was not low. Good for her.

They collapsed inside black bucket seats of soft leather. The boy rolled toward her and coaxed, "Unbuckle my belt, Erin—"

* * *

"GOOD AFTERNOON." GABE BEAMED AT US as he closed the door behind him and eased himself into the upholstered chair at the head of the table.

I was glad class was starting. I'd been dreading it all day. I was half glad Hunter wasn't there. I wondered where he was instead. I hoped he wasn't acting out one of his sexy stories as revenge on me. And I wished I'd finished reading over my story again, picturing what he would think as he read it. I was just getting to the dirty part.

Gabe raised his white eyebrows at Hunter's empty chair at the foot of the table. Beamed at everyone else again.

Footfalls sounded at the bottom of the staircase below us.

"Let's start with Erin's story today, shall we?" Gabe said. "None of us will be able to think about anything else until we get *that* out of the way."

The class tittered. Summer looked over at me, face sympathetic.

The footsteps stomped closer in the stairwell.

"Manohar," Gabe said, "why don't you start—"

Hunter burst through the classroom door, waving my story in my face. Wow, he must have been really angry to take reserve materials out of the library. That was not allowed. He probably had alarm bells ringing and the campus police after him, and he must have left his student ID.

That was what I was thinking as he shouted at me, "Did you want me to watch? Did you want us all to watch? You screamed at me for not writing the right kind of story, Erin, and you have a lot of nerve. Every story you've written in this class, you've calculated to stab me and twist the knife, from casting me as your stable boy to this piece of fucking pornography." He threw "Obedience" down on the table in front of me.

Gabe was yelling at us. Gabe who had never raised his voice in class before or shown any kind of anger at all was standing up in front of his elegant upholstered chair, red faced, shouting about how in forty years of teaching creative writing he had never encountered such insolence. He actually used the word *insolence*.

I stood up, too, because as long as I sat, I was lower than Gabe and lower than Hunter. I told Hunter, "You didn't seem to mind the fucking pornography last night."

"We were doing it, Erin, not writing about it for everybody to read!"

"Well, just fix it, Hunter! You can fix anything with your charm!"

The front of Hunter's shirt rose and fell with his rapid breathing, buttons glinting in the glow from the stained-glass lamps. And in his glare, I saw everything he was thinking. I had overheard what my grandmother had said to him. I had figured out that she was paying him to watch over me, and he'd faked his feelings for me for that purpose. I had slept with him anyway, and faked my feelings for him in turn.

The one thing I hadn't counted on was that at some point during the last few months, or the last week, or the last day, his feelings for me had turned real. He thought mine were still fake.

And Hunter did not like to be taken advantage of.

Gabe was giving us a lecture. Everyone in the room gawked at me. A girl at the other end of the table whispered, "Hunter is Erin's stable boy?"

And I started to cry.

Summer patted my hand on the table. "Go," she said.

"Where?" I asked her. My voice broke.

"Gabe said to go wait for him outside his office," she whispered.

Sure enough, Hunter had turned to leave, and Gabe glowered at me with his arms folded.

I'd never been to Gabe's office. I followed Hunter's stomping up to the third floor of the building. When I emerged from the stairwell, I spotted him at the far end of the hall, backpack slung over one shoulder, arms crossed on his chest, staring out the window onto the street. Beside him was a comfy-looking chaise longue, the only seat in the hall. I took one step toward it to wait there for Gabe, but Hunter turned and glared at me.

I backed down the stairwell, deciding it might be better to wait out class in the basement snack bar.

By the time class ended, I had scribbled twenty pages of a new story and stopped crying. Ascending the staircase again, I saw that Hunter hadn't budged. He stared out the now dark window and shouldered his burden of books. This time I would not let him scare me away from the chaise longue. I trudged down the hall, plopped on the chaise, and opened my history book, like that would fool anybody.

"Well." Hunter's voice cracked as he said this. He cleared his throat. "There goes your internship."

"Which is exactly what you and my grandmother wanted," I said without looking up from my book. After a moment I said brightly, "Maybe I still have a shot. I seriously doubt Gabe is on the committee. He won't give me a stellar rec from class, but I can try to sidestep him and submit my portfolio to the committee—"

"He *is* on the committee," Hunter said.

"He's *not* on the committee," I insisted. At least, I *hoped* he wasn't on the committee. I had assumed he wasn't, but it would be like Hunter to know something I didn't know. I stammered, "Only the bigwigs in the English department are—"

"I'm telling you," Hunter said, "he *is* on the committee. He's the *head* of the committee. He's won the O. Henry and the Pulitzer."

"Gabe?" Even as I gaped at Hunter, I realized he must be right. A university English department with this good a reputation wouldn't hire a washed-up junior college reject to teach honors creative writing. He didn't dress like a beach bum because he was so low on the totem pole that he could get away with it. He dressed like that because he was so high. I put my shaking hand up to my mouth, speechless for once.

Hunter sat beside me on the chaise. "You're not the only one with something to lose. If Gabe flunks us, I can kiss med school good-bye. I'll still be dragging my GPA out of this hole when I'm a senior."

"You're being a little melodramatic," I said faintly.

"*Me?* You're the one writing stories about—" He stopped himself. "It doesn't matter now. Just tell me about Whitfield." His face was white stone.

"What do you care?" I snapped. "Every single thing you have done to, for, or with me since you've been in New York you've done because my grandmother paid you. You are not my boyfriend. You are not even my real friend, and it's none of your business."

"You made it my business last night," he insisted.

I looked into his intense blue gaze for a moment. "My story is fiction."

He scowled at me. "Your name is in it."

"What? No it isn't. I wrote it in the third person about a nameless girl."

"Your name is in it, Erin," he insisted. "Freudian slip."

Uh-oh. "I mean, it's sort of nonfiction," I backtracked, "but it happened a while ago. Not this weeken—"

He closed his eyes and put up his hand. "Just. Stop. Talking."

I was about to point out to him that *he* was the one who'd started talking to *me*, when I heard quick steps toward us down the hall—too quick to be Gabe. Isabelle jogged up to us and panted, "Erin. Gabe will be here any second. I don't know what will happen to you or whether I'll see you again, so I thought it was important to tell you something."

"Okay," I said, careful not to stare accusingly at Hunter. This had to be about him.

"I love your stories," she gushed, bending to put her hand on my forearm. "Love them. I look forward to them every two weeks. I've told my whole family about them."

"Thank you," I said instead of what I really meant, which was, *I don't believe you. I would have believed you at the beginning of the semester, but not now. This must be a joke. Where is the camera?*

"I haven't defended you in class because Manohar seems so sure of himself," she said. "He's hard to argue against and I've felt awful that I've failed you. But you have inspired me. I didn't know an English major was allowed to write a story like that."

"Apparently we're not. That's why I'm in trouble." I patted her hand. "I appreciate this, Isabelle." Gabe's white head appeared in the stairwell. I stage-whispered, "I'll write you stories from prison."

"Okay!" She laughed like I was joking and passed Gabe on her way back down the hall.

I tensed as he approached us, and I could feel Hunter's muscles draw taut, too, even though he didn't touch me. But Gabe was back to his friendly self. He even grinned at us as he unlocked his office door and ushered us into two chairs in front of his cluttered desk.

He grew scarier again as he wedged himself into his chair and leaned on his elbows on his desk. With a stern look at me and then at Hunter, he said, "I do not lose my cool. Do you understand me?"

"Yes, sir," Hunter said. I grimaced and nodded.

"We are going to talk this out so it never comes up in my class again." Gabe shifted his weight back in his chair and steepled his hands. "So. Hunter. You're Erin's stable boy?"

Neither of us wanted to spill our guts or our family secrets to an old man who would probably flunk us both. But when I explained the impetus for my stable-boy story, Hunter had a dissenting opinion. When Hunter defended his bathroom story, I piped up that he wasn't telling the whole truth. We went round and round like this until Gabe finally said, "I'm from California and I thought those people were screwed up, but Kentucky takes the cake, doesn't it? You could write a story about this." He laughed.

Hunter and I did not.

Gabe rubbed one eye. "Which brings us to Erin's story today, and what happened over the weekend that finally broke Hunter."

Hunter frowned. He did not like that characterization one bit.

I kicked while Hunter was down. I asked him, "What exactly was your directive from my grandmother?"

I thought he would deny it, even now. But Gabe stared at him expectantly, too, and with a slow look up at Gabe and a slow look down at his hands again, Hunter began to speak.

"I was supposed to get into some of your classes." He glanced up at Gabe, looked away. "Try to become friends with you again. Become friends with your friends so I could keep tabs on you. Take you out to eat as often as possible so you didn't starve. Keep you away from any no-good piece of shit who tried to get in your pants."

"Come on now," I said. "My grandmother said 'piece of shit'?"

"She may have said 'scalawag.'"

That sounded more like her. "Is that all you had to do?"

He shook his head no. "Bring you home for the Breeders' Cup."

"Even if that meant lying to get me there?"

"We didn't discuss methods. I was desperate at that point." He turned to face me for the first time in an hour. "I'm sorry."

"Speaking of methods," I said, "were you supposed to sleep with me?"

His eyes widened, then slid to Gabe and back to me. "No. I mean, I knew already that your grandmother doesn't think I'm good enough for you. But in case that wasn't clear, she spelled that out specifically."

I grinned devilishly—which was only fitting, because I felt like hell. "So, all I have to do is call her—"

"You don't have a phone."

"—and tell her we slept together, and you're as cut off as I am."

"I already did," he said.

I gasped audibly. "When?"

"This morning, before my anatomy test." Sighing, he closed his eyes and put his elbow on the armrest of his chair and his chin in his hand. He had looked tired the past few weeks. Now he looked beaten.

I studied him, this handsome, brilliant young man whose life should not have been so hard.

Remembered him staring at himself in the mirror at my grandmother's house. At least, that's what I'd thought at first. I'd taken a few more steps and realized his eyes were closed, perhaps examining himself from inside.

"Hunter," Gabe said, "why don't you get us a couple of sodas?"

Hunter nodded shortly and stood.

"Hold on." Gabe sat forward, drew his wallet out of his back pocket, and waved a bill between his fingers. "Sounds like you may need this."

"Funny," Hunter said. But he took the bill. As he backed out the door and closed it behind him, he was watching me.

"Erin," Gabe said, turning to me.

"Yes, sir?" I asked in my best imitation of Hunter.

"You have a problem with authority."

"Yes, sir."

"You can't take criticism."

"What do you mean, I can't take criticism?" I demanded. Gabe did not laugh, so I said, "Ha-ha, joke."

"But I'm trying to give you the benefit of the doubt," he said. "Lloyd Peters tells me you're a brilliant student and wrote a phenomenal paper for his early American literature survey."

"Bleh!" I said automatically. "I mean, I am thrilled that Dr. Peters enjoyed my paper."

"He said you tore Nathaniel Hawthorne a new one."

"Like shooting fish in a barrel," I said gravely.

"And in my class," Gabe said, "though your demeanor has on occasion been less than professional, you've given terrific advice to your fellow writers. In fact, according to the statements of your peers, you've been more helpful than any other student. Brian has commented to me on how much your suggestions have helped him. Summer. Isabelle. Hunter." He snapped his fingers. "What's-his-name, what-do-you-call-him, Wolf-boy."

"Kyle."

"And very recently, Manohar. I was particularly amazed by that. If I'd been you and Manohar had said those things about my first story, I would have knocked his block off."

All of this was said with a jovial smile on his cherubic face.

"And you have a gift," he said.

Those words meant much more to me now, after everything that had happened, than they had when he'd written them on my stable-boy story. I let the words hang in the air between us like the unexpectedly lovely scent of an aromatherapy candle in a funky SoHo shop. I had a gift.

"I think your original story was your best," he said. "The class's criticism of that story sent you on a journey you didn't want to take. Sometimes it's good for our foundations to be shaken. What doesn't kill us makes us stronger."

"I guess," I said bitterly. I still didn't understand why Manohar always got to comment first.

Gabe continued, "You were writing what you thought was a good story. You didn't know Hunter would be in the class, so you weren't trying to make a point to him. You weren't exorcising demons or recounting your family history. You were concocting an enjoyable fantasy for yourself. We all do our best work when we write the story we want to read."

I squinted, determined not to cry again. "I'm not sure this one ends well."

"It ends the way you say it ends," Gabe said gently.

"I think Hunter might have something to say about that."

Gabe's chair creaked as he leaned forward. "We're not talking about your life, Erin. We're talking about your writing. Your imagination. Your creativity. And it's time you learned there's a big difference between your writing and your life. To do it right, your writing takes an incredible amount of work. Your life takes more."

I nodded slowly. "Believe it or not, I've been trying to repair my life. I've planned to apply for the publishing internship."

Gabe raised his white eyebrows at me. "Really."

"Yeah. From your tone of voice, it sounds like you're telling me I don't have a snowball's chance in hell, and I shouldn't bother."

He pried his mouth loose from its grim line to say, "That's what I'm telling you."

I held my breath. I could not cry in front of him. Not again. I tried not to think about my life in New York, my internship, my whole writing career fading in front of me, all because of my tangle with Hunter, whom I'd also lost. I would think about this later and let loose with the waterworks. Not now.

"But, Erin." Gabe tapped his finger on his desk to the beat of his words. "If you are trying to make a writing career for yourself, you will get rejected again and again and again and again." Tap. Tap. Tap. Tap. "You must keep going. You have to learn not to take no for an answer."

I left his office unsure whether to feel better or worse about my chances at the internship, my chances at publishing my writing, and the incredible amount of work it would take to be friends with Hunter again.

He sat on the chaise longue, three bottles of soda beside him on the cushion. As I passed him, he handed one to me.

I downed big swigs of soda while walking down the dark street, thinking hard. I was halfway to the coffee shop when I realized I was ninety minutes late for work, and I had been fired.

18

A week and a half later, we read Hunter's story for class. I was afraid it would be some kind of recrimination, about a man who takes revenge on the bitch who ruined his life. But it seemed to be about reconciling his relationship with his dad. I hoped it was true and I thought it was beautiful, but the rest of the girls in the class didn't hide their disappointment that it wasn't about his sex life. The biggest topic of discussion was Manohar's hilarious story about an Indian stockbroker joining a bluegrass band, which the class argued was unrealistic—everybody but me.

After class, I went back to my room and found a new tube of my expensive face cream on my bed. Summer did not know where it had come from, and she had not let anyone into the room. Jørdis said the same thing, but she looked guilty.

After Hunter left for the hospital late that night, I sneaked up to his room and stuck my New York City magnet on his doorknob.

Jørdis's art project was installed in the college gallery the following week. Everybody she'd roped into cutting faces for her—meaning pretty much everybody in the dorm—was there to admire our handiwork. One of the huge collages held thousands of photos that at a distance formed a portrait of Summer and me. An even larger collage, titled *Watchdog,* showed Hunter curled up asleep on Jørdis's bed with my belly-dancing outfit hanging on the door in the background.

Hunter was at the opening. In fact, at one point we gazed at each other across that collage. When I arrived back at the dorm, a gift card for the restaurant around the corner from the dorm had appeared on my bed.

Summer wanted me to go home with her to Mississippi for Thanksgiving, but neither of us had the money to buy me a plane ticket. Even Jørdis was headed to the home of a friend from Brooklyn. Summer tried to get Jørdis to take me, too. I waved them off. I would go to the dining hall for the sad Thanksgiving dinner for foreign students who couldn't go home and had no local friends, and I would meet some new and fascinating people. No biggie.

"I know you," Summer said. "There is no way you would spring for Thanksgiving dinner in the dining hall. You'll be right here in the room, boiling ramen noodles in your hot pot."

I had thought I would be relieved when Summer and Jørdis left on Tuesday, not because they bugged me, but because it would be nice to have the place quiet and to myself, and I could get some writing done. Since my talk with Gabe, I'd been working on my end-of-semester portfolio. I'd figured out a way to save my grade, save Hunter's grade, and get my internship after all. I'd included my stories from the class, plus Hunter's stories that I'd copied in the library. And around them, I'd filled in the real journey Hunter and I had taken. The stories themselves might still be exploitive and debauched, but the portfolio as a whole made some sense out of the experience, and—I hardly dared say—some art.

All I had to do was get Hunter's permission.

I worked hard at first, halfway glad I'd been fired and determined to make the most of this windfall of time before I found a new job. But the hours and the silence weighed on me. I found myself lying on my bed, staring out the window, wishing for someone interesting to walk by, waiting for any noise upstairs, just to know there was someone in the building with me, keeping me company. I gripped both sides of the bed whenever I heard footfalls in the stairwell.

They didn't sound like Hunter. I wondered if he had gone home.

Wednesday morning I woke with my laptop open on my tummy. Hunter was rummaging through my dresser, packing my suitcase.

I yawned and sat up. My laptop tumbled closed on the pillows. "Is my dad going to be there?"

"Absolutely not," Hunter said without looking up from his neat folding. "But I hear you're out of a job, so that's no excuse for staying. There's lots to fly to Louisville for."

"The end of the fall meet," I murmured. I missed the horses.

"There's the end of the fall meet," he agreed. "And there's, you know, Thanksgiving, which you usually spend with the people you love the most. And then there's me."

He stopped folding. We exchanged a long look.

"Have you bought the tickets already?" I asked. "I thought my grandmother cut you off when you told her we were together."

"That was the deal," he said. "But she's been calling me for updates about you. I guess I'm still employed for now."

"Even after you were so naughty?"

"Even after that. She can't admit this, but all she ever really wanted was to know you were okay and didn't hate her."

I blinked. "I don't hate her," I said, realizing this for the first time.

"Come with me to Louisville, and tell her."

"All right." I feigned reluctance. "Give me a few minutes to wrap up this writing and get ready."

He nodded and pointed toward the larger bedroom. "I'll wait for you out there. Jørdis needs a lot more faces cut out for her project next semester."

"Oh joy."

After he left, I opened my laptop. While I was showering, I would print out the collaboration I'd been working on so Hunter could read it on the airplane. I hoped he approved. I prayed he would get it. There was a small, glimmering chance he would love it.

Thankfully it was almost ready to go, but it had no title page. Thinking of Hunter, whose opinion mattered to me even more than Gabe's at that moment, I typed, LOVE STORY.

And laughed.

In the larger bedroom I plugged the laptop into Summer's printer, then stepped out the door with my bucket of toiletries, headed for the shower. As I looked back, Hunter glanced up from his magazine and scissors and grinned at me. This smile was for real.